Praise for the works of Gerri Hill

Red Tide at Heron Bay

One of the best things I love about Ms. Hill's writing is she takes the time to describe the environment and surroundings within the story, not so much as to stall the storyline but more to enhance the feeling of really being there with the characters... Ms. Hill does a wonderful job of blending mystery with a love story (reminds me of *Devil's Rock* and *Hell's Highway*) and she did it justice again in this book.

-Carol C., NetGalley

Love the Hawaiian shirts and the person wearing them. This romantic intrigue had my attention from the beginning. Detective Harley Shepherd, upbeat yet sad as she deals with the loss of someone close to her. Lauren Voss, resort manager, shying away from relationships as she continues to deal with a relationship that went off the rails. Both women "ran" to Heron Bay to heal. Little did they know that tragedy would be waiting for ░░░ ░░░ ░░░ ░░░ ░░░ corner. I enjoyed the flirting and tea ░░░ ░░░ ░░░ ░░░ ░░░ ░░ me chuckling and laughing ou

-Kennedy O., NetGalley

The Stars at Night

The Stars at Night is a beautiful mountain romance that will transport you to a paradise. It's a story of self-discovery, family, and rural living. This romance was a budding romance that snuck-up and on two unsuspecting women who found themselves falling in love under the stars and while gazing at birds. It's a feel-good slow-burn romance that will make your heart melt.

-Les Rêveur

Hill is such a strong writer. She's able to move the plot along through the characters' dialogue and actions like a true boss. It's a masterclass in showing, not telling. The story unfolds at a languid pace which mirrors life in a small, mountain town, and her descriptions of the environment bring the world of the book alive.

-The Lesbian Review

Gillette Park

This book was just what I was hoping for and wickedly entertaining. The premise of this book is really well done. Parts are hard to read of course. This book is about a serial killer who targets mostly young teenagers. The book isn't very graphic, but it still breaks your heart in places. But there is also a sweet romance that helps to give the book a sense of hope. Mix that with some strong women, the creepiness of the paranormal factors, and the book balances out really well. There is a lot of potential with these characters and I'd love to see their stories continue. If you are a Hill fan, grab this.

-Lex Kent's Reviews, goodreads

Hill is a master writer, and this one is done in a way that I think will appeal to many readers. Don't just discount this one because it has a paranormal theme to it! I think that the majority of readers who love mystery novels with a romantic side twist will love this story.

-Bethany K., goodreads

It was suspenseful and so well written that it was anyone's guess what would happen next! The characters—all of them, as you'll learn, were perfectly written.

-Gayle T., NetGalley

Gerri Hill has written another action-packed thriller. The writing is excellent and the characters engaging. Wow!

-Jenna F., NetGalley

...is a phenomenal book! I wish I could give this more than five stars. Yes, there is a paranormal element, and a love story, and conflict, and danger. And it's all worth it. Thank you, Gerri Hill, for writing a brilliant masterpiece!

-Carolyn M., *NetGalley*

After the Summer Rain

...is a heartwarming, slow-burn romance that features two awesome women who are learning what it really means to live and love fully. They're also learning to let go of their turbulent pasts so that it doesn't ruin their future happiness. Gerri Hill has never failed to give me endearing characters who are struggling with heartbreaking issues and beautiful descriptions of the landscapes that surround them.

-*The Lesbian Review*

Gerri Hill is simply one of the best romance writers in the genre. This is an archetypal Hill, slightly unusual characters in a slightly unusual setting. The slow-burn romance, however, is a classic, trying not to fall in love, but unable to fight the pull.

-*Lesbian Reading Room*

After the Summer Rain is a wonderfully heartfelt romance that avoids all the angsty drama-filled tropes you often find in romances.

-*C-Spot Reviews*

Moonlight Avenue

Moonlight Avenue by Gerri Hill is a riveting, literary tapestry of mystery, suspense, thriller and romance. It is also a story about forgiveness, moving on with your life and opening your heart to love despite how daunting it may seem at first.

-*The Lesbian Review*

...is an excellent mystery novel, sheer class. Gerri Hill's writing is flawless, her story compelling and much more than a notch above others writing in this genre.

-Kitty Kat's Book Review Blog

The Locket

This became a real page-turner as the tension racked up. I couldn't put it down. Hill has a knack for combining strong characters, vulnerable and complex, with a situation that allows them to grow, while keeping us on our toes as the mystery unfolds. Definitely one of my favorite Gerri Hill thrillers, highly recommended.

-Lesbian Reading Room

The Neighbor

It's funny...Normally in the books I read I get why the characters would fall in love. Now on paper (excuse the pun), Cassidy and Laura should not work...but let me tell you, that's the reason they do. I actually loved this book so hard. ...Yes it's a slow burn but so beautifully written and worth the wait in every way.

-Les Rêveur

This is classic Gerri Hill at her very best, top of the pile of so many excellent books she has written, I genuinely loved this story and these two women. The growing friendship and hidden attraction between them is skillfully written and totally engaging....This was a joy to read.

-Lesbian Reading Room

I have always found Hill's writing to be intriguing and stimulating. Whether she's writing a mystery or a sweet romance, she allows the reader to discover something about themselves along with her characters. This story has all the fun antics you would expect for a quality, low-stress, romantic comedy. Hill is wonderful in giving us characters that are intriguing and delightful that you never want to put the book down until the end.

-The Lesbian Review

The Great Charade

Other Bella Books by Gerri Hill

About the Author

Gerri Hill has over forty published works, including the 2021 GCLS winner for *Gillette Park*, the 2020 GCLS winner *After the Summer Rain*, the 2017 GCLS winner *Paradox Valley*, 2014 GCLS winner *The Midnight Moon*, 2011, 2012 and 2013 winners *Devil's Rock*, *Hell's Highway* and *Snow Falls*, and the 2009 GCLS winner *Partners*, the last book in the popular Hunter Series, as well as the 2013 Lambda finalist *At Seventeen*. Gerri lives in south-central Texas, only a few hours from the Gulf Coast, a place that has inspired many of her books. With her partner, Diane, they share their life with two Australian shepherds—Rylee and Mason—and a couple of furry felines. For more, visit her website at gerrihill.com.

Bella Books, Inc.
P.O. Box 10543
Tallahassee, FL 32302

Printed in the United States of America on acid-free paper.

First Edition - 2021

Editor: Medora MacDougall
Cover Designer: Heather Honeywell

ISBN: 978-1-64247-339-1

PUBLISHER'S NOTE

The Great Charade

Gerri Hill

BELLA
BOOKS

2021

CHAPTER ONE

Abby nearly cringed when "Mom" popped up on her cell. Normally, that would bring a smile to her face. But it was November, after all. Her call could only mean one thing.

"Hey, Mom," she greeted, forcing some cheerfulness into her voice.

"Good morning, Abigail. Am I catching you at a bad time?"

Abby eyed the three monitors on her desk, all with different data and spreadsheets. Could she lie and say she was absolutely swamped and had no time to chat? No. That would only delay the inevitable.

"No, it's good." She paused. "What's up?"

"Well, it's almost Thanksgiving."

"So it is."

"And you know what that means."

"Yes. Christmas is right around the corner." Again, the forced cheerfulness hid her chagrin. "Can't wait." The words were out before she could disguise them, and she sighed. "I meant that sincerely, of course."

"Oh, Abigail. Are you *still* not over it?"

"I'm over it, Mom."

"You can't blame your brother, honey. It's as much Holly's fault as anything."

She closed her eyes as if that would make the situation go away. "Do we have to talk about it?"

"Of course not. We'll sweep it under the rug like we did last year. We'll all have a joyous Christmas, just like last year," she said sarcastically.

"Oh my god! You're blaming *me*, aren't you?"

"I said no such thing."

"I can tell by your tone." She grabbed the bridge of her nose. She wondered what her mother's reaction would be if she knew that she and Holly had slept together last Christmas? But no, she couldn't blurt that out. She was too embarrassed by the whole thing to ever tell her mother about *that* transgression.

"So, Aaron and Holly are coming up on that Thursday, the twenty-third. I know that's when you normally come too, so—"

"Surely to god you're not suggesting we ride together?" she asked sharply.

"Well, it seems a waste. You all live in Dallas. Why take two vehicles on a ten-hour trip?"

"Because if we took one vehicle, one of your children would not survive the trip and there'd be a funeral to plan."

"Oh, Abigail, so you're really *not* over it?"

"Have they set a date yet?" she asked in a clipped tone. "I mean, it's been two years. What are they waiting on?"

"Well, he did hint that they might have some news. I can only hope that means they're finally getting married." Her mother cleared her throat. "I know you don't want to talk about that. So…when do you plan to come up?"

She could opt for the day after. The later she got there, the less time she'd have to be around them. Or she could go the day before and get settled in and establish her territory before the happy couple arrived. She leaned her head back and slowly shook her head.

"I don't know yet, Mom. I'll let you know."

"But, honey, it's only six weeks away. I have meals to plan. Your father is going to take a few days off from the ski lodge, or so he says. I wanted him to take the whole ten days off—I mean, he is retired, after all—but he insists they need him there. I swear, he's working more than ever. Do try to come on that Thursday, honey. We'll do our annual Christmas lights tour on Christmas Eve. Of course, we'll do our fancy Christmas Day dinner, like always. And you'll need to let your father know what days you want to ski. He'll get lift tickets in advance for you."

Whatever days Aaron and Holly weren't skiing, that's when she'd go. But she would save that request for later.

"I better get back to work, Mom."

"That's it? But we haven't decided anything yet."

"I will be there on or before the twenty-third. How's that?"

"Before? Oh, that would be wonderful. I'll tell your father."

She smiled at her mother's exuberance. "Love you, Mom. Talk soon."

She rested her head in her hands, wondering what in the world she was going to do. It had been nearly unbearable last year. That is, until the morning she'd found herself in bed with Holly, her ex of two years now. That had pushed her stress level to new heights, and she'd fled Red River four days early, blaming some crisis at work that demanded her attention. She'd not seen nor spoken to her brother nor Holly since then.

And now Christmas was rolling around again. *Oh joy.*

CHAPTER TWO

At noon, Abby hurried into the courtyard, the common area between the three towering office buildings, hoping Sharon had beaten her there. The lunch crowd was crazy today as the first real cold front of autumn had chased away the lingering summer heat that had been holding on for dear life, it seemed. She saw a few empty tables but instead of grabbing one, she scanned the area, finally seeing someone waving at her. She smiled at her friend, then sidestepped two men who rushed to grab one of the remaining tables.

"I almost like the heat of summer better. At least we get our pick of tables then." She looked longingly at their usual spot, the table under the big oak that provided them shade even during the hot summer months. Four chatty ladies were there, all talking at once as they gossiped.

"It's like they just crawled out of the woodwork. I don't even recognize half these people."

Abby eyed Sharon's lunch as she sat down. "You went to the cafeteria?"

"Yeah, I slipped out early. What did you bring?"

"Same old boring turkey sandwich." She pulled it from her backpack along with the small snack bag of chips. Instead of eating, though, she let out a heavy sigh. "My mother called this morning."

Sharon stabbed a fork into her salad. "And?"

"And it's November."

"And?"

Abby rolled her eyes. "She wanted to talk about Christmas."

"You love Christmas."

Abby looked at her pointedly.

"Oh." Sharon waved her hand in the air. "Because you can't control yourself with your ex, you're afraid to go?" Then she laughed. "Can't believe you slept with her last year."

"I can control myself. I told you, she flirted with me the whole time I was there. Right in front of my brother, too. What was I supposed to do? Ignore her?"

"Umm, yeah. Or tell your brother what she was doing." Sharon shook her head. "That whole thing is so messed up. I can't really see you two together anyway. Can't believe you're still hung up on her."

"You've never even met her."

"I saw pictures and I've heard stories. She's not you. You didn't fit together. I see you with someone a little more…sporty."

Abby smiled at her friend. She and Sharon first met out here seven years ago and became fast friends. "Courtyard friends" is what Sharon called them. They knew everything about each other's lives, yet they'd never once met up after work or on weekends. They were the epitome of work friends, even though they not only worked for different companies, but they also worked in different buildings.

"Yes, you're right. We didn't fit. We had little in common, true." She finally opened her sandwich. "It was just one of those things. Besides, we were together all of six months. I'm over it."

"If you're over it, then why are you dreading Christmas for the second year in a row?" Sharon grinned at her. "Afraid you'll end up in bed with her again?"

Abby groaned. "Yes. I'm…I'm still attracted to her, I guess. But it's been a year. Maybe it's gone away. Regardless, I had too much wine and, like I said, she flirted with me nonstop . I finally broke."

"Are you sure you didn't sleep with her just to get back at your brother?"

"Get back at him? If Aaron is stupid enough to date a lesbian, then it's his own damn fault that she cheated on him."

"Cheated on him with *you*, let's don't forget."

Abby held up her hand. "I don't want to talk about it. That was a year ago. My problem now is *this* year."

"So don't go. Simple as that."

"I can't not go for Christmas. My mother would kill me. Besides, I love Christmas." She leaned her elbows on the table, her sandwich forgotten. "I've kinda been thinking…maybe I should take a date along."

"To Red River? Are you dating someone that you didn't tell me about?"

"You know I'm not. And, yeah, that could be a problem. But what I was thinking was, I'd just get a fake date. Someone to keep me accountable and not let Holly get to me."

Sharon stared at her. "That's weird, Abby. Even for you."

"I think it would be perfect. I won't have to worry about Holly flirting with me then. I won't have to go out of my way to avoid her and my brother. I know my mother would love it. Did I tell you how stressful it was last year? It's like everyone was walking on eggshells the whole time."

"I imagine so. This would be, what? The third Christmas with her?"

Abby sighed. "Yes. I took her with me two years ago. She and my brother hit it off so much so that they slept together. She broke up with me on the last day and rode back to Dallas with him."

"And last year she and your brother came as a couple, yet she flirted with you, and you ended up sleeping together. Crazy, I tell you."

"And this year, I want to go armed. If I have a date, then nothing out of the ordinary should happen. I don't care how much she flirts with me."

"I remember you dreaded going last year. If you think having a fake date will be better, then go for it."

"My brother and I—well, there's always been this edge to our relationship. He's four years older than I am, yet there's this competition there. I'm convinced that's the only reason he went after Holly in the first place."

"So, is she gay or not?"

"Who the hell knows? I only know that in six weeks, I'll have to see them. Her. I don't plan to go alone this time."

"Who are you going to take? One of your friends?"

"I don't know. I've been thinking about who I could ask, and it just seems weird to pretend to be in love with one of my friends. I'm not sure we could pull it off." She took her first bite of her sandwich, then put it down. "What if I hired someone?"

Sharon picked out a piece of chicken from her salad. "Hire someone? You're insane. Who does that?"

"I want to enjoy Christmas. I want to enjoy my time with my parents. I don't want to have to worry about being alone with Holly or having her flirt with me whenever Aaron is not around. I'm weak when it comes to her. I'll break. It's too stressful. It took years off my life, I'm sure."

"And like I said, if you really don't want anything to do with her, call her on it."

"That's just it. I don't know if I don't want anything to do with her. Right now, of course, I can say emphatically no. But when we're alone and she makes it clear that she wants to sleep with me, who knows?"

"So tell him what she does. Hell, tell him you slept together last year." She waved her hand in the air. "You're making too big a deal out of it."

"He would never believe me. He thinks I'm obsessed over the fact that they are seeing each other."

"And aren't you?"

"I am not! I don't even give them a thought." That much was true. It was also true that she and her brother no longer had a relationship, but that was irrelevant.

Sharon tapped her arm. "What about that one? She looks like she's gay."

Abby frowned. "That one what?"

"For you to hire." She casually motioned to Abby's left. "Two tables over."

Abby slowly turned, seeing a young woman sitting alone. She was wearing shorts and what appeared to be very dirty sneakers. Her hair was dark, cut short over her ears, and she was wearing sunglasses. The side view she had of her wasn't enough to assess her looks, but she didn't have to. She'd seen the woman before, earlier in the summer. And within the last month or so, she'd seen her about once a week, out here in the courtyard, always eating alone, always wearing shorts and dark sunglasses. Definitely not dressed for one of the offices that called the Las Colinas Towers home.

"Where do you think she works? I've seen her out here before."

Sharon shrugged. "Her knees are dirty. Maybe she's crashing the place. Looks like she's got a tray from the cafeteria, though."

Abby shook her head, pulling her gaze from the woman. "Anyway, no. When I said hire someone, I didn't mean a complete stranger. I meant, you know, maybe a friend of a friend or something like that."

"And they wouldn't be a stranger to you?"

She took another bite of her sandwich. "You think I'm crazy?"

"You think?"

CHAPTER THREE

Abby paced in her small office, cell phone in hand. "What about Jessica?"

"Jessica? Christine's ex?"

"Yes."

"First of all, Christine would never speak to you again," Beth said.

"It would just be a fake date!"

"Second of all, Jessica is psycho. You do not want to spend ten days with her. You'd be better off with Holly."

"God, how hard is it to find a fake date?" she groaned.

"Okay, I wasn't going to come right out and say it, but, Abby, this plan of yours is really kinda weird."

"Oh, Beth, I know. Don't you think I know? I only have four more weeks. Isn't there *someone* you know who would go with me? Free room and board. Free skiing. A white Christmas. Don't you know *someone*? *Anyone*?"

"I told you I would go with you."

Abby laughed. "Yes, but you haven't asked Jenna. I'm fairly certain she would nix that idea."

"Yeah, she would. Speaking of Jenna, I should go. We have a lunch date and I'm up to my eyeballs in reports."

"Okay," she said with a sigh. "Talk to you later."

"Bye, Abby. Oh, and don't forget, we're putting up our tree on Saturday. Come over if you want to get in on the holiday cheer. There'll be eggnog."

She sighed again. "Maybe." She knew she probably wouldn't go though. She simply had *no* holiday cheer yet and she wasn't in the mood to get any. Besides, she hated eggnog.

She placed her phone on her desk and went to stand by the window. She looked out over the courtyard, watching a few people milling about. It was only ten thirty. Too early for the lunch crowd.

Maybe her friends were right. It was a ridiculous plan, wasn't it? Maybe she should just go alone and deal with Holly—and whatever came up—like an adult. Maybe she should make amends with her brother. They both lived in the Metroplex. How had they avoided seeing each other for nearly two years now?

She was about to turn away from the window when she saw her—the woman from the courtyard. She was wearing jeans today, not shorts. Well, it was nearly December, even if it was sunny and warm outside. The woman came from between the other two buildings, pushing a wheelbarrow. Inside were colorful flowers. Her first thought was, who plants flowers this late in the year? Then she remembered that the courtyard was filled with seasonal flowers all year long—yes, even in winter.

So, who was this woman? Was she on the maintenance crew? No, she didn't think they tended to the grounds. Maybe she worked for a landscaping company or something. She watched her for a moment longer, surprised that she was picturing the woman in shorts and not jeans. The woman stopped then and—as if sensing her watching—tilted her head up, glancing in Abby's direction. She didn't turn away. She knew no one could see in the tinted windows. The woman finally went back to her task and Abby moved to her desk. It wasn't like she didn't have any work to do.

The consulting firm she worked for employed over one hundred people, with most of them housed here in Las Colinas. While she'd started out as a business analyst, her degree was in marketing, and she'd been promoted to marketing manager last year. The "manager" title was a bit ambiguous seeing as how she only had six people who reported to her. She, on the other hand, was one of eleven managers who reported to the vice president.

She slid her laptop closer to her, opening the file she'd been looking at earlier. It was an analysis of the quarterly sales report her team had put together on one of the companies they represented. Depending on the trends, she would either recommend they go with a different advertising firm or give the current one another quarter. That is, if she could negotiate a contract for only one quarter.

She was deep into it when the reminder on her phone sounded. Lunch. With a quick glance at the clock—it was 11:55—she closed the laptop and slid her chair back. She looked out the window as she passed, seeing some of the tables filling up already. She hurried to the tiny breakroom on their floor to get her lunch bag and a bottle of water from the fridge.

She ignored Clara, the older woman who always sat inside the breakroom at lunch. As was the norm, Clara had her nose stuck in a book and never looked up, her cue that she didn't want to be interrupted.

Abby went back out into the hallway to wait at the elevator with several others. She smiled and nodded at them, but they were all in their own groups, talking among themselves. Once she'd been named a manager, she found her circle of work friends had changed. That circle had gotten quite a bit smaller. When the elevator dinged, everyone stood back, letting her get on first. Well, being a manager had its perks, she supposed.

As usual, Sharon had beat her outside, and she'd snagged their favorite table under the oak tree. Today she was eating an apple.

Abby raised an eyebrow as she sat down.

"I read that if you eat an apple before your meal, it'll help in weight loss," Sharon said as she bit into it.

"Are you on a new diet again? I thought you were doing that Paleo thing or something."

"I tried it for a month. Did you know you can't eat grains or beans?"

She took out her sandwich. "Yes, I remember you complaining about that."

"You know how I love my rice and bean burritos."

She took a bite. "From El Arroyo, yes."

"Yes. So I decided that the Paleo Diet was not for me."

"So now what? The apple diet?"

Sharon glared at her and pointed the apple in her direction. "Look, just because you're thin as a rail doesn't mean—"

"I am not thin as a rail. Your problem is, you skip breakfast and then you eat rabbit food for lunch. By dinner time, you're starving and go on a food binge. Eat some damn breakfast."

"I'm not hungry in the mornings."

"That's because you've stuffed yourself silly the night before." She opened her bag of chips. "So, listen, what are you doing for the holidays? Want to go to Red River with me?"

Sharon laughed. "Still haven't found a date, huh?"

"No."

"Well, I think my husband might miss me. You think?"

"I suppose."

"You still have a few more weeks." She tapped the table. "There she is again."

Abby knew who she was talking about before she turned her head. "Yes, she's cute, but she looks a little too earthy for me."

"Earthy?"

"That's a polite way of saying she has dirt on her knees, like usual. Not my type."

"Do you need a type? I thought it was a fake date." She motioned to her. "Go ask her."

"I will not! She's a stranger. How would that look? I proposition her? She'll think I'm crazy."

Sharon smiled. "No doubt. But you're the one who thinks you need a fake date."

"I've accepted that I'll go alone and endure whatever happens. Alone. And no, I won't sleep with Holly. No matter how much wine I've had or how much she flirts with me. I won't do it. There! I've said it. So, I'm okay with it. I have to be." She turned her head to look at the "earthy" woman. Yeah, she was cute. She was sitting at a table near one of the flowerbeds, out in the sunshine. She had on sunglasses again today. Her jeans had dirt stains on each knee and some on the side, as if she'd wiped her hand there. Instead of a cafeteria tray, she had a white bag with orange stripes advertising Whataburger, and she had her meal spread out before her. "She is attractive, though," she said, voicing her thoughts. Then she held up her hand. "But no, I will not ask her to be my fake date. Even *I'm* not that crazy."

As she stared, the woman turned her head, looking right at her. Or so she thought. The dark sunglasses shielded her eyes and Abby quickly turned away.

CHAPTER FOUR

Two weeks later, Abby stood there—like an idiot—staring at the woman. Sharon had talked her into it. Sharon had sent her away from their table in a near fit of giggles at the prospect. It was the phone call that did it. Her mother again. And yes, as expected, Aaron and Holly would be announcing their wedding plans over the holidays. Her response to the news had been feigned nonchalance and indifference. As she'd told her mother—and herself—she couldn't care less about it all. She was fairly certain that Holly wouldn't be the first lesbian to get married. It was the second bit of news, though, that threw her.

"I think they want to do an early summer wedding. I hope it's here in Red River since that was where they met, but they may want to do it in Dallas where their friends are. And honey, now don't take this wrong, but as a thanks to you for introducing them, Aaron thinks you should be the maid of honor. Holly is in agreement. Isn't that wonderful?"

Abby had literally spit out her coffee, spraying her laptop in the process. *Maid of fucking honor? Are they out of their freakin' minds?*

So here she stood, about to make a fool of herself in front of a complete stranger. If the woman didn't call the police and charge her with solicitation, it would be a miracle. The woman turned to her, arching one eyebrow above the rim of her sunglasses. A smile followed, and Abby found herself returning it.

"May I help you with something?" the woman asked.

Abby thought she was much more attractive up close like this than she'd previously imagined. Another arch of an eyebrow—a move that she found infinitely sexy—brought her out of her stupor.

"I'm...I'm Abby Carpenter."

The woman nodded. "Nic Bennett. And what can I do for you, Abby Carpenter?"

She took her sunglasses off, and Abby was surprised to find blue eyes looking back at her. With the woman's dark hair, she'd expected equally dark eyes, but no, a deep and vivid blue stared at her.

"Well, let me start by saying, I'm not really crazy."

A smile. "That's good to know. Not sure if that's a great opening line or not."

Abby looked behind her to where Sharon was still sitting. Sharon gave her a wide grin and a thumbs up. Abby turned back to the woman—to Nic Bennett. "I...I have a proposition."

That statement was met with both eyebrows raising. "Okay," she said slowly. "Are you asking me out?"

"Out?"

"Like on a date? Because I've seen you out here before, thought you were watching me."

Abby tilted her head back and looked into the sky, cursing Sharon for making her do this. "I'm not really asking you out on a date, no. Not like a *real* date. That's not why I was watching you."

Nic motioned to the extra chair. "Why don't you sit down? You can tell me why you've been staring at me."

"I have not been staring at you!"

The woman grinned. "We both know you have." She motioned again to the chair. "Have a seat."

Wow, she was a bit arrogant, wasn't she? Something told her she should turn around and leave. But those blue eyes were smiling at her, and Abby sat down, her hands clasped together nervously in her lap. God, why hadn't she rehearsed this? Why had she let Sharon talk her into this? Oh, yeah. Maid of fucking honor.

"So, if I *was* going to ask you out…do you date women?"

"I do."

"Okay, good," she said with relief. "So, Nic, do you have plans for Christmas?"

"Plans?"

"Oh, crap," she sighed. "Look, I'll just come out and say it, okay. And yes, I am kinda asking you out. But not on a real date," she said again. "And I know you're going to think I'm crazy, that's why I told you up front that I wasn't." She paused only a beat. "I need a date. A girlfriend. For ten days. In Red River, New Mexico. For the holidays. With my family. And my ex."

Nic simply stared at her, not even blinking. Abby rushed on.

"My brother is dating my ex. Dating, living together, whatever," she said with a wave of her hand. "Two years ago, I brought Holly with me at Christmas. My parents live in Red River. That's where we spend the holidays. Holly met my brother, slept with him, broke up with me on New Year's Eve. Then last year, they came together as a couple. She flirted with me until I broke. So I slept with her." She held her hand up. "Yes, that was foolish on my part, I admit, and I'm certainly not proud of that. Now, *this* year, I have it on good authority that they are going to announce their wedding plans. Early summer. Since I introduced them, I get to be the freakin' maid of honor." She paused. "Did I mention they live here in the Metroplex and I no longer speak to my brother?"

Nic's lips twitched in a smile. "Wow. All of that? For real? I mean, if you want to ask me out, just ask. You don't need all of this."

"You think I'm making this shit up?"

Nic leaned back in her chair, a smile still on her face. "Okay. So you need a girlfriend…why?"

"Well, a couple of reasons. One, so that she won't flirt with me and try to get me into bed again. And two, so I'm not the pathetic jaded lover, daughter, and sister who everyone feels sorry for. And maybe three, so that everyone doesn't walk on eggshells every time Holly and I are in a room together."

"Why did you sleep with her?"

"Because I'm an idiot. And I had too much wine. And I'd not really dated anyone since we broke up, so…"

"So, sex with your ex sounded like fun?"

"At the time, yes," she said through gritted teeth. Why, oh why had she listened to Sharon?

Nic scratched her neck absently. "Okay, let me just talk this out so I can wrap my head around it. You brought your girlfriend with you for a family Christmas thing. She and your brother had sex. I'm assuming you didn't know."

"Of course I didn't know!"

"And you were also having sex with her? Ew, that's gross."

Abby sighed.

"Okay, so she breaks up with you and is now dating your brother. But last year, even though she's with your brother—having sex—you sleep with her too. Again, gross."

"Must you?"

"And now they're getting married, and you still think she'll try to sleep with you?"

"Of course. Why wouldn't she?"

"Why *would* she?"

Abby narrowed her eyes. "What are you saying? That I'm not good enough?"

Nic held her hand up. "I meant no such thing. I meant, if she's planning on marrying your brother, why is she still trying to get into your bed?"

"Because she's insane, that's why!" Abby snapped.

"And you're not over her? Still dream about her? Still love her? Still—"

"No, no, no. No, I do not still love her. We were together only six months. I don't know if I was *ever* in love with her. It's just…" What? She sighed. "Yes, I'm over her." Surely to god she was.

"Then? What's the problem?"

"She doesn't think that I'm over her. She'll flirt incessantly with me, just to prove it. I'll cave and sleep with her again and she'll have won once again. It's a freakin' game with her."

"So it's a competition thing and you're weak?"

Abby narrowed her eyes. "Yes. Okay. Let's go with that. I'm weak." It was the truth, wasn't it?

Nic leaned her elbows on the table. "So to combat all that, you need a date. And you want *me* to be your date?"

"Yes."

"Why? You're attractive and, dare I say, seemingly sane. Sort of. I doubt you'd have a hard time finding a date. Why me? A stranger."

"Because it would just be pretend and if I took someone I might actually consider dating someday, then that would complicate things too much. And I thought about asking a friend, but how do you pretend to be in love with one of your friends? It would never work." As soon as she said the words, she realized how it sounded.

"But you could pretend to be in love with a stranger? Me?"

"Okay, look, I already asked all of my friends, and none will do it and none of their friends will do it. They all think I'm crazy. And now I'm desperate." She paused. "You're probably seeing someone, aren't you? Of course you are. That could be a problem, I guess. But if you explain that it's all pretend and—"

"I'm not really dating anyone, no."

Abby frowned. "You're not? Why? What's wrong with you?"

"Me?" Nic laughed. "You're seriously asking what's wrong with *me*?"

Abby smiled sheepishly. "Sorry. You're right. I'm the crazy one here. But it's a legitimate proposition. It's all expenses paid. My father works at the ski lodge and gets lift tickets free. My mother will provide all the meals. It's a chance for a white Christmas and as much skiing as you can stand. Snowmobiles, too, if you want. A trip down to Taos if you like shopping. It'll be like a free vacation for you."

Nic smiled at her. "A free vacation and I'll get to share your bed? Tempting."

"I'm desperate." She met those blue eyes. "Please? I'm running out of time. And options."

"Well, I will admit I'm intrigued. Let me think about it. What days are we talking here?"

"We would drive up on either the twenty-second or twenty-third. Come back on New Year's Day, if you'd like. I usually stay until the second of January, but we can come back earlier than that even."

Nic nodded. "Okay. I'll think about it. I'll be back here next week on Thursday. Is that soon enough?"

Abby frowned. "Where do you work, anyway?"

"Bennett Landscaping. My uncle's company. We have a contract here at Las Colinas Towers. I come by once or twice a week."

"I've seen you around, yes."

"I know. I've seen you looking at me."

"Again, I've *not* been looking at you."

"Right. So we'll hook up next week, then."

Abby stood. "Yes. Okay. Thank you for considering my proposition. I know it's…well, a bit outrageous. I'll see you next week."

She hurried over to Sharon without looking back at Nic Bennett. She wondered if Nic was short for something. Nicole maybe?

"So? What did she say? What did she say?"

"She said she would consider it." Abby reached into the bag of chips and pulled one out. "I'm pretty sure she thinks I'm borderline nuts. Hell, *I* think I'm teetering on the edge myself." Then she leaned closer. "She's really cute. She has blue eyes." She sighed. "Something must be terribly wrong with her. She's single. Women who look like that aren't single."

"You're single."

"I have trust issues. Can you blame me?"

"What's her name?"

"Nic Bennett. She works for a landscaping company."

"That explains the dirty knees." Sharon made a face. "Not really your type, though."

"I don't care. At this point, I simply don't care. I just need a girlfriend." She paused. "She was kinda flirty. Kinda conceited."

"Conceited?"

"She thinks I've been staring at her. Watching her."

"And haven't you?"

"Not like that. Not like I'm ogling her or anything."

"Well, she is cute."

"Yeah. Conceited like that. She's cute and she knows it. Women like that are nothing but trouble. I would never date someone like that." Of course, Holly came to mind. Holly with her perfect hair and perfect teeth. Her expensive clothes and expertly done makeup.

"But you would fake date her?"

"I'm desperate."

"Even if she agrees to it, I still don't see how you're going to pull this off."

"Oh, please. How hard can it be?"

CHAPTER FIVE

Nic stood beside the grill, watching as Eric cleaned the grate before adding the burgers. Addison, his wife, had just brought them two beers—a Bud Light for him and a Shiner Bach for her. While she thought she'd be better served having this conversation with Addison, she'd already gone back inside to get the patties. Eric might be more receptive to the idea, though. They'd gotten into their share of mischief in college, double dates and all. Of course, now that he was married with a baby on the way, he'd settled down quite a bit. He might not think of this offer as the possible adventure she did.

"So…I had a proposition the other day," she started.

He glanced at her, then turned his attention back to the grill. "Something good?"

"Depends how you look at it, I suppose."

He turned to her then. "And?"

"Some woman—a stranger—invited me to Red River for Christmas."

He frowned. "New Mexico?"

"Yeah. For skiing and stuff."

He took a swallow of his beer. "You don't ski, Nicky."

"Well, yeah, there's that. She wants me to pretend to be her girlfriend."

"*What?*" He held his hand up. "Okay, wait, start over. *What?*"

She laughed. "So this really cute woman comes up to me, out of the blue, and says she needs a fake date for Christmas. With her family. For ten days."

"Are you serious? Who does that?"

"Right? No one does that."

"So, is she a weird psycho type?"

"I don't think so. At first, I thought it was just her attempt to ask me out."

"And we all know *you* like to be the one doing the asking."

"I know. I'm picky that way. But anyway, no, she looked perfectly normal. Attractive, in fact."

He shook his head. "Don't do it. She's probably a crazy woman." He pointed his finger at her. "I know you! You're thinking about doing it, aren't you?"

She smiled. "Could be kinda fun."

"For ten days? With a family you've never met? With a woman you don't know? That's insane." He looked up as Addison came back out. "Babe, listen to this. Nic got invited to go skiing in Red River for ten days. At Christmas."

"How nice." Addison patted her arm. "You don't know how to ski, do you? That could be a problem, Nicky."

"She was really cute, though."

"Oh, well, that makes all the difference. Don't ski into a tree."

"That's what you tell her?" Eric held his hands up. "I told her she was insane."

Nic smiled at him. "And here I thought you'd be all in favor of it."

He shook his head. "Why can't you do normal dating? You meet someone, you go out, you fall in love. Why do you always have these weird dates?"

She stared at him. "Because I don't want to fall in love. I've told you that a hundred times."

"And I've told you a hundred times, you can't use your parents as your role models. That whole situation shouldn't define your future."

She sighed. "But it does."

"Who's it with?" Addison asked.

"Yeah. Tell her that part, Nic."

She glanced at Addison. "So, I don't actually know her. At all. In fact, I just met her the one time when she approached me at lunch."

Addison drew her brows together. "What? Wait." She held a hand up. "A strange woman came up to you and asked you to go skiing with her for Christmas? Is this one of your stalkers?"

"I don't think so, but yeah, I have noticed her watching me."

"Tell her the rest," Eric prodded. "Tell her about the girlfriend part."

Nic grinned. "Well, she kinda needs a date. Her ex is now dating her brother and last year at Christmas, she slept with the ex. So this year, she wants to avoid that scenario." She pointed at herself. "I'm to pretend to be her girlfriend."

"Oh my god! No! You're so not going! Nic, that's just weird. Who goes up to a complete stranger and asks them to pretend to be a girlfriend? Eric is right. You're crazy to consider it. What if she's a serial killer or something and she's trying to lure you away?"

"You guys, no. It wasn't like that. I didn't get any bad vibes from her at all. She was really apologetic about the whole thing. She knew it sounded weird, she said that several times." She smiled at Addison. "Did I tell you she was really cute?"

Addison squeezed her arm. "I'm with Eric, Nicky. I wish you could meet someone *normal*. I wish you'd stop all this crazy stuff you've been doing."

"I don't want to meet anyone normal. I don't have anything to offer anyone normal," she said. "But I wouldn't mind another beer."

"So this woman intrigues you and you've already made up your mind?"

"Well, it'll be something different." Sure it would. But she did remember the look of desperation in her eyes—Abby Carpenter. "It might be fun."

"But it's Christmas. Would you really leave your uncle alone for the holidays?"

"It's perfect, really. One of his buddies wants him to go to Vegas with him, but he's hesitating because he doesn't want to leave me alone. I told him to go, that I could hang out with you two, but he hasn't made up his mind." She shrugged. "You know me and Christmas. Just a day to get past."

Addison squeezed her arm. "I hate that you still feel that way."

"Oh, it is what it is. I think I'm too old to change."

Addison took the empty beer bottle from her. "We'll miss you being around." She paused before going back for more beers. "What's she like?"

Nic shrugged. "Don't know anything about her. Abby Carpenter. Kinda dirty-blond hair, about to her shoulders, light brown eyes." She smiled. "Cute. That's all that matters to me."

It could be fun, she reasoned. A game. Abby needed a girlfriend. She could play along. Wonder how long it'll take to *really* get into her bed? Two days? Maybe three, she conceded. They could have a little fun. No attachments to worry about. Not like real dating where she had to keep her distance and run when she felt they were getting too close. She wouldn't have to worry how she'd untangle herself from this one. Ten days. Then they'd part company and go their separate ways. It could be perfect.

She smiled at Addison. "Maybe I'll actually find some holiday spirit there. It'll be my one and only white Christmas. Who knows? Maybe I'll come back a changed woman. I may actually *like* Christmas from now on."

CHAPTER SIX

Abby was too anxious to eat, and she tapped the table with her fingers nervously. Sharon finally stilled her hand.

"What is wrong with you?"

"What if she says no?"

"Then you still have a few days to look for someone else."

Abby met her gaze. "What if she says yes?"

Sharon frowned. "Isn't that what you want?"

"Sharon, I don't even *know* this woman. What if she turns out to be a lunatic or something?"

"Says the woman who asked a stranger to be her date."

"Right. It was crazy. So if she accepts, what does that say about *her*?" Sharon actually rolled her eyes at her. "What? I'm just sayin'."

"If you make it through the holidays with your sanity it'll be a miracle." She stabbed part of a boiled egg from her salad. "I'm really starting to worry about you."

Abby blew out her breath. "If she says no, then I've just got to suck it up and go alone. It won't be the end of the world. It'll be a horrible Christmas, but I'll get over it. And I'm going to take your advice. If Holly flirts with me, I'm going to tattle to Aaron about it." She grinned. "Or maybe I'll sleep with her."

Sharon laughed. "Well, it's been a year. Unless there's been someone you've not told me about."

"Sadly, no. But—oh, there she is! She's looking for me." Abby ducked her head down. "What should I do? Should I hide?"

"You should wave at her and get her attention. Geez, you're losing your mind."

Abby watched as Nic Bennett made her way through the courtyard, glancing around as she went. She was wearing baggy jeans again today and a long-sleeved T-shirt. Maybe she wasn't looking for her. Maybe she was trying to decide where she wanted to sit. But no. She *was* looking for her. Oh god. What if she said yes? Was it too late to take back the invitation? She should, shouldn't she? Beth had told her she was completely insane to even consider taking a stranger as her date. With all her friends tossing around the "crazy" and "insane" words, she was starting to question her mental stability.

But then Nic Bennett found her and smiled at her. Abby stared as she came toward their table. Her blue eyes seemed brilliant today. Her smile was friendly. She found herself returning it.

"Hi."

"Hello, Abby." Nic turned to Sharon. "Hi. I'm Nic."

"Sharon. Nice to meet you." Then Sharon looked at her and winked. "I'm done with this scrumptious salad," she said dramatically. "I think I'll go see if I can find some low-calorie dessert. You want anything?"

"No thanks. See you later."

Nic claimed Sharon's chair when she left. They both sat there, looking at each other without speaking. Abby wondered how she could gracefully get out of the deal. If it was necessary, that is. Maybe Nic was going to say no. Yes, that's what she hoped. Wasn't it?

"I…I should apologize for this crazy scheme I came up with. You've had time to ponder it and you probably think I'm nuts. I don't blame you."

Nic smiled at her. "Well, some of my friends thought you were nuts, yes."

"Oh, mine too! Well, I don't mean about me, I meant the plan." Then she paused. "Okay, so yeah, some thought *me*, but most were warning me that you might be…well, a serial killer or something."

"That's funny. That's what Addison said about you. She and Eric are my best friends. College buddies." Then she leaned forward. "But I'm not the one who invited *you* on a trip so the serial killer thing probably wouldn't apply to me."

Abby held her hand up. "Look, I'm really not crazy. I was desperate, that's all, and dreading the whole holiday thing so—" Let's forget it, she was about to say. But no. Nic was apparently thinking something entirely different.

"I think it'll be fun."

Abby's eyes widened. "What? Are you seriously considering it?" She stared as Nic actually winked at her. *A wink?* Why was she winking at her? What did that mean?

"It's almost like it's an invitation I couldn't possibly turn down."

"Oh my god. So you'll do it? Seriously?"

"Sure. I mean, I guess so. It's certainly the most entertaining proposition I've ever had. And I've had a few." She tossed a business card her way. "My cell number is on there."

Abby didn't know what to say. Should she say thank you? Should she say she'd changed her mind? *Had* she changed her mind? Or was she really going to go through with this? She glanced at the card, then shoved it into her pocket.

"So…I'm not really sure how this works," Nic continued. "Do we do a crash course on getting to know each other? Or do we pop in as new girlfriends, so we really aren't that familiar with each other?" Nic eyed her suspiciously. "Do you have a plan?" She raised an eyebrow. "You do, right? A plan? You have one?"

"Honestly, I didn't expect you to say yes. So my plan was to go alone and try to avoid Holly and Aaron as much as possible and hope she left me alone." She mindlessly pulled a chip out of the bag. "Are you sure you want to do this?" She turned the bag toward Nic, offering her some. She took a handful on her first grab.

"Sure, why not? I've never had a white Christmas before."

"You haven't? We've been going to Red River for as long as I can remember. It was my grandparents' place. It's a huge mountain lodge and very beautiful. But they wanted to go somewhere warmer, and my parents were…well, they needed a change—they were both in real estate here in Dallas—so they bought the house from them, and the Christmas tradition continued. My grandparents live in Tempe now, and they'll come up for a few days too."

"Wow. So the whole family, huh?"

She smiled at her. "Having second thoughts?"

"No, no. I'm good. Always up for a challenge."

Abby gave an exaggerated smile. "I find alcohol helps. That's my stress relief while I'm there."

"Is it that stressful?"

"Yes. Well, ever since the whole Holly thing." She paused. "Although me and Aaron, we've never been warm and fuzzy. There's always this tension between us. I'm not really a big drinker normally and I don't know that Aaron is, but for these few days, yeah, we indulge. My mother is all wine, all the time. My father hates wine, so there is always scotch or bourbon. My brother likes beer, but he'll join my father for a cocktail too. And…" —she paused a beat— "And Holly likes wine too, but margaritas are her favorite. They make her *frisky*," she said with a shudder. "Her word, not mine."

Nic laughed. "I like tequila too. Not a big fan of wine. I may join your father for a cocktail."

Abby stared at her. "Do you think we can pull this off?"

"Oh sure," Nic said with a smile. "But maybe we should go with the new girlfriend thing."

"Like we just met?" She shook her head. "My mother would be suspicious. I'm usually very cautious when I meet someone new."

"Cautious?"

"Yes. Like I don't just jump in right away."

"Ah. Like no kissing on the first date?"

"I'm saying, if we just met, I'm not very likely to invite you to meet the family. Not for a ten-day stay, that's for sure. I think we should go with we've been dating for a couple of months, at least."

"Okay. That's still new-girlfriend territory. That means we're having sex and lots of it." Nic wiggled her eyebrows. "We'll have to be a little more handsy, but that's certainly okay with me."

Abby stared at her blankly. *Handsy*?

"And you'll need to tell me what to pack. I've not been in the snow before. Ever."

Handsy? Abby shook that away. "You've not? So you don't ski?"

"Afraid not. Now, I can water ski. Is it similar?"

"Umm, I don't know. I've never been water skiing. But they do offer lessons, of course. You look athletic. I'm sure you can learn."

Nic took another few chips without asking. "How cold will it be?"

Abby moved the bag before Nic stole all of them, and held her hand up. "Okay, wait. Why are you agreeing to this?"

Nic frowned. "Because you asked."

"I'm a stranger. Why would you agree to go somewhere for ten days with someone you don't know?"

Nic met her gaze. "Okay, is this like a test or something?"

"No, it's not a test!" She leaned closer. "What did you mean about being handsy?" Then her eyes widened. "Oh my god! You think we're going to have *sex*? Like for *real*? Are you out of your mind?"

"I'm beginning to think one of us might be," Nic murmured just loud enough for her to hear.

Abby took a deep breath. "You're right. I was completely out of my mind when I asked you. I admit, I freaked out a little, especially about the maid of honor thing." She waved her hand in the air. "We should forget the whole thing. Forget I asked. I'm sure you're a very lovely person, but—"

"Well, you see, I've already cancelled my Christmas plans with my uncle. So, I've got like ten or twelve days free." She smiled at her. "And I am a very lovely person, yes. And sex? Well, yeah, I assumed. I mean, we're going to be kissing and touching and all that stuff. I assumed that would carry over to our bedroom. For real."

Abby's brows drew together sharply. "*What?*"

"What?"

"Are you serious?"

"Well, yeah." Nic smiled at her. "I thought that was your plan."

Abby sat back, almost dumbfounded. "What the hell are you talking about?"

Nic gave her a charming smile. A charming smile that bordered on arrogant and conceited, both. Was she really thinking that they'd be *real* girlfriends on this trip?

"I thought you needed a girlfriend. Someone who was head over heels in love with you. You know, to make Holly realize you were so over her."

"Yes. That was my plan." She leaned closer. "That doesn't mean we're going to have sex, for god's sake!" she hissed.

Nic spread her arms out. "Then what's in it for me if not sex?"

"Oh my god," she muttered. She shook her head. "Obviously we're not on the same page. We're not even in the same *book*. What was in it for you was a ten-day vacation to a winter wonderland. Sex was *never* part of the equation," she said pointedly. "So forget the whole thing. I'll find someone else."

She got up abruptly, nearly knocking the chair over.

"I think it's a reasonable tradeoff, Abby. Call it a counteroffer if you will."

"Counteroffer? *Reasonable?* You're out of your mind! We don't even know each other. Why in the world would you assume I'd have sex with you?"

Again, the charming—conceited—smile. "I've never had any complaints. I'll make it good for you. It'll be a Christmas you won't forget."

"Oh my god," she murmured again, holding up her hand. "I'm leaving now. I hope you have a wonderful Christmas. It *won't* be with me."

CHAPTER SEVEN

"Please. Don't you know *anyone?*"

Marcos reached over and stole a fry from her plate. "It's not like I have unlimited lesbians at my disposal, you know."

Abby let out her breath. "I can't believe no one wants to go with me."

"I thought Beth said you had someone lined up."

Abby leaned forward. "Oh my god. She wanted to have sex. She thought I was inviting her along to have sex!"

"And?"

"And? I don't even know this woman! She's a stranger!"

"Yet you invited her on a ten-day trip?"

She held her hand up. "Look. I thought I'd made it clear. Free vacation. That's all. Ten days pretending to be my girlfriend. *Pretending*," she said again with emphasis.

"Have you not slept with anyone since Holly?"

Abby pushed her burger away. "I have deep scars. I'm jaded. I have no faith in mankind any longer."

Marcos rolled his eyes. "So I guess that's a no. Maybe that's your problem. Lack of sex. Go out. Have some fun. Take this stranger with you to Red River and fuck her brains out. Loosen up!"

Abby stared at him. "You've lost your mind too. Because that is *so* not me."

"Well, what do you want? You want me to go with you? Try to convince your family you've fallen for a gay man?"

Abby groaned as she buried her head in her hands. "It shouldn't be this complicated, should it?"

"No, it shouldn't. You're letting Holly—a royal bitch, I might add—get into your head. If you go alone, surely you're strong enough to tell her to fuck off," he said dramatically. "But if I were you, I'd take some cute-ass girl along and rub it in her face. Because I hate that woman. She's caused you nothing but misery. I still don't know what you saw in her, and I still can't believe you slept with her again."

Abby squeezed his arm. "Oh, Marcus, I know. I'm letting it all get to me. I should just go alone—like the grown-ass woman that I am—and deal with it. And tell her to fuck off, like you say." She leaned her elbows on the table, wondering if she could actually say that to Holly. No, most likely, she'd cave as she'd done last year. "Did I tell you about the maid of honor thing?"

He laughed rather loudly. "No, but Beth did. They can't be serious."

"I know, right? It's like they're *trying* to piss me off."

"I say, take the stranger with you. If she's as cute as you say, rub it the hell in Holly's face. Give her a taste of her own medicine."

She finished off the last of her margarita. "Yeah, Nic's really cute. She's got that arrogant bad boy attitude, though. Like the kind of person your parents warned you about but the one you can't resist."

"Oh? So are you—"

"I didn't mean it like that. I *can* resist her. I'm just saying, she's kinda—"

"Like a rebel dream? A woman you'd never consider dating but one you wouldn't mind having a fling with just for sex?"

"Yes. Only, as you know, I don't have flings."

"Well, maybe you should start. It could be fun. No strings." He gave her an exaggerated wink. "You should seriously consider it."

"Oh, Marcos, you know me better than that."

"So you'd rather fall into bed again with Holly?"

"Well, at least Holly's not a stranger," she reasoned.

"No. She's your brother's fiancé. I'd say that's worse."

CHAPTER EIGHT

Abby headed out to the courtyard where Sharon was sitting at their normal table under the oak tree. She smiled at her friend, then sat down across from her.

"Hey. How was your weekend?"

Sharon shook her head. "Michael's parents popped over unannounced on Saturday. The house was an absolute wreck and not primed for company."

"Did they stay the weekend?"

"No. We went out for a very early dinner, and they went back to Waco. I spent all day yesterday cleaning house, doing laundry, and changing the sheets on our bed. I sent Michael to the grocery store to get him out of the house. So, not a fun weekend." She stabbed a fork into her salad. "What about you? Do anything exciting?"

"Marcos took me out for burgers and margaritas yesterday. That was fun."

"You haven't been out with him in a while, have you?"

"No. I hadn't seen him since Thanksgiving."

"And the girlfriend search?"

Abby waved her hand in the air. "No. I've given up on that plan. I'm going alone. As I told Marcos, I'm a grown-ass woman. I can handle it."

Sharon laughed. "If I were you, I'd take Nic up on her offer. It might be the only way you ever have sex again."

Abby gave her a humorless smile, wishing she'd not told Sharon about Nic's offer. Or rather, her counteroffer, as she'd called it. "Very funny. I'm sure I will meet some cute, charming woman someday who will sweep me off my feet." She sighed. "At least, that's my dream. Of course, I'd thought that about Holly once, didn't I?"

"Yes. You thought you'd found your Princess Charming."

"More like wicked stepsister." Then she groaned. "And soon she'll be my wicked sister-in-law."

Sharon pointed her fork at her. "Whatever you do, do *not* sleep with her again. I'm not sure either of us could take that. I think you'd need a professional therapist then, not just me pretending to be one."

Abby laughed. "No. I'm going with the mindset that I will not sleep with her, no matter how much she flirts with me. I won't do it," she said with confidence. "I admit, I was weak last year. I won't make that same mistake again." Right?

"Oh, look! There she is."

Abby turned, finding Nic strolling through the courtyard, holding a tray from the cafeteria. She was wearing jeans. Tight jeans today, not the loose, baggy ones she'd seen before. No, these were curve-clinging, and Abby found herself staring.

"She's cute."

Abby pulled her glance away. "Yeah. And she knows it. You can't trust people like that."

"It seems like she's been here a lot lately. Thursday last week. Here it is Monday and she's already here." Sharon smirked at her. "I think she's here for your benefit."

"What? Parading around in tight jeans so I'll see what I'm missing out on?"

"I saw you staring at her. So that would be a yes."

Abby shook her head. "You know me well enough to know that I don't do anonymous sex."

"Oh, I know. You like to thoroughly vet the person first. So romantic," she said sarcastically.

"It may not be romantic, but it's the sensible thing to do."

"Worked out so well for you with Holly, hmm?"

Abby's comment died on her lips. It was the truth, wasn't it? She'd gone on four dates with Holly before she'd felt comfortable enough to move things past a goodnight kiss. Six dates before they slept together. By then, she felt like she knew Holly, knew who she was and what she was about. Oh, how wrong she'd been. She mentally shook her head. She did not want to rehash the whole Holly thing, even with herself.

"Well, as I said, maybe someday I won't have to be so careful. I'll be swept off my feet by someone without having the chance to dissect them."

"I hope you're right. Because *that* would be romantic."

She sighed. Yeah, it would be nice. Had she ever had romantic? Had she been wined and dined and pampered in a relationship? Certainly not with Holly. Holly was the one who needed pampering. Who else was there? There was Cynthia in college. They'd dated for nearly a year, but she wouldn't call it romantic. It was more just…well, hanging out. Devin? No. That lasted all of ten weeks.

She nibbled at her sandwich. Maybe it was her. Maybe she was expecting too much. Or maybe she was hard to live with. Maybe she was boring and predictable and no fun.

"Why are you frowning?"

She sighed again. "I'm going to be single forever and end up a bitter old woman."

Sharon reached over and patted her hand. "I think you try too hard."

"What does that mean?"

"It means, you meet someone new, and you do your thing, trying to see if they fit into this box that you've designed. You're too rigid, never flexible."

"How else are you supposed to know if someone is right for you? You just can't go date willy-nilly and see what happens. Talk about a waste of time."

"Okay then. You're going to be single forever and end up a bitter old woman." Abby tossed a chip at her which Sharon scooped up and popped into her mouth. "Thank you very much."

"I'm sorry," Abby said sincerely. "I'm a little on edge."

Sharon laughed. "Just a little. Hopefully, when you get back from vacation, you'll be in better humor."

Yes, hopefully she would be. For a few months, at least. Until the freakin' wedding came around, that is. *Maid of honor*, she thought with disgust. *My ass*.

CHAPTER NINE

Abby stood at her window, looking down on the courtyard. Well, she was at the corner of her window with her face pressed against the glass. It was the only way she could see down to where the flowerbeds were. When she'd walked back to her building after lunch, she hadn't seen Nic anywhere. Not that she'd been looking for her. But she'd found herself here, at the window, staring out. Nic and some guy had come from between the buildings, both pushing wheelbarrows loaded with...with something. Dirt or mulch or something. They'd moved to just out of her sight. Well, out of her sight unless she pressed her face against the glass like she was doing now.

She blew out a breath and moved away from the window. "She thought we were going to have sex. *Please*," she muttered as she sat down.

Her phone dinged and she glanced at it, seeing a text message. She picked up the phone, her eyes widening as she read.

Looking forward to seeing you in Red River. We have some catching up to do. Yes?

The message was followed by a winking smiley face. She dropped the phone on her desk as if she'd been clutching a hot coal. Still, she stared at it, finally picking it up and reading the message once again.

"Unbelievable. She's freakin' unbelievable."

She leaned her head down, slowly banging it against her desktop.

* * *

Nic was on her knees, spreading mulch between the pansies and snapdragons. She enjoyed planting flowers, but dressing them up with mulch was a little too tedious for her liking. If it had been anywhere else but here, she would have assigned someone else. But when Cody hadn't made it to work this morning, Jeff needed a partner. She got there right at noon, knowing that was when Abby Carpenter took her lunch break. She didn't know why, but thoughts of the other woman had crept in all weekend long.

She'd obviously been too presumptuous regarding Abby's invitation. But really, had Abby expected her to agree to this trip simply because it was a *free* trip? A free vacation, sure, but it was still taking ten days of her time. She thought she'd be compensated in some way.

She smiled as she dumped out more mulch. Yeah, she'd assumed she'd be compensated in bed. But no. Abby's eyes had turned fiery hot when she realized that she'd been talking about sex. Well, it was a shame Abby felt that way. She thought they could have had fun together.

"Hey, there's some chick coming over," Jeff said from beside her.

Nic sat back on her heels and turned her head, finding a rather flustered-looking Abby Carpenter heading her way. The smile was on her face before she could temper it.

"Wow. To what do I owe the pleasure?"

Abby met her gaze without returning her smile. "Do you have a second?" she asked in a clipped tone.

"Sure."

Then Abby glanced at Jeff. "In private?"

Nic got up and brushed off her knees. "I guess I can take a break." She took her gloves off and knocked them against the side of her jeans to clean them. "Messy job today," she explained.

"Mulch?"

"Yeah. One of the guys called in sick so I thought I'd help out." She smiled at Abby, a charming smile, she hoped. "How nice to run into you. Or rather to have you running into me, I guess."

Abby moved away and she followed. Abby seemed tense and she'd swear that her teeth were gritted.

"Everything okay?"

Abby turned to her then. "I'd like you to…to reconsider going with me to Red River."

Nic frowned. "Umm, I offered to go. I believe it was you who turned me down. So, in essence, it would be *you* who would need to reconsider." Yes, Abby was definitely gritting her teeth.

"I mean, I'd like you to reconsider your reason for going. Your…your counteroffer."

Nic gave a quick laugh. "You mean sex?" Yep, clenched jaw and gritted teeth. She laughed again. "You want me to waste ten days of my life celebrating Christmas with you and your family—all strangers to me—so that Holly doesn't try to get into your bed. And all I get out of the deal is a free ski vacation, which would be great and all if I actually knew how—or wanted—to ski. So basically, I'm getting cold weather, snow, ski lessons—hopefully I won't bang into a tree—and having to pretend to enjoy a holiday I absolutely loathe. You want me to reconsider all of that?"

"You don't like Christmas?"

Nic shrugged. "It was always a crappy, depressing day when I was a kid. It holds no fond memories for me, that's for sure."

"You said you'd cancelled plans with your uncle," Abby reminded her.

"He likes to pretend it's a tradition with us. I usually play along with him."

Abby tilted her head. "Why uncle and not parents?"

Nic stiffened a bit. "They're not in the picture anymore. Long story." She twisted the gloves in her hands. "So?"

Abby sighed, then pulled her phone from her pocket. She held it up to her. Nic read the text, then glanced at Abby. Then she read it again. Then she smiled.

"That's from Holly?"

"Yes. Please go with me."

Nic met her gaze. "My offer is still on the table. When are we leaving?"

"Seriously? That's my choice? I go alone and chance Holly sneaking into my bed, or I go with you and…and…"

"And have *me* in your bed. If I were you, I'd choose the latter. Much less stressful than sleeping with your brother's fiancé."

Nic was shocked to see Abby blinking tears away. Then Abby folded her arms across her chest protectively and nodded.

"Okay. You win. We leave on Wednesday. I'll call you with details."

Abby turned and left without another word. Nic watched her go, wondering at the despair she'd seen in Abby's eyes. Did this Holly person really have that much of a hold on her? Apparently so.

Well, it looked like she was going to have a white Christmas. It might actually be a fun Christmas too. That would be a first for her, wouldn't it?

CHAPTER TEN

"You're really going?"

"Yep." Nic sorted through Addison's coats. "Maybe I should be looking through Eric's closet," she said as she tossed a brushed suede coat back on the bed.

"Too girly for you?" Addison teased.

"Just a tad."

"What about ski pants and stuff?"

"Abby said I could rent them there in town." She paused. "You think I'm crazy?"

"What part? The skiing part? Or the running away from home at Christmas part?"

Nic shook her head. "I'm not running away. Uncle Jimmie is going to Vegas. And I know I could hang out here with you, even though your mother only tolerates me. Now that you're pregnant, I think she's afraid I'm going to be spreading my gayness to your baby or something."

Addison laughed. "Sadly, I think you're right." Her face turned serious. "Eric wants you in the delivery room with him. That'll freak my mother out."

Nic's eyes widened. "Oh my god. Like *in* the room? While it's happening?"

"Yes."

Then she smiled. "He only wants me there because he's afraid he'll pass out or something."

"I'd like you to be there too, Nicky. If not for you—"

"Yeah, yeah, I made him ask you out when he was interested in…what was her name?"

"Erica."

She laughed. "How could I forget? He thought it would be so cool to be Eric and Erica." Her smiled faltered a little. "But really, you want me in the delivery room?"

Addison hugged her. "I would love for you to be there. You're family. You're going to be Aunt Nicky. And you're right. Eric is afraid he'll pass out." She went to Eric's closet and opened the door. "So, tell me about this woman. Abby is her name?"

"She seems nice. Normal." Then she laughed. "Well, you know, normal is relative, considering this scheme she's got going on. But yeah, we talked and came to an understanding." She smiled. "An understanding as to how I would be compensated."

"Do I want to know what that is?"

"I get to be her *real* girlfriend for ten days. Won't that be fun?"

Addison shook her head. "Oh, Nicky. Why do you play these games?"

The smile left her face. "It's easier."

"Easier? No commitments, you mean?"

"No commitments, no fighting, no stress, no—"

"No love, no emotion," she countered.

"Like I've been telling you for years, I'm not looking for love. I don't need that in my life. I'd rather be alone."

"Your parents—"

"I don't want to talk about them." She reached into the closet and pulled out a heavy coat. "Does he ever wear this?"

"Rarely does it get cold enough. Take it." Addison touched her arm. "We worry about you, Nicky."

"Well, don't. I'm fine. You and Eric are my family. And I've got Uncle Jimmie. That's all I need. I'm happy."

She found herself in a tight hug. "We'll miss you."

"Thanks. I'll miss you too."

Addison took a deep breath. "So? She's cute?"

"Yes. Quite."

"Do you need gloves?"

"I've got some nice leather ones. And if I need something, I can always buy it up there. I think I'll be okay."

"When are you leaving?"

"Wednesday morning, very early. Her brother is coming on Thursday, and Abby wants to get there first to 'establish her territory,' as she put it. It's an eleven-hour drive. We'll spend that time getting to know little tidbits about each other so we're not totally lost when we meet the family."

Addison smiled at her. "I'm surprised. You sound like you're excited to be going."

"Trust me. My excitement has nothing to do with having a traditional Christmas with her family. I'm more interested in the nighttime activity, if you know what I mean."

"Oh, you better be careful, Nic. I can imagine all the snow and colorful decorations. It'll be like a fairytale Christmas. The Grinch in you might finally be quelled."

"I highly doubt it."

"Hey, you two," Eric called from the living room. "Nachos are ready."

They smiled at each other. Eric's specialty was his supreme nachos, laden with both chicken and beef, beans, olives, tomatoes, onions, and jalapenos and smothered in a Colby-Jack and mozzarella cheese mix. And of course, there was guacamole and sour cream on the side. He baked them in the oven on an extra-large pizza tray and they were enough to feed six. They were sinfully good and the three of them almost always finished them off.

"I love his nachos, but they make me want to have margaritas," Addison complained. "This has been the longest pregnancy."

"April will be here before you know it." She reached out and rubbed Addison's protruding stomach affectionately. "And I can't wait to be Aunt Nicky."

CHAPTER ELEVEN

"She sent you a text? And so then you went and begged Nic to go with you?"

"Something like that."

"And the sex part?"

Abby groaned. "I don't want to talk about it. Besides, I'm pretty sure I can get out of it." Or at least she was going to try like hell. She fumbled with her phone, pulling up the text from Holly. "Here. Read this crap."

Sharon laughed. "Oh my god! She's got some nerve, doesn't she?"

"Oh, she was always so sure of herself. I'm actually looking forward to seeing her reaction when she meets Nic."

"You're leaving in the morning? At what ungodly hour?" Sharon asked as she snapped a carrot in half with her teeth.

Abby bit into her sandwich. "Four," she mumbled around a bite. "It's a ten-hour drive. Well, eleven by the time you count stops along the way. We'll pick up breakfast and lunch and eat in the car. We gain an hour when we cross time zones, so, with luck, we should be there by two thirty, three at the latest."

"Are you nervous?"

Abby jerked her head up. "Yes," she said honestly. "I don't know if it's because of Nic and our agreement or if it's Holly. She's so competitive, I can see her ignoring the fact that I brought a girlfriend—fake girlfriend, but still—and trying to get me into bed with her. And what if I break? What if I do it? Then I'll have cheated on my fake girlfriend. Can you imagine the drama then?"

"And what about Nic? How are you going to get out of having sex with her?"

She shrugged. "I'll just say no."

Yes, that was her plan: to renege on her agreement with Nic. Just because she'd agreed to her counteroffer—to sex—didn't make it so. Once they got up there, what was Nic going to do if she refused to sleep with her? Well, she supposed she could spill the beans about the whole charade, but would Nic really do that?

When she'd called her with the details, Nic had seemed almost normal. There'd been no mention of her compensation. In fact, she seemed rather nice and maybe even a little bit excited about going. Or maybe that's what she wanted to read into Nic's demeanor.

"We talked," she said. "I called her yesterday and we talked. I think it'll be fine."

"But what will you talk about for eleven hours stuck in a car together?"

"We're going to get to know each other so that when we are around my family, it won't be quite so obvious that we're strangers. And we're going to rehearse our dating history and how we met and all that." She put her sandwich down. "Aren't you sick of salads?"

"Yes. And my diet stops on Christmas Eve. I—like millions of others—will start it again on New Year's Day."

Abby stared down at her sandwich. "I'm sick of these too." She took a chip from the bag. "How old do you think she is?"

"You don't know?"

"I didn't think to ask. I don't care, really. I'm guessing she's around my age. Thirtyish."

"Probably so." Sharon stole a chip from her bag. "Are you packed?"

"Yes. Pretty much. A few little odds and ends." She smiled. "At least I'm not dreading the holidays any longer. Nic may be a stranger, but at least she's an ally."

"What did your mother say when you told her you were bringing someone?"

"I haven't told her yet. I've been putting it off because I know she'll have a million questions. But my mother is a planner, and planners don't like to have an extra guest sprung on them. I'll call her tonight."

Yes, she would call, and she could already guess at the questions. *Why am I just now hearing that you're dating someone? How did you meet? Is it serious? What's her favorite meal? Is she allergic to anything? What should I get her for Christmas?*

That thought made her eyes widen. If they were dating—a couple—then they would exchange gifts.

"Oh, shit."

"What?"

"I don't have a gift for her."

"For your mother?"

"No, for Nic. I can't get her what I give everyone else."

"What's that?"

"Amazon gift cards."

"Are you *still* doing that?"

"Yes, I've told you before, I'm a terrible gift giver. But what am I going to get for Nic?"

Sharon grinned. "How about a ring? That would probably put Holly in her place."

CHAPTER TWELVE

"Hi, Mom."

"Abigail? Shouldn't you be in bed? I thought you were leaving very early in the morning."

"I am in bed. I'm just not used to going to bed at nine and I'm not sleepy." She took a deep breath. "I completely forgot to tell you…I'm bringing a…a…well, my…my girlfriend."

"*What*?"

"Yeah, so I'm bringing Nic with me. I hope that's all right."

"Who is Nic?"

"She's someone I've been seeing."

"And why am I just now hearing about her? How long have you been dating?"

Abby closed her eyes. "A few months."

"*Months*? Why didn't you tell me? Is it serious?"

"Mom, we can talk all about it when I get there. I forgot to tell you the other day when we talked, that's all. She wasn't sure she could get off work for that long so…"

"What's her name? Nic?"

"Yes."

"Is that a nickname? What's her real name?"

Oh, crap. Was it a nickname? "Her name is…Nicole." At least she hoped it was.

"Good. Because you know I'm not fond of nicknames. I still can't believe you didn't tell me you were seeing someone. William, can you believe that Abigail is dating someone?" her mother called loudly to her father.

"Mom, it's not a big deal really. It's only been a few months. I wasn't even sure I was going to invite her but, well, she's never had a white Christmas before." That much was true, at least.

"It's just such great news, Abigail. I was afraid Holly had scarred you for life. I can't wait to meet her."

"Okay, then," she drew out. "I guess I need to get some sleep. I'll see you tomorrow afternoon."

"Do drive carefully, honey. I'll plan a special dinner for the four of us. What's her favorite meal?"

Oh, good lord. Abby squeezed her eyes shut. "Don't go to any trouble, Mom. Really."

"Nonsense. What does she like?"

"Um, she likes…hamburgers."

"Hamburgers? I said a special dinner."

"She likes chicken, Mom." Everyone liked chicken, didn't they? "Do some kind of a chicken dish. Like chicken parmesan or something."

"Well, I do have a good recipe for that. What kind of vegetables does she like? I normally serve that with steamed broccoli, but not everyone enjoys broccoli. I could—"

"Mom, how about you surprise us? Make whatever you want. I'm going to bed now. Goodnight."

She disconnected before her mother could protest. She gave an exasperated sigh and put the phone on the nightstand. She punched her pillow a couple of times, then rolled to her side. This was a stupid plan, she thought as she closed her eyes. Stupid, stupid, stupid.

No. What would be stupid would be to go alone. Because, yes, she was weak. A stupid plan beat trying to ward off Holly's advances for ten days. Because, yeah, she'd probably break again, and be humiliated once more. So, a stupid plan with a fake girlfriend it was.

CHAPTER THIRTEEN

"What's your name?"

Nic arched an eyebrow as Abby pulled out of the parking lot of her apartment complex. It was fifteen minutes after four and there were only a handful of cars on the road at this early hour.

"So…it's Nic. And I think you're Abby." She smiled. "Unless something has changed since we last spoke."

"It's my mother."

Nic looked around. "Where?"

Abby laughed. "It's early. I know I'm not making sense. I had a hard time going to sleep. I think I was still tossing about at eleven. When the alarm went off, I nearly threw my phone across the room."

"I'm used to getting up early. Most jobs, especially during the summer, we try to start work at daybreak. I'm in the office well before that, getting everyone's schedules together." She took a sip of the coffee in her travel mug. "But getting up at three is a little early."

"I know. I'll be a zombie by tonight."

"I can share driving duty," she offered.

"Good. I'll take you up on it." Abby glanced at her. "Nicole?"

"Huh?"

"Your name? Nic. Is it short for Nicole?"

"No."

"No? Crap."

"Why?"

"My mother."

"Again?"

Abby laughed. "My mother asked what Nic was short for. I assumed Nicole."

"Oh. No, it's actually short for Nicky."

"Really? Your given name is Nicky? That's cute. Why do you go by Nic?"

"I don't know. That's just what everyone always called me. You?"

Abby groaned. "It's Abigail. And my mother is the *only* one who calls me that. And Holly," she added, before blowing out a breath. "Okay. So, what's your favorite meal?"

"Are we practicing being girlfriends?"

"Yes."

"Okay." She took another sip of her coffee. "I don't guess I have a favorite meal. My mother didn't cook much. Well, not unless you consider making Hamburger Helper cooking. We ate a lot of KFC, a lot of burgers. Pizza." She shook her head. "I was a fat kid. Really fat."

"No way."

"Yep. When I moved in with my uncle, I lost a ton of weight. He cooked for us each night and he got up early and made breakfast too. Oatmeal and toast."

Abby laughed. "And you hated it?"

"I did. But it grew on me, I guess. He'd pile blueberries or strawberries on top and usually a banana too. And sometimes he'd let me put peanut butter on my toast." She thought back to those days, days when at first, she'd felt so lost and alone. "I guess back then my favorite meal was smothered pork chops on top of rice. He'd make that once a week. It was something my aunt used to make for him."

"His favorite meal then?"

"Yeah."

"Why did you live with your uncle?"

Nic stared into the darkness for the longest time. "I just did."

"And is the aunt in the picture?"

"No. She died about a year before I moved in with him. They had no kids." She glanced at Abby, wanting to steer the conversation away from her. "What about you? Favorite meal?"

"Oh, I don't know. My mother *did* cook. It was a passion of hers. I told you they were both in real estate."

"Successful?"

"Yes. My father specialized in commercial property, my mother in residential. They worked for different companies so they were competitive. But she was almost always there when we got home from school. If she wasn't, then he was. And we always ate dinner together as a family." Abby glanced over at her. "I'm assuming you didn't."

"No. Food was put on the table, and everyone ate when they wanted. I usually took mine into my room and ate there. But go on. What was your favorite?"

"She used to make this sinfully delicious chicken tetrazzini. It was full of sour cream and butter and cheese and spaghetti noodles, and I don't think I'd touch it today, but as a kid, when it was served, it was a treat. But as far as normal meals, I liked her meatloaf and mashed potatoes. That was a once-a-week thing, usually."

She nodded. "Yeah, Uncle Jimmie made that weekly too."

"What about now? You cook?"

"Oh yeah. I'm a pretty good cook, actually. I'll usually cook a couple of times a week and make enough for leftovers. And I still have oatmeal for breakfast most mornings. Eggs and bacon are a treat."

"I have cereal with almond milk."

"Do you get up just in time to get to work or do you get up early and linger over coffee?"

"Early. Two cups while I get online. Shower. Eat breakfast in a rush and sit in traffic for forty minutes. You?"

"I do a quick workout—stretches and some floor exercises and stuff—and one cup of coffee. Shower, coffee to go, and fifteen minutes, no traffic. I'm usually at the office by five."

"Until?"

"I knock off about three, most days. Hit the gym and try to make it home before traffic is too unbearable."

"And why aren't you dating?"

They were now on Highway 287, heading toward Decatur. There were more cars on the road now, but most were heading in the opposite direction as people drove into the city for work. Nic had looked at a map yesterday and knew they'd stay on this road until they got to Amarillo, then they'd head north on Highway 87 to Clayton, New Mexico. At least she thought that was the route Abby would take.

"I don't really date," she said honestly. But she knew that would garner more questions if she didn't elaborate. "I had shitty role models, so the idea of being in a relationship scares the crap out of me," she said with a laugh. "I avoid attachments at all costs. But you're not dating either. What's your reason?"

"I could say that I'm still wounded from Holly, but that's only partially true. Honestly, I'm a little bored with the whole thing. No matter which nightclub we go to on Saturday nights, it feels the same. Like it's the exact same people there. And I'm just not sure I want to seriously date someone I met at a bar."

"Guessing, but you met Holly at a bar?"

"Yeah, I did."

"At a gay bar?"

"Yes."

"Yet she's dating your brother."

"Engaged to be married, let's not forget."

"Oh yeah. Maid of honor." She laughed at the look on Abby's face. "I'd tell them to kiss my ass, I think."

"Oh, I so want to do that. My mother would kill me, though. She wants us all to be one big, happy family. No quarrels, no drama."

Nic sighed. Growing up, quarrels and drama was all she knew. What would it be like having a traditional Christmas celebration? Would they have a special meal? Probably. She could envision a big, beautifully lit tree, a house decorated to the hilt, maybe some candles and Christmas music.

"What are you thinking?"

"What will Christmas be like?"

"What do you mean?"

"We had this little fake, tabletop tree. No lights, just some old, mismatched ornaments on it." She didn't add that on a good year, they'd have a gift or two wrapped. Other years—most years—the gifts would still be in their Walmart bag. If there were gifts at all, that is. "We opened gifts on Christmas Eve. On Christmas Day, we'd have Chinese food."

"Why Chinese?"

"Back when my parents first got married, it was the only thing open on Christmas Day. My mother liked to say that it was tradition." She sighed. "It was a crappy tradition."

"I'm sorry."

"So, tell me what Christmas will be like."

"Well, it's very Christmasy, that's for sure. It's a big, two-story log house and my mother will have every inch of it decorated."

"Fireplace?"

"Huge fireplace. And there'll be stockings hung there. A large tree—never artificial—that will make the living room smell like the forest. It will be decorated to an obscene degree, so much so that there'll hardly be any green showing and it's quite beautiful." She paused. "I'm sorry. I sound like I'm bragging. It's—"

"No. My mother wasn't into all of that. Nothing for you to apologize for. When I moved in with my uncle, things were more normal, I guess. I think it was too late, though. My impression of Christmas was that it was just another day with a little more glitz than usual. Some years, anyway." She glanced over at Abby, wondering how much to tell her. Hell, they'd just met. Do you blurt out that your parents were drunks? No. Her past really wasn't any of Abby's business. "What else? Special meal?"

"Yes. We have a more informal meal on Christmas Eve. Usually an early buffet. Then we'll pile into their Suburban and drive around and look at lights. Back home, my father will play the piano, and we'll have cocktails and sing carols. We open our presents on Christmas morning. My mother will usually make a quiche or something light. Then we'll have our main meal about one o'clock. She likes to get all fancy with it and brings out the 'good china' as she says. The evening meal is very informal again—usually leftovers—and it's usually a short day. Skiing starts in earnest after that. And they like to take us all out to eat once or twice too."

She stared out at the lightening sky, picturing all Abby had described. It sounded like, yes, a fairytale of a Christmas, something she knew absolutely nothing about. How lucky had Abby been to have enjoyed all of that growing up. And now here she was, forever jaded—and quite cynical—with the holiday. What was going to be her reaction to all of it? Would she secretly mock their family traditions? Would she be envious? No, not envious. Just indifferent, probably. That was how she normally felt when she joined Eric and Addison on Christmas Day. Indifferent.

Maybe she could fake it this year. Seeing as how she was a fake girlfriend, surely she could pretend to enjoy the holiday with all its pomp and gaudy decorations.

CHAPTER FOURTEEN

Abby turned sleepy eyes to Nic, then closed them again as she leaned her head back. "You okay?" she mumbled.

"Yes. Go back to sleep. We're about ten miles from Amarillo."

"Mmm," she murmured. Amarillo was a little more than halfway.

They'd stopped for breakfast at six—McDonalds. By seven, she was struggling to stay awake and Nic had offered to drive. That was the last thing she remembered. She'd apparently fallen asleep immediately. She opened her eyes a tiny bit, enough to watch Nic. There was a smile on her face as she drove, and Abby wondered if Nic knew it was there.

Nic had turned out to be an engaging partner to drive with. There was none of the awkwardness she'd feared and thankfully no mention of the arrangement they'd struck up. They'd actually chatted as if they'd known each other for years, although Nic tended to skip over anything that had to do with her childhood. Perhaps she was estranged from her parents. She talked about her uncle a lot, the man who Abby guessed was the father-figure in her life. Nic also said she knew his landscaping business would be hers one day, but that subject, too, she didn't linger on. She seemed more interested in asking questions than answering them.

And she asked a ton of questions about Red River and what the snow would be like and whether they could take a sleigh ride. And Nic had her describe the house to her. Abby found herself sharing little tidbits of her early life, stories she'd not shared with anyone in years, if ever. For a pretend girlfriend, Nic was being extremely attentive. But they only had another four or five hours on the road. There was still so much to go over.

"What's your favorite color?"

"Blue," Nic said without taking her eyes off the road. "And I thought you were sleeping."

Abby sat up and stretched her arms out. "I feel better. Do you want me to drive?"

"I can make another hour."

Abby reached for the water bottle that was in the console. "My mother will ask you a lot of questions. She's nosy that way. You'll need to set the ground rules right away with her or she'll get way deep into your business."

"Okay. So where did we meet?"

"How about the truth? She already knows I have lunch out in the courtyard most days."

The smile left Nic's face. "So where do I work?"

Abby studied her. "How about the truth?"

Nic shook her head. "Not very glamourous. What does Holly do?"

Abby sighed. "She's an attorney, works for her father's firm."

"See? Now that's glamourous. You don't want your new girlfriend to be a common laborer. That's stepping down several notches for you."

"Okay. So, what do you want to be? Doctor? Professor?"

Nic laughed. "How about we tell them I own the business and we have a fleet of twenty or thirty crews that branch out all over Dallas?" Nic glanced at her. "And I never have to get my hands dirty."

"I'd guess that you like getting your hands dirty and you'd be bored silly working in the office all day. Right?"

Nic gave a heavy sigh and nodded. "Right."

"How many crews do you have now?"

"Eight. We could do ten or twelve easily—we have to turn down business all the time—but Uncle Jimmie is afraid we'll get too big, and he won't be able to manage it."

"Are you embarrassed about what you do for a living, Nic?"

They were in Amarillo traffic now and Nic didn't look at her. Abby saw the slight clenching of her jaw, though.

"Sometimes, yes. It's not a very exciting life. I mean, I have a business degree. Shouldn't I be doing something with it?"

"Do you want to?"

"No. I'm happy there. I love it, actually. And I know I can put my degree to use someday. The business will be mine eventually. It's just in the meantime, there are so many things I'd change, so many ways we could grow, but Uncle Jimmie is set in his ways. He's content with the way things are. And so I guess I have to be too."

"But?" she prompted.

"Well, like I said, it's the very opposite of glamorous."

"Oh? And being stuck inside an office all day is?"

"It's more acceptable."

"Ah. So we're talking dating now and not passing muster with my mother." She smiled at that. "Because I think my mother will be intrigued by your job. She'll probably hit you up on tips for growing flowers. But for dating, it's not acceptable?"

"I don't date, remember. But I was thinking of you. Someone like me is probably the last person on earth you'd go out with."

"Why? You're very attractive."

Nic blushed at her words and Abby was surprised. Nic obviously knew she was attractive. She was arrogant and conceited that way, she reminded herself. Although today, during their drive, there'd been no sign of that arrogant and conceited person she'd met back in Dallas.

"I don't date. But I do go out occasionally. I don't have a problem meeting women. But once they find out what I do for a living, things change. It no longer matters what I look like. I think it's because, in the back of their mind, they're picturing having to introduce me to their friends."

"And what? You won't measure up?"

"Right. Not quite good enough. Not that I care. I don't normally stick around long enough to get introduced to friends anyway."

She felt a tiny twinge of guilt. When she'd first seen Nic—with her dirty knees—hadn't she indicated to Sharon that Nic wasn't good enough? She certainly wasn't her type, she'd said. Nic had dirty knees and worked in the dirt. No, not her type at all. How arrogant of her, though.

Nic looked at her then. "But it's up to you. If you want to introduce me to your family, to your ex—who's an attorney—as a landscape artist, I'm fine with it."

Nic's mouth twitched in a smile, and Abby laughed. "A landscape artist, huh? I love it."

"Okay. So, I'll tell the truth then. But is that something they'll question?"

"What do you mean?"

"Who do you normally date? Will this be drastically different for you?"

"Oh." She hadn't thought of that. Yes, it *was* drastically different, all right. Had she ever dated anyone who wasn't a professional of some sort? God, how snooty did that sound? But she waved it away. "It doesn't matter. Maybe drastically different is what I need. I'll tell my mother Holly drove me to it."

"Drove you to the dark side? This could be fun."

Abby smiled. "Yeah, it might be. It'll drive Holly crazy, that's for sure. She's got this haughty attitude. She'll probably go out of her way to prove her superiority and—"

"And try to get into your bed?"

"Judging by her text, isn't that what you inferred?"

Nic nodded. "Yeah. But I think I've got dibs on your bed. Not her."

Abby's smile faded a little. Yes, Nic had dibs, didn't she? Because they had an agreement. She pushed that thought aside as she leaned back against the seat, trying to relax. She pictured Holly's face then. She could already see the scorn there. Holly would be perfectly dressed, as was her style. Since she'd been dating Aaron, she wore more makeup than when Abby had first met her. More makeup, longer nails, and higher heels. And while Holly would no doubt think that Nic was attractive, she would make it be known that Nic's social standing was several rungs below hers. That, she could count on.

Abby turned and stared out the window, absently watching cars and concrete speed past as Nic maneuvered them along I-40. Was she any better than Holly? Or was she just as shallow? So Nic worked in the dirt. So she didn't have a glamorous office job, as she called it. Abby would never call her mundane eight-to-five job on the sixth floor of Las Colinas Towers glamorous. It was just a job. It was her chosen career, she was good at it, she was comfortable there…but it was just a job.

She turned to Nic then. "I need to apologize."

"For what?"

"You had dirty knees."

Nic arched an eyebrow. "Yeah. That goes along with dirty hands. I usually start out with gloves on, but that doesn't last."

Abby motioned up ahead. "Take Highway 287 to the north, toward Dalhart."

"Got it."

Abby nodded. "Sorry. I guess you can see that on the navigation screen. I know my way there blindfolded, but I always like to have the map up."

"So what about my dirty knees?"

Abby sighed. "Sharon and I were talking about my dilemma of not being able to find a date and she pointed you out. And I'd seen you before. Anyway, you were having lunch like we were. And…"

"And I had dirty knees?"

"Yes. And I basically dismissed you for that reason alone. And now I feel terrible about it."

Nic didn't seem upset by her confession. No, she smiled at her instead. "I knew you'd been checking me out. I told you I'd seen you."

"I was *not* checking you out!"

"No? Well, I guess I shouldn't have been mingling there with you all anyway. Probably should have stayed in my truck until after the lunch crowd."

She didn't know Nic well enough at all to try to read her, but the tone of her voice—while sounding the same—had a wounded feel to it. It was as if Nic was saying she should have stayed in her truck *where she belonged*. She likened it to her schoolyard days where everyone would be playing and there, on the fringes, stood Kara Butka—the "butt" of all their jokes—alone and unwelcome, never invited to join in. It simply tugged at her heart, and she reached across the console and touched Nic's arm.

"Please forgive me for being so…well, so shallow," she said, thinking of her earlier word. "I'd like to say that's not who I am, but…"

"Oh, don't worry about it. I'll try not to embarrass you with my lowly standing."

She released her arm, not knowing if Nic was teasing or not. "You won't embarrass me. I think it'll be fun. It'll certainly confuse them all, that's for sure."

"I'm the opposite of Holly, in other words."

"The complete opposite." She smiled at her then. "And that's a good thing, I think."

The truth was, last year at Christmas, she wasn't really *over* Holly. Oh, she said she was, and she pretended that she was, but once she was around her again, Holly had turned on the charm and Abby had found herself responding to her once again. She'd pushed aside the fact that Holly was sleeping with her brother. She'd purposefully shoved the memory of the breakup scene to the back of her mind. Because Holly was attractive and dynamic, and she was flirting with her. And when Holly made it clear that she wanted to sleep with her, Abby only half-heartedly fought it. Oh, hell, that's a lie. She didn't fight it at all.

She knew then that Holly was only using her, yet she wasn't strong enough to deny her. She'd been disgusted by it all the next morning. Holly had slithered back into her brother's bed, and Abby had felt dirty and emotionally abused. She remembered sitting at the edge of the bed, wondering what had ever drawn her to Holly in the first place. She had a conceited air about her—condescending, really. How had she ever been attracted to that?

She turned to glance at Nic. She'd thought her conceited, too, hadn't she? In a totally different way than Holly. Nic seemed sure of herself, comfortable with who she was. She certainly didn't put on airs. She was quite the opposite of Holly in that regard. Shocking, really, but Nic had turned out to be a nice, normal, and unassuming person.

Well, if she ignored this little charade they were playing, that is. That, and the compensation she was expected to dole out as payment for Nic's participation in this game. That thought made her close her eyes with a sigh. Oh, she could get into some predicaments, couldn't she?

CHAPTER FIFTEEN

"Do you have a pet?"

Nic shook her head. "No. You?"

"No. Do you like pets?"

"I've never had one," she lied.

Abby glanced over at her. "No pets growing up?"

She shook her head but didn't elaborate. Yeah, there had been a cat. A stray that had hung around long enough for her to tame. She'd snuck food out to it in the back corner of the yard. She hadn't worried that her mother would find out. Her mother never set foot out there. It was a big orange tabby, and she named her Sally. Every day when she came home from school, she'd go out there and Sally would be waiting. She'd sit and the cat would crawl into her lap, purring constantly. Then Sally started getting fat. Really fat. There would be babies soon. Then one day Sally wasn't waiting for her anymore, no.

"We had a dog," Abby said, interrupting her thoughts. "He was a Boston Terrier and he used to sleep with me. Buster."

Nic could hear the smile in Abby's voice, and she tried to picture the dog sleeping at the foot of a young Abby's bed. She didn't know what a Boston Terrier looked like, though.

"He died when I was a senior in high school. It was traumatic for us all and my mother couldn't bring herself to replace him. She still has pictures of him displayed." She laughed lightly. "There'll be one on the mantel. He's got a red Christmas bandana on and an elf hat. I remember the Christmas she took that picture. It was the year I got my first 'big kids' bike."

"What was that?"

"Before, I had the cutesy little pink girl's bike with those frilly things hanging from the handlebars. This was a real road bike with lots of gears and I thought I was hot shit when I took it for a spin around the neighborhood." Abby laughed again. "And then I fell and scraped my knee pretty bad." Her smiled faltered a little. "Aaron saw me. He carried me back home."

"So, you used to be closer?"

"He's four years older than me. We were closer when we were kids, I think. As we got older, we seemed to drift apart. Not sure why, really. He was already in college when I got into high school, and he didn't come home all that much. He worked in Houston while I was in college, so we rarely saw each other except for holidays." She waved her hand. "And then the whole Holly thing."

"Is she your age?"

"No, she's three years older. And we were only together for about six months. I had known her several months before we went on our first real date." Abby glanced at her. "She's very attractive and charming. Or she *was*. After a couple of months, she announced that we were officially a couple, which was fine by me. I'd told myself I was falling in love with her, so it all seemed perfect to me."

"Yet months later—"

"She's sleeping with my brother. But they've been together for two years now, so I guess it's the real thing. I should be happy for them."

"How real can it be if she slept with you last Christmas?"

"You're right. Truth is, I don't feel happy for them. Mostly, I feel sorry for my brother. I know how she is, and I also know she was most likely the one who initiated things between them. And it speaks volumes as to mine and Aaron's relationship that he would sleep with her." Abby waved a hand in the air once again. "And I know how that sounds considering I slept with her last year." She glanced over at her. "It's a complicated mess and I'm almost sorry you're being brought into it."

"Oh, it'll be fun to mess with her."

Maybe fun wasn't the right word, but she certainly wouldn't feel any stress by being there. She wouldn't ever see these people again. Whether she made a good impression on them or not was beside the point.

Abby glanced over at her. "You know, I think it will be kinda fun. Even though you and I don't know each other, I'm really glad you're with me. And if Holly wants to play games, we can play them too. You seem like the type not to take any shit from her."

She laughed. "I can hold my own, I think."

"I'm looking forward to having a normal Christmas again. Last year was anything but that. And it'll be fun to show you around. If you want to, that is. I know you weren't really all that keen on the cold and snow."

"And skiing," she added. "But yeah, I'd like for you to show me around. My first time in the snow, my first—and probably only—white Christmas. Something different for me. I'm trying to keep an open mind about the whole holiday and all."

CHAPTER SIXTEEN

Abby smiled, watching Nic as she stared around them, the white landscape nearly blinding in the bright sunshine. They'd first seen patches of snow when they'd entered Cimarron Canyon. Most of the canyon was part of the state park and she'd pulled into a picnic area. Nic had been out before she'd even stopped her Explorer. She'd walked into a snowbank, bending over to scoop up a handful of snow with childlike laughter. Abby had been completely charmed by her antics, something she would have never thought possible with Nic Bennett.

Now, though, as they were crossing Cimarron Pass, the snow was more widespread and the higher peaks around them were covered. Nic seemed to be in awe of it all.

"Is this what it'll be like in Red River?"

"Around the ski area for sure. The town itself is in a valley, but it's still over eight thousand feet. Most years there's snow on the ground from December through March. My parents' place is west of town, in the foothills. My mother said they had over five inches the other day."

"Do you think it'll snow while we're here?"

"I'm sure it will. I don't remember a time when it didn't snow at least once during the holidays. December and January are the snowiest months here. Late February and early March get a lot of snow too. I've come up here in March a couple of times for spring skiing. It's not quite so cold then."

Nic touched the window with the back of her hand and nodded. "Yeah, it feels really cold."

Abby glanced at the touchscreen. "It's twenty-eight. But with no wind and lots of sunshine, it's not too bad."

"You probably think it's silly—a grown woman like I am getting excited about the snow."

Abby laughed. "Not silly, no. I'm excited too and I've been here dozens of times in the winter. But I would think you'd be nervous."

"Yeah, speaking of that, you're not going to leave me alone with your mother, right?"

"Not for a second, no. She's really very nice, though. Just nosy. And I think you'll love my grandparents. As you'll see when you meet them, my mother takes after hers."

"What about your father?"

"My dad? Oh, he's always got to be doing something, so you won't find him sitting idly at the breakfast table drinking coffee or anything. When they quit the real estate business and moved up here, Mom thought they'd travel and see the western states. I think they were barely here six months when he applied for a job at the ski resort," she said with a smile, remembering *that* argument between her parents.

"Winter job?"

"No, the resort is open all year. They have lots of summer activities too. Actually, they're busier in the summer than winter. There's competition for skiing in the area. There's a resort in Angel Fire too and it's only thirty miles from Red River. Taos has skiing too."

"And I guess this area isn't exactly on a main route either."

"Right. If you're on this road like we are, you're either going to Red River, Angel Fire, or Taos." She pointed up ahead. "We're coming up on the intersection. Left will take you to Angel Fire. I'm, of course, partial to Red River because that's where I grew up skiing, but I've done Angel Fire too. They're similar but Angel Fire is better suited to beginners," she said, glancing at Nic. "It also has some nice alpine skiing. If you find Red River too challenging, I won't mind taking you over to Angel Fire. And if you don't want to ski at all, that's perfectly fine too."

"Oh, we'll see. If we need an escape, maybe you can take me out and show me around."

She slowed when they got into Eagle Nest, which was a tiny village that catered strictly to tourists. At the intersection, she stopped.

"Eagle Nest. Not much to it. The lake over there," she said, pointing to their left, "is great for seeing elk in early evenings. We can take a drive over one day if you're interested."

"Sure."

She turned right, heading to Red River—and her mother. Even if Nic wasn't nervous, she certainly was. Because the only thing worse than being here alone—having to endure Holly and Aaron together—would be for them all to find out that Nic was only her fake girlfriend. How humiliating would that be?

"What's wrong?"

Abby glanced at Nic, then back at the road. "Nothing."

"You have a death grip on the wheel."

Abby smiled and made herself relax. "So, you're not nervous. But I am."

"I think we'll be fine. And if your mother asks questions that we're not prepared for, we'll just make something up and go with it. It'll be okay."

"Well, you certainly sound confident." She took a deep breath. "I just need to relax. I'm sure after the initial introductions, I'll be fine."

They rode on in silence, Nic still looking around at the surrounding forest, the snow now more widespread as they approached Red River. She slowed as they came to the old mining town. A resort town with less than five hundred full-time residents, it swelled with tourists during the summer months and during ski season. It was bustling with activity today as cars and Jeeps crowded Main Street, the road that housed most of the pubs and shops in town.

"During the summers, all of these restaurants and bars have outdoor patios open. The brewery over there has a second-floor patio too that's quite fun." Abby smiled at her. "That may be an escape for us one day. They also have killer burgers."

"Sounds like fun. I don't really go out to places like that much."

"What do you mean?"

"I mostly hang out with Eric and Addison, my best friends. College buddies, like I said. I'm usually at their place twice a week for dinner."

"Twice-a-week dinner date? Must be nice to have close friends like that."

"Yeah, he and Addison are the best. She's pregnant, so I'll get to be Aunt Nicky pretty soon. What about you? Any close friends I should know about?"

"Beth and Jenna are my best buds, I guess. We don't have standing dinner dates, but we get together two or three times a month. I have a group of single friends that I mostly go out with on Saturday nights. Used to, I should say. I haven't made one of those outings in a month or more."

"That's right. You met Holly at one of those nightclubs."

"Do you ever go?"

"Oh, sure, when I go out, that's where I go. To be honest, I much prefer hanging out with Eric and Addison than that scene. Much less stressful."

"Are you going to tell me why you don't date? Other than you're not interested in a relationship." She heard Nic take a deep breath before answering.

"Love is not for me. I've been quite skeptical that it even exists, but Eric and Addison have proven me wrong. But it's not me. I don't have that burning desire to settle down with someone."

"Bad experience?"

"You could say that."

"I don't think being ready to settle down or not has a bearing on with whom and when you fall in love. But I suppose you have to be receptive to it. If you're not ready to settle down, you probably aren't looking for love. Therefore, you won't find it. Is that your goal?"

"And you're receptive?"

"Sure. I'm also cautious." She pointed to her left. "The ski resort is down that way. A little ways up here, you'll be able to see the ski lift."

Nic leaned forward, looking around to where Abby had pointed. While the roads were clear, snow was piled along the sidewalks where it had been plowed.

"My parents' place is just outside of town. We'll turn left and cross the river."

"So it's out in the forest?"

"Yes, but it's not like it's on a huge plot of land or anything. Less than two acres, but it's still private, lots of trees. Most of the homes around them are seasonal, meaning no one lives there full-time."

"It's like second homes then?"

"Yes. One of their neighbors is from Louisiana. A retired couple. They come up each May and stay through Thanksgiving. The neighbor on the other side is from Houston. It's going to become their retirement home someday, but right now, they only come for a few weeks each summer and occasionally, they'll come up for Christmas. There are others that come for the summer that my mother has made friends with." She turned to the left, and she felt her heartbeat increase. "Here we go," she said.

"Is this the river?"

Abby laughed. "This is it. All of ten or fifteen feet wide," she said as they crossed the bridge.

"It's beautiful. Crystal clear."

"Yes, it is."

"So, this isn't the same Red River that separates Texas and Oklahoma?"

"No. This little river flows south. It actually splits into two forks, then eventually ends in the Wheeler Peak Wilderness."

The pavement ended and they continued on the dirt road—a road covered with slushy snow—a little ways before turning to the right. Tall pine trees lined the road, and she slowed as she approached her parents' entrance. The metal gate was opened and inviting. She drove through and they got their first glimpse of the two-story house.

"Wow," Nic murmured. "It's beautiful."

Abby smiled at her, noting that Nic was taking it all in—the cutout reindeer pulling a wooden sleigh, the big cedar tree at the corner that was decorated with edible treats for the birds, the oversized Santa that would glow red come nighttime, and the real snowman with a red scarf that her father had most likely made earlier that morning. Nic may have professed that she wasn't all that into Christmas, but her eyes were wide with wonder.

"Okay, so now I'm nervous. I'm going to be like a kid because all of this is just…wow."

Abby laughed. "The few conversations I had with you, I never thought this would be your reaction."

"I know. I thought I would be indifferent to it, just like I am to the holiday itself."

"Well, there's nothing wrong with being excited. This is all new for you. You don't have to try to temper your enthusiasm, Nic. This trip isn't all about me, you know."

"Oh, yeah, that's right. My free vacation." She wiggled her eyebrows. "And other things."

Abby met her gaze. "Let's don't talk about it, please."

"Okay, I'll play nice. I'll also try not to embarrass you."

"You won't embarrass me. I hope my mother doesn't ask anything to embarrass *you*." She took a deep breath. "I guess it's showtime."

She reached into the backseat for her jacket before getting out. The air was cold and fresh, and it smelled like the forest, the fragrance as intoxicating now as it had been when she was a child. The driveway was clear of snow, and she walked around her Explorer, opening the back so they could get their bags. They had two each, and she handed one to Nic, who slung it over her shoulder before taking the smaller duffel bag.

"It doesn't feel as cold as I thought it would."

"No. The air is dry and with the sun shining, it's almost pleasant." She glanced to the house, seeing her mother at the door. "I guess she heard us." Abby met Nic's eyes for a moment. "You ready?"

Nic took a deep breath, then nodded. "Sure…honey."

Abby laughed, releasing some of the tension she felt. "You can call me any endearment you want except 'baby' or 'darling.'" She nearly cringed. "Holly used to call me those. I told her I wasn't fond of them, but she ignored me."

"Why don't you like them?"

She shrugged as she headed toward the house. "I don't know. They sound condescending to me. Especially darling. It sounds so haughty, which fits Holly perfectly."

"You're right on time!" her mother called as she opened the door fully.

Abby walked up the steps to the front porch, feeling Nic behind her. "Hi, Mom," she greeted as her mother pulled her into a hug. When she was released, she smiled broadly, hoping it didn't look forced. "This is Nic Bennett." She turned to Nic. "And this is my mother, Sandra Carpenter."

"Such a pleasure to meet you, Nicole. I'm so happy you were able to come for Christmas."

Her mother drew Nic in for a hug too, and Abby tried to hide her smile as Nic's eyes widened.

"Nice to meet you too, Mrs. Carpenter."

"No, no. Call me Sandra."

"Well, then, you should call me Nic."

"That's lovely, dear, but I think I'll stick with Nicole. Now come inside. There's a roaring fire that your father got going for me earlier."

"Is he not here?" Abby asked as she followed her mother inside.

"I sent him into Taos for some last-minute shopping. He should be back within the hour."

"Oh my god," Nic murmured as she looked around in awe.

Abby smiled at her mother. "I tried to prepare her."

Nic set her bags down where she stood and walked over to the tree. "I think this is the most beautiful thing I've ever seen."

Her mother nearly beamed as she went over to Nic. "I do love people who appreciate the holiday spirit. Abigail will say I go overboard, but I say, is there such a thing?"

"I never had much of a Christmas growing up," Nic said. "This is kinda what I dreamed a real Christmas tree would look like."

Nic was staring up at the tree as she spoke, and her mother smiled broadly as her gaze followed Nic's. "Then I am so happy you are here to experience our Christmas tradition. I am all about decorations, as you can see." Her mother turned to her. "Take Nicole up to your room, Abigail. Get your things settled. Because...well, Aaron called."

"And?" she asked suspiciously.

"And they decided to come up early too."

"You have *got* to be kidding me."

Her mother looked quickly at Nic. "I assume she's aware of the Holly situation?"

Abby nearly rolled her eyes. *Situation?* "She is."

"I'm looking forward to meeting her," Nic said easily.

"You knew all along they were coming early, didn't you?" she accused.

"I did not," her mother said defensively. "He called me this morning. I think they are maybe an hour behind you."

"Great," she said dryly. "An hour of peace."

"That's why I sent your father to the store. I had planned dinner just for the four of us. I wasn't expecting six." Her mother looked at her pleadingly. "Let's all try to get along, huh?"

"Why are you saying it like *I'm* the one who can't get along? I'm not the one who—"

"So, babe, why don't we go get unpacked before they get here?"

Abby turned to Nic, eyebrows raised. *Babe? Did she just call me babe?* She saw the smile flitting on Nic's mouth, and before she could stop herself, she found herself returning it. Okay, so she could live with babe, she supposed.

But it was all so very odd, wasn't it? She'd gone groveling to Nic, pleading with her to come up here, all the while hoping she'd drop the "compensation" clause she'd added. Nic hadn't, of course, and Abby had accepted anyway. Because it beat dealing with Holly, she reasoned. And she stubbornly told herself that she didn't *like* Nic Bennett, and she would have nothing to do with her when this little charade was over with. However, spending eleven hours in a car together told her that she did like Nic and her first impression of her was wrong. Of course, that didn't mean she wanted to sleep with her. God, why was there always drama?

"Yes, go up to your room," her mother urged. "Relax."

"Okay. Some time to unwind would be good." She glanced at her mother. "I'll need something alcoholic, please."

"Of course. You know your father has the bar stocked." She waved them away. "Now go. Get settled."

As they went toward to the stairs, Nic's gaze landed on the fireplace with its crackling fire and all the Christmasy knickknacks that her mother had put out. Abby nearly laughed as a new stocking had been added. *Nicole.* Nic glanced back at her with such a cute expression on her face that she did laugh. Nic grinned back at her.

"What's funny?" her mother asked.

She looked at her mother, still smiling. "The stocking is nice, Mom."

"Well, we must all have a stocking."

"Very few people call me Nicole—in fact, no one that I can think of," Nic said, a smile still playing on her lips. "I doubt Santa will know who it's for."

"Oh, you girls with your nicknames. In school, everyone wanted to call me Sandy. Well, that's not my name. It's Sandra. And my husband. It's William, yet everyone calls him Bill. Well, my daughter is Abigail, and you are Nicole. So there."

Nic smiled at her. "I love it. Thank you."

"You're welcome."

Abby found she was still smiling when she reached the second floor. She glanced behind her, finding Nic smiling too. "Do I need to apologize?"

"I don't mind being Nicole. Just not sure I'm going to remember to answer to it."

She pushed open the door to her room, then laughed. It, too, was bursting with Christmas cheer.

"I think she's trying to make a good impression on you. She never decorates my room."

"We even have our own tiny tree." Nic walked over to it. "This was about the size we had at home." She touched a red ball. "It wasn't ever this pretty, though."

Abby put her bags on the bed and moved closer to her. "Do you want to talk about it?"

"Talk about what?"

"About why you dislike Christmas so much?"

Nic shook her head. "No."

Abby stared at her a bit longer, trying to read her eyes. Of course she didn't know her well enough to read them. "Is this all going to be an overload for you?"

"I'll manage. I'm kinda looking forward to it. I'm certain it will be a Christmas I'll remember always." She laughed lightly. "I mean, who could forget the year I played a fake girlfriend named Nicole?"

Abby returned her smile, then moved to sit on the bed. "Thank you for interrupting down there. I guess I get too defensive with my mother, but I always feel like she's blaming me for everything. Like it's my fault there's this rift between me and Aaron."

"Maybe she finds it easier to corner you than to deal with both Aaron and Holly."

"Maybe." She took a deep breath, then stood up. "Do you want to shower? Change?"

"Do you mind?"

"Of course not. I want to, too." She motioned to the bathroom. "Use ours. Each room up here has a private bath. I'll use my grandparents' room. They won't come until Friday."

"Okay." Then Nic smiled. "Is it bad that I'm looking forward to meeting Holly?"

"Well, the way my luck runs, you'll probably love her. Everyone else does."

Nic stared at her "I won't love her, Abby. You can count on that."

CHAPTER SEVENTEEN

Nic stood at the window, looking out at the expanse of snow. It was a scene she was trying to imbed in her memory, and she wasn't quite sure why. She was here playing a part, that's all. She didn't imagine there'd be much about this trip that she'd truly enjoy. She smiled at that thought. Well, she could think of one thing, perhaps. What surprised her was how much she'd enjoyed Abby's company on the ride up. She'd found her pleasant and, well, engaging. Spending ten days with her wasn't going to be such a chore after all.

She slid her gaze to the white SUV which had pulled in a few minutes earlier. It nearly blended in with the snow, but she'd watched as a man and woman—Aaron and Holly, she assumed—got out. She hadn't paid much attention to him as her gaze was locked on the woman. Thick brown hair reaching past her shoulders, the woman paused to flip it back from her neck as she surveyed her surroundings. She was in tight black jeans and a red Christmasy sweater, and she appeared—at least from this distance—to be quite attractive. She'd watched them until they disappeared from her view. Now, though, she was simply enjoying the landscape, her eyes darting over snow-laden trees, then to the Christmas decorations, back to the trees, then farther still as she looked into the thick forest. All so different than anything she'd ever seen before.

She turned around quickly when the door burst open. Abby, looking a bit frantic, closed and locked it, then leaned back with a sigh.

"That was close." She pushed away from the door. "I heard their voices right when I came out of my grandparents' room."

Nic pointed out the window. "Yeah, I saw them drive up." She smiled at her. "Holly is attractive, yes."

"She's also evil." Abby put an armful of clothes on the bed. "You look cute."

Nic looked down at herself. "I wasn't sure if jeans would be appropriate for dinner. That's kinda all I brought, though."

"Yes." Abby came closer, surprising her by reaching out to straighten her shirt collar. "Your button-down and sweater dress it up too. But no, the only meal I take care to dress for is the Christmas Day event."

"With the good china," Nic supplied.

"Yeah." Abby sighed. "I'm tired. Are you?"

"I am."

"Driving all day always does that to me. Warning you now, I'll be in bed by eight." Then she held her hand up quickly. "And please, let's don't talk about it. I haven't forgotten your stipulation for coming with me. Believe me, it's never far from my mind."

Nic watched her as she neatly folded the clothes she'd carried with her—the clothes she'd been wearing all day while driving. Abby looked nervous and she wasn't sure if it was because of her or Holly.

"Abby, my stipulation, as you call it, doesn't involve me forcing myself on you, if that's what you're thinking."

"No? So if I tell you I have no intention of having sex with you, we'll just leave it at that and call it good?"

Nic walked closer to her. "No, we won't." She reached out to still her hands. "Relax."

Abby must have realized what she was doing, because she tossed the clothes down with a shaky laugh. "So, I'm nervous."

"Me or Holly?"

"Both."

"I'm your girlfriend. There's nothing to be nervous about with me."

"What if they find out we're faking?"

"We'll be fine. I'll be a doting girlfriend and Holly will be jealous she let you go."

With a sigh, Abby sat down on top of the jeans she'd just folded. "I don't know why I'm getting all stressed about this. I *hate* that she does this to me. It's not like I have feelings for her or anything. It's just that last year, I felt like such a wretched, lovesick fool, you know."

Abby met Nic's gaze. "I let her play games with me. I knew she was doing it and I did nothing to stop her. I played along with her. I flirted back. I told myself it was because I was lonely. I was feeling unloved." She made a fist and hit her thigh. "And then I slept with her. We didn't talk afterward. No. She got out of bed and tiptoed back to Aaron's room, leaving me alone to dissect everything that had happened. Then over breakfast, she was so overly affectionate with him, it was nauseating. And she was doing it for show, for my benefit. Just to let me know that she was madly in love with Aaron and that she'd only slept with me out of pity."

"Pity?"

"Yes. Talk about a blow to your self-esteem, that will do it. I made up some crisis at work and escaped that very day." Abby lay back on the bed, staring at the ceiling. "I cried a lot on the drive home. I was feeling sorry for myself and disgusted with myself at the same time. And I was depressed."

"You never talked to her about it?"

"No. Not one word. Even back when she broke up with me that day, we didn't talk. I was stunned speechless. I'm not certain I said anything to her. So, no, we didn't speak last year either. There's been absolutely no contact at all until she sent that damn text." Abby leaned up on an elbow. "If you weren't here, do you think I'd fall into that trap again?"

"I don't know. What do *you* think?"

"I'd like to say no. But what has changed? I'm still single. Still alone and lonely."

"And she's familiar?"

"Yes," Abby groaned. "God, I'm pathetic."

"You'll be fine, Abby. We're in a new relationship and we're falling in love. We'll be attached at the hip. I won't give her the chance to get you alone." She moved over to the bed and sat down too. "Are you sure you don't want to just talk to her about it, though? Get it out in the open?"

"Oh, no. No, no. That would be the adult thing to do, so no. She wouldn't be adult about it. That would only give her an opening to rub it in my face. To remind me of how very weak I was. And to deny that her text meant anything sexual." She shook her head. "I don't want to talk to her. Not about that."

Nic patted her thigh lightly, then squeezed it. "Okay, then let's get to it. Give me a tour of the Christmas decorations, show me some pictures and stuff."

"The first thing I'm going to do is guzzle down a glass of wine."

CHAPTER EIGHTEEN

Abby was absolutely *dreading* the first encounter with Holly. She feared Holly would see through their guise and know they were faking it. How humiliating would that be? Right. As if this whole situation wasn't already humiliating.

She found everyone—including her father—gathered in the living room, standing around the fireplace. It seemed that conversation ceased, and all eyes turned their way. She felt her heart hammering nervously in her chest and she wanted to turn and run back up the stairs. But then she felt Nic's fingers wrap around her own and she heard Nic's voice, sounding perfectly normal and at ease.

"Hello, everyone, I'm Nic Bennett," she said, holding her hand out to her father first.

"Welcome, Nic. I'm Bill. Nice to meet you."

"Come in, Nicole. Come meet my son, Aaron, and his fiancé, Holly."

Her mother's voice sounded odd to her ears, but Abby watched as Nic gave them an easy smile, shaking her brother's hand, then Holly's.

"A pleasure to meet you," Nic said. "How was your drive up?"

Yes, it was all so perfectly normal as they exchanged pleasantries. She hugged her father tightly and got a kiss on the cheek. Aaron's greeting to her seemed warm and genuine, and Abby grudgingly returned it. Yes, normal. That is, until Holly slid her gaze over to her. It was as if everyone in the room was holding their collective breaths.

"Hello, Abigail. So good to see you again." Her voice was sultry and velvety, and she remembered how it used to whisper into her ear. Her hair seemed to be a little longer than last year, long and thick and wavy. The red sweater clung to her curves and the tight black jeans left little to the imagination. "I see you brought a friend with you this year. How nice."

Nic was the one to laugh. "Well, we're friends too, yes. I've heard a lot about you, Holly." Then Nic leaned closer to Abby, nudging her shoulder. "You were right, babe. You and Aaron look nothing alike. Other than he's as handsome as you are beautiful."

Relieved laughter from her parents followed, and Abby met Nic's eyes, hoping her smile looked affectionate. She was fairly certain she had not ever described Aaron to her. She relaxed then, seeing a quiet—and calm—confidence in Nic's gaze. Yes, they could do this. Nic seemed to be a natural at it.

"So…who wants a drink?" her mother asked, the smile on her face not quite as forced as it had been earlier. "Wine? A cocktail? Beer?"

"Wine," Abby said automatically. "A big glass. A really big glass."

"I'll have a beer, I guess," Nic said.

"Me, too," Aaron said.

"William, will you do the honors?" Her mother turned to Holly. "And what about you, dear? Should we whip up a batch of margaritas?"

"It's a little early for margaritas. I'll have wine too. A red, please, Abigail. Whatever you're having. You know what I like."

In defiance, she turned to her mother. "I'll have white, I think. Do you have a chardonnay?"

She went with her mother into the kitchen, relieved to get away from the others. She glanced over her shoulders, seeing Holly's attention fully on Nic. She sighed.

"Gonna be a long ten days."

"Nonsense. Nicole seems to fit in just fine." Her mother pulled a previously opened bottle from the fridge. "Let's finish this one before we open another. The wine cooler is stocked, and your father added several reds to the wine rack at the bar."

Abby poured a generous amount into a glass and took a large swallow before adding more, then she emptied the bottle into her mother's glass.

"I can't believe you didn't tell us you were dating. And she's attractive to boot."

Abby smiled at that. Yes, Nic was cute, she couldn't deny that. More importantly, she was turning out to be really nice. It seemed she'd hit the jackpot with her fake girlfriend.

They heard a chorus of nervous laughter from the other room, and they jerked their heads around. Then their eyes met. Her mother arched an eyebrow.

"What do you think that laughing was about?"

"I can't imagine."

When they went back out with their two wineglasses, they found Aaron and Nic holding beer bottles. Her father had opened a bottle of red wine for Holly, and he was holding a tumbler in his hands. He paused to shake the ice cubes a bit before drinking. A whiskey, she guessed. Here it was, barely four in the afternoon and they all held drinks. What did that say about her family? Were they all as stressed as she was?

"So, Nicole, how did you and our Abigail meet?"

Abby knew that would be her mother's first question, and despite her inclination to intervene, she let Nic answer it as she may.

"At her office, actually. Well, out in the courtyard." Nic glanced toward her with a smile. "At first, she wouldn't give me the time of day. I had dirty knees."

It was Holly who asked the question.

"Why on earth did you have dirty knees?"

"Hazards of the job," Nic said easily. "I do landscaping. I'm on my hands and knees a lot."

"What kind of landscaping?" her mother asked.

"We do both commercial and residential. It's my uncle's company. I've been working for him since I was a teenager. I call myself a landscape artist."

One of Holly's perfectly plucked eyebrows arched into her hair. "So you…plant stuff? Or do you mow lawns and such?"

Abby nearly choked at the question, but Nic merely smiled.

"Yes. Both. All over the Metroplex. Are you in need?"

"No, no. Aaron has a yard service. We are going to be building a home soon. A custom home. Perhaps we could talk to our builder about using your little company." Holly slid her glance over to Abby before looking back at Nic. "So you met in the courtyard?"

"Yes. I asked her out three or four times before she said yes." Nic smiled at her adoringly. "It was the best day of my life."

Abby found herself returning the smile, and she moved closer, tucking her hand beneath Nic's arm. "Best decision I made too," she said, playing along.

"Although our dinner date wasn't all that romantic," Nic continued. "I couldn't afford a fancy restaurant, so I took her to a little neighborhood dive that serves up barbeque—we had ribs and brisket—on paper plates."

"Oh, that was so good," she chimed in. "We should go again. I loved it."

They looked into each other's eyes. Nic's were swimming in amusement as she was sure hers were. She couldn't seem to get the grin off her face. Who knew?

"I don't recall you liking barbeque, Abigail."

Nic turned to Holly. "Oh, that's right. You two used to date, didn't you? Abby has a fondness for ribs. My uncle has this huge smoker and he'll put on several racks of ribs and slow cook them all day. Abby fights me for them."

"Well, if that's a favorite meal, there's a barbeque place in town we could go to for one of our outings," her mother offered. "We've been several times. It's quite good."

"Sure. If everyone else wants to." Abby dared to look at Holly. "I can't see you eating ribs with your hands, though."

"I'm sure you remember that I'm not fond of barbeque. It seems so uncivilized. How about that nice steak restaurant we went to last year?" Holly turned her gaze to Nic. "It was very nice and quite expensive. I'm sure a filet mignon would be a treat for Nicole."

Abby was floored by the callousness of her statement. Even her mother seemed taken aback. But Nic's smile never faltered. In fact, her eyes widened enthusiastically.

"A filet mignon? Oh wow. I've never had one. That *would* be a treat."

"Then we must go," her mother said. "And speaking of eating, I need to check on dinner. I hope everyone likes chicken parmesan. I'd planned to eat early. I know the four of you must be exhausted after driving all day."

They all murmured something in the affirmative, then silence ensued. It was broken by her father.

"It just occurred to me. We have two guests with holiday names. Nic and Holly. That's pretty neat."

Holly gave a fake smile as she looked at Nic. "Yes. Old Saint Nick. That's flattering."

"Yeah. About as flattering as being named for a poisonous shrub," Nic fired back.

Again, a chorus of nervous laughter ensued, and her mother took that opportunity to dart from the room. Her father moved to the bar to freshen his drink. Aaron opened the mini fridge and pulled out another beer. Holly openly stared at them. Nic smiled charmingly as she sipped from her bottle. Abby downed the rest of her wine in one gulp.

CHAPTER NINETEEN

"That was endless," Abby said as she locked their bedroom door. "Torture."

"Was it?"

Abby laughed quietly. "You were so good. Perfect, in fact."

"You're right. Holly is evil."

"Oh, I know. I can't believe I once thought I could be in love with her."

"I like your mother. She's pretty. You look just like her. But your father and Aaron didn't talk much. I didn't get a good feel for either of them."

"No. My father is always preoccupied with something. Idle chitchat bores him. Always has. And Aaron? He seemed a little flustered, almost. I'm not sure why. Holly was being Holly, but I think I saw him cringe a few times."

"She certainly wasn't shy about acknowledging that you two used to date. That had to be uncomfortable for Aaron. But then Holly was being a bitch," she said bluntly, causing Abby to laugh.

"Yeah, she was. Nothing surprising there." Abby walked closer to her. "She was so condescending. Why did you let it go on?"

"What should I have done? Should I have told her that Eric grills a mean filet mignon once a month for me? Or that the neighborhood barbeque joint is so popular they run out of food each day and you're one of the lucky ones if you get inside?" She pulled the sweater over her head. "Their ribs *are* fantastic, by the way."

"So you're one of the lucky ones?"

She smiled at that. "I know the owner. Scooter. He lets me in the back door."

"Well, I think Holly was making everyone uncomfortable. Do we really care how many clients she has or how big her raise was? Do we care that they plan to have Jacuzzi tubs in all *five* of their bathrooms? Do we care how obscenely big their new house is going to be?"

"You know why she was doing that, right?"

Abby frowned. "Other than showing off?"

"She was separating herself from me. I'm like the hired help and she's queen of the castle. Everything she said was to highlight the differences between us. I think she wants to make sure you know how far down you've sunk with me."

"Oh, Nic, she's—" But Abby paused. "You're right. She was."

"And you were right. If I wasn't here, she would be trying to get into your bed. By the sound of it, she may even try it with me here. Because she's not happy in her life. She and Aaron *together* are not happy."

"I have to agree. I didn't see it last year, but yeah, they don't really seem to be in love, do they?"

"No." She shrugged. "But what do I know about it? Maybe they have a different definition. They have lots of money— Holly mentioned that *several* times—and they're building an elaborate new house. Maybe those are the things that make them happy." She went to her bag and rummaged inside for one of the oversized shirts she'd packed. "Are you shy?"

"Huh?"

She held her shirt up. "Would you rather I change in the bathroom?"

"Oh. I take it you're *not* shy?"

Nic gave her a quick smile. "Not at all. That's one of the perks of being at the gym nearly every day."

"I see. Well, if you want to change out here, that's fine." Abby grabbed a small overnight bag and what looked like flannel pajama bottoms. "I'll take the bathroom."

Nic watched her as she hurried away and closed the door firmly behind. Damn, was she scared of her or what? With a shrug, she went back to her bag. She had no flannel, but she did bring a couple of pairs of sweats. Of course, she'd be much more comfortable without them. She slipped out of her jeans and folded them neatly. Instead of putting them back into her bag, she put them into one of the drawers Abby had offered. They were going to be here ten days. No sense in leaving her clothes shoved into a bag.

She'd just finished unpacking when Abby came out. She was wearing the brown and beige pair of flannel pajama bottoms and a white T-shirt. No bra. Her feet were bare and Nic smiled at the red nail polish Abby sported. *How sexy is that?* she thought.

"I got a pedicure after work the other day. Christmas red," Abby explained.

Without another word, she went around to the other side of the bed. She stopped before pulling the covers back.

"Do you have a preference for sides? I usually sleep on this side, so…"

"That's fine."

She took a turn in the bathroom, brushing her teeth and splashing water on her face. There was a tiny, foot-tall Christmas tree in the corner by the sink and mirror, and she stared at it, the glitter on its limbs seeming to twinkle in the lights. Then she looked up, meeting her eyes in the mirror.

What in the world was she doing here? She was in a house among strangers, about to crawl into bed with a woman she'd known a few days, and she was going to celebrate a holiday that had been nothing but a blip on her radar as a child. Uncle Jimmie had tried to make it into something special, but she'd already been scarred. The first Christmas with him had been difficult, to say the least, despite the multitude of gifts he'd had under the tree for her.

This year, though, would be different. She wouldn't have the comfort of home. She wouldn't have Uncle Jimmie there to remind her that she was okay. She wouldn't have the closeness of Eric and Addison. Christ, what had she been thinking?

Well, she'd been thinking that it was fifteen years ago, and it was damn time she put all of that in the past. And maybe, just maybe, Addison's words had struck a chord. Was she secretly hoping to have a fairytale Christmas? This house certainly had the makings of it, decorated as it was. And the snow outside was picture-perfect.

Only now—right now—she was feeling a bit lonely. A lot lonely, actually. Maybe it was a mistake to accept Abby's invitation. Because, yeah, Holly was putting her in her place all right. Making sure everyone, especially Abby, knew that she wasn't good enough for this family. At first, it was a bit of a game, sure. But why had she played along with it? Why had she made herself out to be so second-class? She could have told them she managed her uncle's company. She could have told them she ran the office and that she rarely went out on job sites. She could have made up some story about how she'd taken Abby out to The Oasis on Lake Travis for their first date and that they'd sat out on the patio and enjoyed the sunset views. That would have been romantic. She hadn't thought of that, though. No, because she wasn't a romantic person. Barbeque ribs that were dripping in sauce was right up her alley.

Maybe she'd let Holly go on like she had because, in truth, she didn't think she was good enough. She'd had a dysfunctional childhood, that was for sure. She didn't really remember the early years. Were they normal? All she remembered was the drinking, the fighting. On any given night, you never knew which one of them would be the most lit. If it was her father, then she and Sean would hide. He would just be looking for an excuse to lay into them. If it was her mother, they'd retreat to the farthest room—Sean's room—because the yelling and screaming would be so bad, it was the only place they could attempt to escape it. She sighed. Yeah, those were the good old days, weren't they? Because later, things really got ugly. She stared into her own eyes, seeing the hollowness there. Was it always there? She didn't know. It wasn't often that she did this self-perusal.

And she didn't want to do it now. That was in the past. She didn't want to relive it. She'd moved on. She had a new life now. A normal life. *Yeah, right.* Her uncle was much like she'd always wished her father had been. He was warm, friendly. Caring. Who knows? Maybe her father used to be that way too. Before the drinking. Before the fighting. Or maybe not.

With a heavy sigh, she turned away from the mirror. She looked once more at the tiny tree with its flickering glitter, then she turned the light out. Back in the bedroom, Abby had the lamp on beside her bed, but she was tucked under the covers, her eyes closed. She was about to walk around the bed to turn out the lamp when Abby's eyes fluttered open. There was a hint of fear in them.

"Sorry I woke you."

Abby stared at her for a long moment. "Are you okay?"

She nodded.

Abby reached an arm out and flicked off the lamp. "Come to bed," was all she said.

Nic took care to stay on her side of the bed, leaving ample room between them. She lay on her back, listening to the silence. Abby's even breathing indicated she'd fallen asleep again. She pulled the covers up a little more and closed her eyes. If she thought she would have a hard time falling asleep—a strange bed, a strange room—she was mistaken. She let herself drift away into a peaceful sleep, the long day finally catching up to her.

CHAPTER TWENTY

She wasn't sure what woke her, but her eyes popped open as if someone had shaken her. She rolled her head to the side, finding Nic still sound asleep. The room was quiet, but cold, and she turned toward the window, seeing the first glimmer of daylight peeking through the curtains. She got out of bed quietly and went to the window, moving the curtains aside. She stared as big, fluffy snowflakes drifted about. Judging by the amount on her dark Explorer, it had been snowing for a while.

She turned to the bed, wondering if she should wake Nic. Would she enjoy the sight? Would she want to go outside? She took a step toward the bed, then stopped. What was she expecting? That Nic would be as excited as a kid and want to go out and play in it? Maybe. She had been quite enthralled with it yesterday on the drive up.

But instead of waking her, she went into the bathroom. She'd brush her teeth and get dressed. If Nic was still asleep, she'd slip downstairs for an early cup of coffee and a visit with her mother. Judging by the tracks she'd seen outside, her father had already left.

When she came out of the bathroom, though, Nic was indeed awake. She was standing at the window, much like she had been earlier, only Nic had the curtains pulled wide apart, letting in the morning light. When Nic turned to look at her, her eyes had that look of wonder she'd seen in them yesterday.

"It's...it's snowing."

"Yes, it is." She moved closer to her. "Several inches, judging by the amount on the cars."

"It looks cold."

"In the teens, I guess. Maybe colder." She moved away. "I was going down for coffee. Should I wait on you?"

"Are the others up yet?"

"My mother is. Looks like my dad left already. Holly and Aaron are late sleepers."

Nic nodded. "Yeah. Go ahead. I'll be down in a bit."

Abby nodded too, then paused. "Did you sleep okay?"

"Oh, yeah. Out like a light. You?"

"Yes. I don't think I woke up once. Will you be up for a trip into town? We'll need to get gifts for each other."

"Right. Sure."

"We can go about ten or so and stay in town for lunch, if you'd like."

Nic shrugged. "Is that normal? Will your mother mind?"

"She will assume we are escaping Holly. Or maybe that we want some alone time."

Nic turned back to the window. "Sure. Whatever you want. I'm all yours, remember."

Abby watched her for a moment, then turned to go. Nic sounded...different. A bit subdued. Maybe she wasn't a morning person. Maybe she didn't get her swagger until after she had coffee. No. She'd been normal—talkative—yesterday morning on the drive up. Oh, well.

She went down the stairs, pausing to listen for voices. There were none so she continued down. The lights on the tree were twinkling and the fireplace was already going. She knew where she'd find her mother. In the sunporch off the kitchen. The sunporch had been rather rustic and not insulated in the least when her grandparents had owned the house. Her father had renovated it, putting in double-paned windows that opened wide in the summer. It was winterized now and there was a cute woodburning stove that kept it warm. It was her mother's "space" and where she spent each morning as she watched activity at the birdfeeders in the back.

She poured a cup of coffee, then went to the porch, finding her mother in the oversized chair, a throw blanket over her knees and a cup cradled in her hands.

"Good morning."

Her mother turned, smiling. "Abigail. Good morning." She looked behind her. "Where's Nicole?"

"She was at the window watching it snow. She'll be along."

Her mother motioned to the chair beside her in a silent invitation to sit. "I like her. Holly was rather rude to her on several occasions last night. I felt sorry for Nicole."

"Let's call it like it is, Mom. Holly was being a bitch."

Her mother leaned toward her conspiratorially. "If I had to hear one more thing about the house they're going to build, I might have vomited."

Abby laughed. "God, me too. And Aaron just sat there and didn't say a word. In fact, he hardly said anything all night. What's up with that?" She held her hand up. "And do *not* blame me. I attempted to talk to him. A couple of times. Well, at least once."

"Who could get a word in with Holly going on and on like she was? I don't remember her being like that last year."

"It's because of Nic. She wants to make sure I know that Nic's not quite on her level."

"Why would she care about that?"

"Oh, Mom…it's complicated."

"You don't still have a thing for her, do you?" her mother whispered.

"God, no! But the way she went on and on, you'd think she has one for me."

"Oh my goodness, Abigail! They're engaged to be married. And it's been two years."

"Exactly. So why does she care who I date?"

"I think you're reading too much into it."

Oh, she itched to show her mother the text Holly had sent her. But no, she couldn't do that, could she? That might cause another family rift and they certainly couldn't have that. The first one hadn't been fixed yet.

"Is this private or can I join you?"

Abby turned, finding Nic standing in the doorway, already holding a cup of coffee. "No, come in."

She nearly dropped her own cup when Nic bent down to kiss her. She was certain her face turned scarlet as her mother watched them.

"Good morning, Sandra." Nic looked out the windows. "It's beautiful. Is this a special spot for you?"

"Good morning, Nicole. Yes, this is my favorite perch in the mornings. William gets the fire going for me in here before he leaves. I have my coffee and spend some time just relaxing and watching the activity at the feeders before I start my day."

"Where is he anyway?" Abby asked.

"At the resort. I swear, the man thinks they can't run the thing without him."

Abby stared at her mother, seeing a bit of sadness there. Bitterness was mixed in too, she imagined. Was it like before in Dallas? Did he have something to occupy his time now and he was neglecting his home and his wife? Well, she couldn't ask questions now, not in front of Nic.

"We'll probably go into town later," she said instead. "We have a little shopping to do. We might stay for lunch, too. Maybe grab a burger at the brewery."

"Oh, that sounds like fun. When we first moved here, we used to go there at least once a week for lunch. Your father can't seem to find the time now."

Abby wondered if her mother knew that, yes, bitterness had crept into her voice. She glanced at Nic, who raised her eyes questioningly. Abby sighed. God, were her parents having marital problems again? *Now?*

She finished her coffee in a last gulp. "So, are you ready to explore outside? Play in the snow?"

Nic nodded. "I'd love to."

"Gloves. Parka."

She got up and looked at her mother. "We'll go out the front door so we don't disturb your birds back here."

Her mother only smiled at her. "I made a breakfast casserole. I knew everyone would be up at different times. Let me get that in the oven. It only needs forty-five minutes to bake."

"Thanks, Mom." When Nic went ahead of her back into the kitchen, she paused. "Mom? Is everything okay? With you and Dad?"

Her mother forced a smile. "Of course, dear. It's Christmas. Everything is fine."

"You want to talk?" she asked gently.

Her mother waved her offer away. "Oh, you know how your father is. He gets involved in something and it becomes the center of his life. I didn't tell you, but he's moved into a manager's position."

"So much for retirement."

"Yes. I guess I knew it wouldn't last. He's bored silly stuck here at the house and those first few years, we did all the touring we wanted to do."

"What about you? Are you bored here?"

"I keep busy. There's always something to do. And if there's not, I bring a book in here to read. I can lose several hours like that."

She went over to her mother and squeezed her shoulder. "I'm sorry, Mom."

"Oh, it is what it is. I guess I knew at the time that we were far too young to retire. I have things here to keep me busy, but your father? No. Now go take that cute girl of yours out for a play in the snow. Breakfast will be ready when you get back."

She hurried up the stairs, finding Nic standing by the window, waiting for her. The bed had been neatly made and the room was tidy. She motioned to the bed.

"Thanks."

Nic nodded. "I'm a bit of a neat freak when it comes to things like that."

"Lucky me," she said easily. Then she stopped. "You kissed me."

Nic gave a quiet laugh. "That was hardly a kiss, Abby. But we are supposed to be girlfriends, aren't we?"

"Yes. It surprised me, that's all."

She got her coat out of the closet and made sure her gloves were inside. Then she took her phone and slipped it into her pocket on the off chance she wanted to take a picture. "Ready?"

"Yes. Lead on."

Between her mother's sullen mood and now Nic, who seemed to be brooding about something, the morning was getting gloomier by the minute. Perhaps being outside in the fresh snow would brighten things up.

They hadn't quite made it out when she heard a bedroom door open upstairs. Without turning around to see whether it was Holly or Aaron, she hurried down the last few steps to the front door. She held it open for Nic, then closed it quickly behind them.

The morning was gray and dull as thick clouds hung low, still dumping light snow on them. She pulled the wool cap from one pocket of her coat and put it on her head. Their boots crunched on the driveway, and she led Nic around the cars, out to the road.

"It's so quiet," Nic said. "You can almost hear the snow falling."

"Yes. Close your eyes. Listen."

She did as she'd just instructed Nic to do. It was cold and still, no wind to disturb the quiet. She lifted her face up, feeling snowflakes hitting her cheeks. She knew she was smiling, and she finally opened her eyes.

"Beautiful."

Abby turned, meeting Nic's gaze. "Yes, it is."

"I was talking about you."

"Oh."

Nic smiled and turned away. She walked out into the snow toward the reindeer. She spread her arms out. "Is this normal? The decorations out here?"

"Yes." She stared at the snow clinging to Nic's dark hair. "Do you not have a cap or something for your head?"

"No."

"We can buy one in town. You'll be more comfortable outside with one."

Nic nodded as she turned in a circle, her eyes filling with wonder as she took it all in. Then she bent down and scooped up a handful of snow. Abby watched her, noting her healthy, tanned skin, even in December.

"Come around here to the side. I'll show you the bird tree up close."

Nic surprised her by taking her hand and pulling her closer in an affectionate embrace. "We have an audience," Nic said quietly. "Someone is peeking out the window by the front door."

"Is it her?"

"I can't tell. I assume."

"She knows we're faking it."

"Why do you say that?"

"Because she knows the type of women I date."

"Ah. And I'm not one of them." Nic stepped away from her. "I guess we should have gone with doctor or professor then."

Abby took Nic's hand before she could walk away, leading her to where the bird tree was. "Like everything else, my mother goes all out for this tree. Air-popped popcorn gets strung with dried fruits. And she makes these suet cakes with cookie cutters shaped like wreaths and Christmas trees and stuff." When they rounded the side of the house, she stopped. "Nic, I'm sorry. I—"

"Wow. That is pretty cool. How long does it last?"

Abby moved her gaze from Nic to the tree. "She has to restock it every couple of days."

"Why over here and not out by the sunporch?"

"She'll tell you because this tree is the perfect size, but I think it's because there aren't any feeders over here and she can see this tree from the living room when she's sitting by the fire."

Nic turned to her. "Your dad is absent a lot?"

Abby stared at her, wondering if she should discuss her parents' relationship with her or not. "He's working again… so…"

Nic said nothing—she only tucked her hands under her arms.

"Are you cold?"

"A little."

"Do you have anything on under your jeans? Tights or leggings or something."

Nic gave her a wry smile. "No."

Abby laughed. "Not your thing, huh? Well, you should get some anyway. No one will know you have them on. You'll be thankful to have them."

"Can we walk a little?"

"Of course." Abby wondered if she wanted to talk. "Let's go down the driveway to the forest road."

"What kind of gifts are we going to get each other?"

Abby shrugged. "I have no idea. I'm awful with gifts."

"What about the others? Should I get something for them?"

"No, no. That's not necessary. Our gift giving is not at all personal or even thoughtful, for that matter. My parents give us money each year. My grandparents give us money. I give Amazon gift cards to all of them."

"What about Holly and Aaron?"

"I got them a gift card to a restaurant."

Nic laughed. "So opening gifts on Christmas morning is not all warm and fuzzy?"

"Oh, when we were kids, it was. Keep in mind that Aaron is four years older than me, so he was already out of the Santa phase long before me. I guess I was in high school when the gifts dwindled to a couple and the money tradition started. Of course, back then and when I was in college, getting a chunk of cash was a lifesaver."

"Like a hundred bucks' chunk or larger than that?"

Abby hesitated. She didn't want to sound like she was privileged or anything, especially considering how Nic had grown up with Christmas as an afterthought. Nic seemed to recognize her hesitation for what it was.

"Sorry. None of my business."

"It was an obscene amount. Still is. My paltry hundred-dollar gift cards pale in comparison."

"Why gift cards?"

"Because I'm a terrible gift giver. I never have a clue as to what to get them. They certainly don't need anything." She shrugged. "I guess I never really learned. And the excuse of a gift card is that they can get whatever they want. The stockings, though, that's usually fun. My mother seems to find cute little knickknacks or something for each of us. Sometimes there'll be jewelry—earrings or a necklace or something like that."

"What about Aaron? Did you used to exchange gifts? Before Holly, that is?"

"Alcohol. He would get me a couple of bottles of wine, and I'd get him a bottle of bourbon or something. But really, we're just not that close. He didn't move back to the Dallas area until three years ago. And, of course, the last two, he's been with Holly. Since I've been in high school, the only time we see each other is at Christmas."

"So as much as I consider my family life dysfunctional, you—"

"God, yes. Totally dysfunctional. Although maybe that's not the right word. Unconventional. My mother and I are still very close. When they lived in Dallas, I had dinner with them at least once a week, sometimes more. It was an adjustment when they moved. We talk on the phone all the time now. My dad? Well, he's—"

"Preoccupied?"

Abby nodded. "He's one of those people who will never retire. He has to have a purpose, a job. There's no idle time with him. He'll have everything organized. Tomorrow we'll take their Suburban to tour the lights in town. He'll have the route planned out precisely. He'll know exactly how long it'll take. And my mother, just to mess with him, will suggest a side street or suggest we stop somewhere. It drives him crazy," she said with a laugh.

They paused at the edge of the driveway, both looking down the forest road, which was covered in snow. The only evidence that there was a road was the break in the trees.

"I have a confession to make," Nic said, her breath frosting around her.

Abby nodded. "Okay."

"Last night, before bed, I was...I was feeling out of place. Lonely. Like I was thinking, what the hell am I doing here." She turned to glance at her. "And wishing I hadn't agreed to this."

"I'm sorry, Nic. It's because of the way Holly treated you, right?"

Nic shook her head. "I think it was because of the way I *let* her treat me. And the reasons for that." She started walking and Abby followed. "I haven't told you much about my childhood. It was crappy all the way around, really. My parents were...well, they weren't normal parents. They drank a lot." Nic turned to her. "Falling down, screaming, and fighting drunk kind of drinking. So I never brought friends around. At first." She looked away again as she walked. "Because later, I really didn't have any friends to bring around. Most of the kids in school made fun of me."

Nic stopped walking and looked up into the trees. "I was in the sixth grade. We were having this...this program. I was in one of the skits. I'd asked her to come. My dad was working nights back then, so I knew he wouldn't make it. So, I don't know, three or four days before the thing, I asked her to come. I don't know why, really. I guess I wanted to be like other kids whose parents were active in their lives." She reached out and touched a snow-laden branch, watching as the snow fell to the ground. "I'd begged her not to drink that day. Begged her." She started walking again. "But no. She showed up late, making a scene. She was stumbling down the aisle, then laughing so loud, everyone stopped to stare. She fell into a man's lap—the father of one of my classmates." She held a hand up, as if to ward off old memories. "Anyway, after that, parents made sure none of their kids came near our house. Kids stopped being friends with me. Instead, they started making fun of me, calling me names."

"Oh, Nic…I'm so sorry."

"Truth was, I was always an outgoing person. Despite my parents, I was a happy kid. I was popular in school. Until that day. After that, I never felt good enough. And I was embarrassed to look people in the eyes. I knew then, even at that young age, that socially I was beneath them."

"And so you think you're not good enough for me? Not good enough to be here with us?"

"You have a normal family. You—"

"What is normal, Nic? Is my mother going absolutely bonkers over Christmas decorations normal? Is me not speaking to my brother for two years normal? Is having a father who's so preoccupied that he sometimes forgets we're around?" She touched Nic's arm and squeezed. "I'm not trying to make light of your childhood, Nic. I'm not. And I'm certainly not saying that I can relate, because I can't. Yes, I had a privileged upbringing. My parents were both very successful in their careers and I never wanted for anything, including their support—both emotional and financial."

This time she started them walking. "So, my father may have been at my school program, but he had one ear to his phone. He didn't miss many of my soccer games, but he was always working. He was there in body only." She sighed, deciding to elaborate. "Their marriage was failing. They were working so much they were like strangers to each other. They didn't really fight. They weren't together enough for that. But it was bickering and callous remarks to each other and putting each other down. I was a senior in high school, and I thought that as soon as I was out of the house, they'd divorce. I was prepared for it. Actually, I was prepared for them to do it sooner than that." She turned to Nic and met her gaze. "So, not all roses and sunshine. Different than what you went through, certainly, but still, not all roses."

"What happened?"

"They still loved each other, I guess. And they knew that their jobs, their careers, were tearing them apart. So they quit. Made a pact that they were out of the real estate business for

good. Moved up here and learned how to live together again."
She kicked at the snow. "Or so I thought. It looks like he's fallen
back into old habits." She held her hand up. "Regardless, please
don't think you're not good enough for this family. Holly was
being a bitch and that's just her."

Nic turned to look at her, meeting her gaze as if trying to
read her eyes. Maybe to see if she was being sincere or not. But
she said nothing as she turned away. Abby felt a tiny tug on her
heart at the look in Nic's eyes. Lonely? Yes. She'd been surprised
that Nic had confessed to that, but she could see it in her eyes.
She was normally so sure of herself. Confident, with enough
swagger for her to have called Nic arrogant. But now? No, that
swagger was missing, wasn't it? Surprisingly, she missed it.

CHAPTER TWENTY-ONE

Abby paused at the front door, turning to look at her. "Holly will most likely be in the kitchen. She's like a four or five cup coffee drinker, so…"

"If you're worried that I'll blow our cover, don't be. I'll smile at you adoringly the whole time."

"We can head to town after breakfast."

"Trying to escape already?"

"Yeah." She opened the door. "Please don't let her talk down to you today, Nic."

Yes, she needed to snap out of her funk, didn't she? Maybe she should have told Abby the whole story. Maybe she should have gotten it all out at once. Over and done with. But really, was it any of Abby's concern? Was there any reason to tell her all of that?

"Nic?"

Nic met her gaze, finally nodding. "I'm good."

Abby smiled at her. "Yes, you are. So don't think otherwise."

She followed Abby inside, taking her coat off like Abby had done and hanging it next to hers on the rack in the entryway. She wasn't nervous, no. She felt a little apathetic, she supposed, and that wouldn't do at all. She forced a smile to her face and took Abby's hand, squeezing her fingers. They were still a little cold, as were hers.

Instead of going into the kitchen, which is where Abby was headed, Nic tugged her toward the fireplace. Abby looked at her questioningly but said nothing. They held their hands out to its warmth for a moment, then both turned at the same time, facing the tree.

"Does she leave the lights on all the time?"

"They're on a timer. I think they go out at eleven or midnight, then come back on in the morning. Except for Christmas Eve—tomorrow—they'll be on all night long." She nudged her shoulder. "You know, so when Santa comes, he'll have lights."

"Was that always a tradition?"

"Yes. I tried to warn you. It's Christmas overload."

"I like it." Which surprised her. "It feels very…I don't know, peaceful in here."

"Why didn't your parents like Christmas?"

Nic stared at the star on top of the tree, watching the white light blink on and off. For some reason, it reminded her of their old porch light, the one with the short in it. It flickered all the time, and she remembered many an occasion when her father would bang on the wall, cursing the damn thing. Bang just hard enough to get the connection going again and it would stay lit for a minute or two, then it would blink at them again in a mocking manner—on and off. On and off. That is, until the day her father took an empty whiskey bottle and slammed it into the light bulb. *"Fixed that son of a bitch finally."* Yeah, he did. No one ever replaced the broken bulb. It never blinked at them again.

"They…they were drunks, like I said. He could at least function and hold down a job. She couldn't." She shoved her hands into her pockets. "He wasn't working shift work any longer, so by the time he got home each day, she'd already been drinking for hours and hours. He'd pour a drink as soon as he got in the door and gulp it down, like he was trying to catch up to her. There was seldom dinner made. He'd yell. She'd yell. They'd fight." She sighed. "Pretty much every day was like that. She always passed out first, then things quieted down. He'd sit in his recliner, a drink in his hand, staring at the TV as if it were on. She'd be either on the couch or slumped back in her chair. Christmas was no different."

She felt Abby's hand tug her own out of her pockets, and warm fingers wound around hers. She turned to look at Abby. "I think my dysfunctional family tops yours."

Abby gave her a sympathetic nod. "Are you an only child? Or do you have siblings?"

Nic stared back at the tree. "I...I had a brother." Then she cleared her throat. "Sorry. I've been in a little bit of a funk today." She motioned with her hand toward the kitchen. "Should we go in?"

"Are you up for it?"

She paused. "I could maybe use a hug."

"Oh, Nic."

Abby wrapped her arms around her shoulders and pulled her tight. Nic closed her eyes, relishing the closeness. No one ever hugged her except for Addison. Oh, Eric did sometimes but his hugs were the one-armed "good to see you" hugs. Not the affectionate ones that Addison gave her. And this one from Abby? Nic slid her arms around Abby's waist, noting the slimness of it. She pulled her closer until their bodies were touching. This caused a contented—relieved—sigh to leave her. This hug was nice. She didn't ever remember getting one quite like it before.

"Oh, there you two are."

They pulled apart, finding Sandra watching them with a broad smile. Abby took a step away from her.

"Sorry. We—"

"Oh, it's all right, Abigail. But breakfast is ready."

"Are *they* in there?"

"They are," she said quietly. "And they're making plans to go into town today too."

Abby groaned. "You've got to be kidding me."

"Maybe we should do a group lunch," Nic suggested.

Abby actually slugged her arm playfully. "Are you out of your mind?"

"Come into the kitchen. Please," her mother said in a quiet voice. "I shouldn't be the only one subjected to more house plans."

"Oh god...*again*?"

But they dutifully followed Sandra into the kitchen. Aaron and Holly were at the table, coffee cups in front of them. Aaron was scrolling through his phone, and he glanced up, offering a quick smile.

"Good morning."

Nic nodded. "Good morning. Have you been out? It's beautiful."

"Oh, that's right," Holly said. "It's your first time for snow. How did you like it?"

"Like I said, it's beautiful. And cold. Abby has promised me a snowball fight later."

Abby laughed as she poured them coffee. "You wouldn't stand a chance. I'm sneaky quick with those things. You'll be beaten to a pulp."

"Maybe we should do teams. Get Aaron and Holly to play too."

Holly smirked. "A bit too childish for me."

"Childish? Or do you mean childlike? I, for one, hope I don't ever lose that childlike enthusiasm. Especially about something as fun and innocent as having a snowball fight. I won't apologize for jumping in with a youthful exuberance." Nic smiled at Abby. "Seeing as how I've only seen a dusting of snow here and there in my lifetime, this is certainly special. I wouldn't want to waste a minute of it."

"Snowball fights are fun," Sandra chimed in. "When Aaron and Abigail were kids, they'd chase each other around outside. Abigail, despite being four years younger, was—like she said— sneaky quick. Poor Aaron got pummeled by them."

Abby glanced at her brother. "I guess I should confess. I used to go out early and make hard, tight snowballs, then stash them in different places."

Aaron laughed. "Like I didn't know that."

"You did?"

"Of course."

Abby actually smiled at him. "And you still let me win? That was sweet of you." She handed Nic a cup of coffee. "Here you go."

"Thanks, babe."

"So, Nicole, tell me more about this company you work for? You know, in case we want to hire you sometime."

Nic slowly slid her gaze to Holly, hoping her expression was as bored as she felt. "Bennett Landscaping. My uncle's company."

"Yes. Your uncle. What is it that you do?"

"Why so interested in Nic, Holly?" Abby asked as she sat down.

"Well, I've just never met a…a landscaper before."

"Landscape *artist*," Nic corrected with a smile. "I thought you said Aaron has a crew that comes to your house now." She sat down beside Abby. "Most companies are pretty much the same. If you've met them, you've met us. We have more commercial contracts than residential, though."

"But what do you *do*?"

"What is it you're asking? I thought we covered this last night. Or did you not get in enough digs about it yet?" She felt Abby stiffen beside her, but she calmly took a sip of her coffee. "For the record, for as much disdain as you obviously have for my profession, I can match that for yours."

Holly didn't seem fazed at all. "Profession? Is that what it is? A job you've had since your teens?" Then she laughed. "Well, I suppose it is a profession by now. A little late for you to go to college and start over. I'm assuming you're over thirty."

There was a long, awkward silence, broken only by Sandra, who flitted nervously about the kitchen. "So who's ready for casserole? It's all ready."

Abby surprised her by leaning closer against her. "Oh my god. You're over thirty? How does Holly know this and I don't? You keep telling me you're only twenty-nine, like me."

"I am twenty-nine. Would I lie to you?" She glanced at Holly. "I'm sure at your age—What? Forty?—it's hard to guess the age of others younger than you."

Abby gave a muted laugh beside her while Holly gasped. "Forty? Seriously? I mean, not that I have anything against forty, I'm simply not anywhere *near* that."

Nic shrugged. "I don't really care." She turned to Sandra. "That casserole smells divine. Can I help with something?"

"Oh, thank you, Nicole, but I'll just put it on the table, and everyone can scoop as they want."

Nic felt Abby's hand on her thigh and its gentle squeeze. She turned to her, meeting her gaze. Without thinking, she leaned closer, kissing her. It wasn't a long, drawn-out kiss, no. They were sitting at the breakfast table, after all. But it wasn't the quick touch that they'd done earlier that morning in front of her mother. Even so, Abby's eyes were still smiling at her, and her hand never left her thigh. Nic returned her smile, feeling all of the…well, the blueness she'd been feeling earlier slip away. Yeah, the hell with Holly. For Abby's sake, if she wanted to make a good impression on anyone, it was her parents. She didn't give a fuck about Holly.

The breakfast was eaten mostly in silence, even with Sandra trying to force the conversation along. It was a great meal, though, and she took seconds. A biscuit batter type of thing with eggs and sausage, spinach and mushrooms, and loads of cheese. She was stuffed when she pushed her plate away, wondering how on earth she could contemplate a burger for lunch after that.

"That was delicious, Sandra," she complimented. "You've got to give Abby the recipe."

"Thank you, Nicole. It's one I've been making for years. It's one of Abigail's favorites too. I'm surprised she hasn't whipped it up for you already."

"Mom, this thing has so many calories and fat grams, I wouldn't dream of having it for anything other than Christmas." Abby turned to her. "So don't get any ideas!"

"Then maybe I should get the recipe then."

"Do you cook, Nicole?" Sandra asked.

"Oh yes. I love to cook. I make this chicken dish with asparagus that's sautéed in wine. It's served over wild rice. Abby loves it." She looked pointedly at Holly, who had been unusually quiet. "Do you and Aaron cook? Or do you get a meal service or something?"

"I fancy myself as a bit of a gourmet cook, actually. Abby can vouch for that. She loved my cooking. Unfortunately, with my busy schedule, I don't get to enjoy that all that much. Aaron dabbles in it, but we mostly eat out or have delivery. Except weekends. Then we do try to put a nice meal on the table."

"Oh, yeah. Weekends are the best. I try to do breakfast in bed at least once." She turned and winked at Abby. "And we like playing in the kitchen together too."

"So, you…live together?" Holly asked. "I'm surprised, Abby. You were always so guarded about that."

Nic shook her head. "Not officially, no. But I've got a really small place, so it's nice to stay with Abby."

"Well, I guess you are practically living with me, aren't you? You're there most nights."

"It's so nice that you have someone, honey, but I wish you'd told me about Nicole earlier. I would have been better prepared," Sandra said.

"Well, after the…the last relationship I had, I wanted to be sure." Abby looked quickly at Holly, then to her. "It's been like a breath of fresh air so far."

Nic barely resisted laughing at the twinkle in Abby's eyes. They were rewarded with Holly pushing her plate away and standing.

"Thank you for breakfast, Sandra. I need to shower and get ready for the day. Aaron is taking me into town for shopping." She motioned for Aaron to get up, which he obediently did. "We'll grab lunch there, so don't bother with it on our account."

"Oh, wow," Nic said. "We're going shopping too. Maybe we'll run into you."

Holly's smile was so obviously forced. "I doubt we'll be patronizing the same shops, Nicole. But you two have fun."

"Thanks. Y'all too."

No one spoke a word as Aaron and Holly left the kitchen. Sandra busied herself with putting the casserole away, and Abby got up, piling plates together to take to the sink. It wasn't until Aaron and Holly were well out of earshot that Abby laughed. A tiny, controlled laugh. Then Sandra joined in. Nic found herself smiling as Abby and her mother giggled like schoolchildren.

"I guess I should set the record straight," Nic said. "I am over thirty. Birthday was in July. I simply wasn't going to give her the satisfaction."

"Six months? That's not fibbing too much. But she's being so bitchy. What did I ever see in her?"

"I wondered the same thing," Sandra chimed in.

"Was she always like that and I just didn't see it?"

"Yes." Sandra loaded plates into the dishwasher. "I would say consider yourself lucky that you're with Nicole now and not Holly. Poor Aaron has to deal with her, not you." Sandra looked back at her. "You held your own, Nicole. Good for you."

Abby touched her mother's arm. "I guess we're going to go up to shower too. What do you have going on today?"

"Oh, I have things to do. And dinner to plan and cook. You go on and enjoy yourselves."

"Do you want to go with us, Sandra?"

"Oh, no. I couldn't. You run along. We'll have a nice dinner. Then tomorrow is Christmas Eve. More informal. A buffet."

"When do Grandma and Grandpa come?"

"Oh? I didn't tell you? They're not coming this year. Four of their friends invited them on a cruise. They'll be back the twenty-ninth so they're planning to come up for New Year's instead."

"Really? Well, I guess that sounds like fun but hardly Christmas. I don't think we've ever not been together, have we?"

Her mother pursed her lips, indicating her displeasure. "We have not. That didn't seem to matter to them."

Abby tried to hide her smile as she patted her mother's shoulder. "Well, at least I'll get to see them then. Do you need anything from town?"

"No, no. I'm going down to Taos since all of you will be gone. I have a few last-minute things to get, and I need to hit the grocery store one last time. Aaron said that Holly wanted to lunch at that new Italian place." Sandra grinned at them. "Hopefully you won't run into them."

"We'll definitely be at the brewery." Abby kissed her cheek. "See you later, Mom."

CHAPTER TWENTY-TWO

"How about this?"

Abby shook her head. "No. How is it possible that we are the world's worst gift givers? How hard can it be?"

Nic pulled out a sweater only to have Abby wrinkle up her nose. "Actually, I don't give gifts," Nic said. "To anyone. I guess now that I'm going to be Aunt Nicky very soon, that'll change."

"Are you looking forward to that?"

"Can you tell?" She laughed. "April. They want me to be in the delivery room. Is that cool or what?"

"It is. I'm sure it'll be a beautiful experience."

"Between me and Eric, one of us will pass out. I hope it's not me."

Abby paused at a rack of assorted knit caps, all different colors, some with balls on the top, others not. Most had *Red River* stitched across the front. "Here. You need a cap. Pick one out. I'll stick it in your stocking."

Nic shuffled through them, finding a blue one. "This one."

Abby nodded. "Your favorite color. It matches your eyes."

She took it from her. "Now, seriously, we've got to find gifts for each other. What do you want?"

"Well, I've had my eye on this really nice food processor. I just haven't pulled the trigger on it yet."

Abby smiled as she shook her head. "How about we stick to something a little more romantic than kitchen gadgets. It *is* our first Christmas together. We should get something special."

"How about an ornament with the year on it?"

Abby shook her head again. "Not romantic and besides, I don't have a tree up."

"You don't? So you didn't take after your mother?"

"I have a few Christmas decorations, I just didn't put them out this year. I don't do a tree, though. I'm always up here for the holidays. Ten or eleven days of this is all I need. By the time I leave, I've had my fill."

"The whole town looks decorated. I bet it'll be pretty tonight."

"Oh, it's beautiful. Like a real Christmas village. There's a couple of neighborhoods in the foothills north of town that go all out. That's where we'll tour the lights. All of the pubs in town are open, but they're usually jampacked. That's why we go home and have our own party and sing carols." She shrugged. "At least, I guess that's still the plan. What with my father being so distant…" She sighed. "You think I should talk to him?"

"What? Find out what's going on?"

"Yeah. I mean, maybe he doesn't realize that he's fallen into this trap again. Maybe he has no clue that he's abandoned Mom."

"Well, not that I know them or anything, but judging by their actions, their demeanors, I'd say they're not exactly in a happy marriage."

She groaned. "Oh, I know. I was thinking back to last night at dinner. He had that faraway look in his eyes, like he wanted to be anywhere but there." She laughed lightly. "Of course, so did I."

"Would he talk to you about something like that?"

"I don't know. I've always been closer to Mom, but Dad and I have always been able to talk."

Nic stopped at a display of snow globes. She picked one up and shook it, watching with almost rapt attention as the snow settled around a gingerbread house that had Red River stenciled across the front. When the snow had all fallen, she shook it once more, then put it back down, still staring as the snow swirled around. Abby watched as Nic's eyes remained glued to the globe. She looked up, almost embarrassed, then walked on.

Abby moved beside her. "I think Dad misses the excitement of his job," she continued. "Closing a big deal, getting the contract signed, coming home with an expensive bottle of something to celebrate. He was good at his job. Too good, maybe. I think he feels like he's wasting away up here."

"How old are they?"

"Dad will turn sixty in March. Mom is fifty-eight."

"How long have they been retired?"

"Oh, this is like, maybe six years now. Or seven. I was still in college when they started the process." She walked on. "At first I felt guilty. I thought they'd only stayed together because of me. Aaron was already out of the house. By the time I was a senior in high school, he was out of college and working. He hardly came around. I felt almost like an only child." She paused. "You said you had a brother. Is he with your parents?"

Nic stared at her for the longest time. "Abby, I'd rather not talk about it if you don't mind."

"I'm sorry, Nic. I'm being nosy. It's absolutely none of my business."

"How about a necklace or something? Or a bracelet?"

Abby nodded. "Okay. But we don't have to do expensive. And I'll of course return it to you when we get back home."

"Good. So what do you like? Silver? Gold?"

"You know what, let's go down the street a bit. Do you mind walking?"

"Of course not."

"There's a place that makes handcrafted jewelry. It's mostly silver. They have a lot of Southwestern designs and stuff with turquoise too. We should be able to find something there."

The snow clouds had started drifting away when they'd first gotten to town but now the sky was clear, and the sun was bright. She handed Nic the blue knit cap she bought for her.

"Here."

"Thanks." Nic put it on and pulled it over her ears. "Much better."

Abby smiled at her. "You've never worn one before, have you?"

"Nope. Why? Do I have it on backwards?"

"I don't think there is a backwards."

They walked on in silence, blending in with the other shoppers on the sidewalks. Despite the earlier snow, the town seemed to be bustling with activity. Each time a shop door opened, bells jingled, and Christmas music could be heard from inside. It was a festive atmosphere and she wondered if it was rubbing off on Nic. She seemed to be taking it all in and there was a smile on her face.

She opened the door to the jewelry store—The Red River Silver Mine—and motioned for Nic to follow. Like the other stores they'd been to, it was decorated for the season and Christmas songs played in the background. She found herself humming along to "Walking in a Winter Wonderland" as she went up to one of the displays.

"Do you wear jewelry?"

Nic peered over her shoulder. "No."

Abby looked at her quizzically. "Then are you sure this is what you want?"

Nic met her gaze and offered a slight smile. "No one has ever given me jewelry before, and I never thought to buy it for myself."

Abby again wondered at her childhood. She had so many questions, but she kept them inside. Nic had made it clear that she didn't want to discuss it. Instead, she reached up and moved the cap aside, revealing her ears.

"Never had your ears pierced? How did you manage that?"

Again, Nic met her eyes, and she wasn't quite sure what she saw there. Regret? Nic didn't answer her question, though. She turned her focus to the display of silver necklaces. She pointed to one that had a small pendant attached—a small blue gemstone encased in a silver ring.

"I like something like that." She pointed to another. "That stone is pretty too."

That particular stone was green. A jade? It was raw. Unfinished and she thought it fit Nic better than the perfectly round and polished blue stone. Of course, with her blue eyes, the jade wouldn't quite match.

"Okay. What about for me?"

Nic smiled and led her down the way, pausing at the necklaces with heart pendants. Some plain, some with small diamonds. She looked at Nic with raised eyebrows. "Really? A heart?"

"Really. Pick one out."

There were no prices and she hesitated, not wanting to pick an expensive one. Nic seemed to read her mind.

"Abby, don't worry about the cost. It's Christmas. My very first gift to someone. Make it special."

"Well, since I'll be returning it to you, maybe you should pick out something you like instead."

"I already did, and I don't plan to return it to you. Same goes with this. Pick out something you'd like to wear. Then you keep it."

"Really? You don't want to—"

"No. I'm going back there to look at some others. Get what you want, Abby."

She watched her for a moment, seeing her leaning over the glass, looking at the different necklaces there. Nic motioned a saleswoman over and Abby turned her attention back to the multitude of hearts laid out before her. In the end, she decided to go with one called Infinity—an open heart with a light blue crystal inside. She held it in her palm, watching as the light reflected off the stone.

Nic picked out an unusual one, yet something that fit her perfectly—a small geode that had been cut, sliced, and polished.

"It's beautiful. What is it called?"

"It's a blue agate and the crystal is called a Druzy crystal."

Abby held hers up. "I got a crystal too, but it looks nothing like yours."

"No. But I love it. Both of them. I think they'll be perfect."

They exchanged the necklaces, then separated so they could each pay and have them giftwrapped. The whole thing took less than twenty minutes. Abby thought if all Christmas shopping were that easy, she might actually enjoy it.

Back outside, she led them across the street. The brewery was a few blocks up, but it was only eleven. She thought they could shop a little longer before going for burgers.

"Here," she said, motioning to a shop that specialized in outdoor clothing. "You can get some leggings to wear under your jeans."

"Like tights?"

"What? Too girlie for you?" she teased.

Nic arched an eyebrow. "Do you wear them?"

"Yes. I have some on right now."

Nic stepped back, perusing her. "You can't tell."

"No. But they're warm. You should get some." She went inside. "Just a couple of pairs. Black ones. You'll be glad you did."

Besides the tights, Nic surprised her by actually shopping. She bought a thick, bulky sweater, a sweatshirt proclaiming *Ski Red River*, and two long-sleeved T-shirts, both with Red River logos on them. Abby got so caught up in shopping, she bought herself a new sweatshirt too. By the time they'd left the store, it was going on noon, and they made their way down the street toward the brewery.

"Dare I ask if you're having fun?"

Nic glanced at her with a smile. "I am. But does it matter?"

"Of course. I told you before, this trip wasn't all about me."

Nic nudged her shoulder. "I remember, of course."

Abby felt a blush light her face. They hadn't mentioned the…the "agreement" as she'd begun to call it. Would tonight be the night? They were both rested. What excuse could she come up with? What if she refused? Would Nic force her?

"So this brewery place. What do they have?"

Abby took Nic's cue and relaxed. The night would get there soon enough. "They're famous for their burgers, not their beer. But I've sampled quite a few of their brews over the years and I think they're quite good. Although I'll admit, I most often get their blonde."

"Lighter?"

"Lighter than their others but not light like Miller Lite or Bud Light. I'm not a big fan of dark beer and that's mostly what they have. What about you?"

"Back home I like Shiner Bach, so I'll give one of their darks a try."

She shouldn't ask, she knew, but it was at the forefront of her mind. "You said your parents drank. A lot. So—"

"Are you asking if I'm following in their footsteps?"

"No. I guess I'm asking if drinking bothers you."

"Not anymore, no. Actually, I never touched it until college when I met Eric." Nic stopped as they stood outside the Red River Brewery. "I don't ever overdo it. I think in the back of my mind, I am afraid I'll—" She shrugged. "I don't want to end up like them." She motioned to the brewery. "This wasn't my parents' kind of drinking anyway. They did theirs at home, behind locked doors where no one could see."

"Except you?"

"Yeah. So this doesn't bother me. It looks festive."

"It is. And in the summer, their patios are hopping. It's probably the most popular place in town." She opened the door and went inside. "They have a deck on the side that is winterized. Let's try to sit there."

The place was buzzing inside, and she watched Nic as her eyes darted around the room, pausing over the big Christmas tree, then up to the garland strung over the bar. She had a contented smile on her face and Abby realized she quite liked it. Nic glanced at her then, nodding.

"I love it. Let's get a beer."

CHAPTER TWENTY-THREE

Abby read the note for a second time. It was addressed "To whoever gets home first" and it had a list of things to do. Like take two pounds of ground beef from the freezer to thaw, start the rice maker at two o'clock—wonder why she didn't just set the timer for it?—and chop onions, celery, and bell peppers, which were already prepped in the fridge.

"I'm guessing she's making the Creole dirty rice casserole for dinner." She smiled at that thought. It had been a childhood favorite and she hadn't had it in years. Of course, after just consuming a huge burger with sautéed mushrooms, avocado, and pepper jack cheese, she was too full to think about dinner.

She went about the business of chopping onions, but her thoughts were on Nic. They'd had such a pleasant time at the brewery she hadn't been in any hurry to leave. While Nic didn't say anything more about her parents, she did talk freely about her time in college and her friends Eric and Addison. And in turn, she had shared some of her exploits with her friends as well. She paused in her chopping. She would say Nic was nice, yes, but she was still a little...what? Mysterious? Well, not mysterious in a creepy sort of way, no. Guarded. Maybe guarded was a better word. Nic was certainly guarded about her younger years. She sliced through the onion again, then paused once more. Actually, she was pretty guarded about her current life too, wasn't she? The only thing she talked freely about was college. She stared out the window and shook her head. No, the only thing she talked freely about was her friends Eric and Addison.

Did it matter? So, she wasn't an open book. Did she have to be? They were fake girlfriends. After this trip, they most likely wouldn't see each other again. Was there a need to be open—transparent—about her life? Not really. She was interested and curious about her, that was all. Mainly because she found herself liking the other woman, which surprised the hell out of her. Spending time with Nic had proven to be painless and, well, enjoyable. In fact—

"So, I finally get you alone," came a sultry voice behind her.

She froze, then whipped around, knife in hand as if it could protect her from Holly. That smile—that confident, sure—cocky—smile was on her face. The smile she remembered from last Christmas. The smile that she thought was sexy and charming. The smile that had finally broken her. Well, the smile and a bottle of wine had crumbled her defenses.

"Grab a knife. You can chop celery."

A throaty laugh was her answer. "Darling, I assure you, I did not come down here to chop celery with you. Aaron is in the shower. And since you're alone, I assume Nicole is as well."

"And that means what, exactly?"

"That means I've missed you. That means I was looking forward to seeing you again. I was hoping we could perhaps get reacquainted," she said with a twitch of her eyebrows. "Last year was such fun."

"Oh my god! You are unbelievable. I am seeing someone, and you are engaged to marry my brother. Remember him?" She turned back around, nearly mutilating the onion as she chopped. Freakin' unbelievable.

"So? Do either of those things matter, Abigail? You and I, we have a connection. We—"

"Oh, give me a break, Holly. We don't have a connection." She held her gaze. "What is it? Is the sex not good enough for you?"

"Let's just say he's not you." She felt Holly move up close behind her. "Can you slip away?" she asked breathily into her ear. "Just for a few minutes, darling?"

Abby felt Holly's body press against hers, and she closed her eyes, trying to decide how she felt. Aroused? Surprisingly, no. She slid to the side, away from her. "I'm seeing someone. So you don't get to touch me. Nic can touch me. Not you." She childishly held the knife between them.

"Yeah, what she said. I'd rather you not touch my girlfriend."

They both turned, finding Nic standing there, watching them. Nic met first her gaze, then Holly's.

"So? What did I miss?"

"Nothing," Holly said tersely. "We were just talking. It doesn't concern you." She went to the knife drawer and pulled one out. "Abigail wanted me to help chop…what was it? Celery?"

Abby didn't know why she felt guilty, but she did. Maybe it was the look in Nic's eyes, because she swore there was a bit of jealousy there. And, as she was supposed to be her girlfriend, there should have been, she supposed. Holly had been pressed against her in the most intimate of ways.

"I can help too," Nic offered.

Abby smiled at her and nodded. "Mom left a note with instructions. You can set up the rice maker."

"Sure." Nic looked around the kitchen. "And the rice is where?"

"The pantry is over there." She pointed with her knife.

When Nic would have walked past her, she paused, meeting her gaze. Again, there was something there, just under the surface. But Nic's eyes softened, and a smile formed a second before she moved closer. Abby was prepared for the kiss this time, and she leaned in to meet her. She was prepared for the kiss, yes—because Holly was watching. Yet she wasn't prepared for the fluttering of her stomach as Nic's lips lingered just a second or two longer than necessary. She felt a bit flushed as she turned back to her onions. She made a couple of slices, then looked up, finding Holly staring at her.

Holly shook her head quickly, her voice quiet. "She is so not good enough for you, Abigail. What are you thinking?"

"She's perfect for me. Not that it's any of your concern."

The vegetables were chopped and put into a bowl. The rice maker was all set up to start at two. Holly had escaped upstairs, and now here they were, alone. Nic seemed more relaxed now that Holly was out of the room. Not that there was anything to stress about. Holly had said very little and, in turn, neither had they.

"So she wants to sleep with you?"

Abby sighed. "Yes."

"Did she come right out and ask?"

"Umm, yeah." Abby went into the sunporch. It was a beautiful, sunny afternoon, and the snow was almost too bright to look at. "She says she missed me, and she wants to get reacquainted." She turned to glance at Nic. "She said you weren't the one for me."

"No." Nic slowly turned to look at her. "No, that's not what she said. She said I wasn't good enough for you."

Abby met her gaze. "You heard?"

"Yes." Nic smiled, a smile that didn't reach her eyes. "And once we break up, she'll know she was right."

Abby moved closer to her, finding one of her hands and squeezing it. "My friend Marcos said I should tell Holly to fuck off." Nic's smile was a little more genuine now and Abby matched it. "He also said we should rub it in her face how in love we are."

"I think I would like Marcos."

Abby nodded. "Yes. And he would like you."

Their eyes held for a long moment. There was absolutely no reason they should kiss, yet Abby knew that they would. She could tell by the subtle change in Nic's eyes. She could have pulled away when Nic leaned closer. Yes, she could have. She probably *should* have. But no. Her eyes slipped closed when Nic's mouth met hers—just like a real kiss. The fact that they didn't *need* to kiss—there was no audience, no one watching— never quite registered with her. Nic's hands cupped her face and Abby's lips parted, the tiniest of moans escaping before she could stop it. She heard the shift in Nic's breathing, felt Nic move closer, bringing their bodies into contact.

The barest, briefest touch of a tongue against hers made her moan again, then it was gone. Nic pulled away, her eyes a dark, smoky blue now. She didn't say anything. She simply went deeper into the sunporch, going to stand near a window. Abby wondered if Nic was really watching the activity at the birdfeeders or if she was reliving that kiss.

Abby stared at her, letting her eyes roam over her body at will. Would tonight be the night? Would Nic collect on that compensation she was owed? Yes. Abby swallowed nervously, knowing she wouldn't put up a fight. No. Not after that kiss. She could almost feel the anticipation—is that what it was?— build as she leaned back against the wall. The thoughts running through her mind made her feel a little naughty.

Oh, who was she kidding? For her, it was way past naughty. It was downright promiscuous, a word she would have never, ever used to describe herself. She was the overly cautious one, always a bit guarded when it came to her love life. Then why now was there this smoldering heat making its way through her body? A smoldering heat that had been missing when Holly had been pressed against her.

She heard the back door open, and she turned, finding her mother coming in from the garage, her arms loaded with packages. Abby hurried over to help.

"Looks like you had fun," she said as she relieved her mother of a bag.

"All the shops were packed. It was a madhouse." She looked around. "You found my note?"

"I did. Actually, Holly helped chop veggies too."

Her mother's eyes widened. "Whatever in the world was wrong with her?"

"I'm not quite sure. She went back upstairs. I've not seen Aaron."

Her mother nodded, then looked past her as Nic leaned in the doorway of the sunporch. Abby met her gaze, surprised to still see a lingering desire there. That made her breath catch.

"Nicole, were you enjoying the sunporch?"

"I was. No wonder it's your favorite room. You had quite a few customers at your birdfeeders."

"Oh, speaking of which, would you mind terribly getting the birdseed out of the trunk of my car? There are two metal trashcans next to the door that leads out back. Just put the bags in there."

"Sure. No problem. There's one feeder that is almost empty. Would you like me to fill it?"

"Thank you, Nicole. Yes, that one gets emptied every day. It's sunflower seeds. Put a scoop or two in there, if you don't mind."

Instead of going out the back door, Nic pointed toward the living room. "Gonna get my coat."

Abby smiled at her. "Excuse to get out in the snow?"

"Yeah. It looks inviting."

Her mother turned to her when Nic walked out. "She's so nice. I trust you had a good day in town."

"We did. Ended up at the brewery for burgers. It was fun." She opened one of the bags and peered inside. "You want this in the pantry or is it for tonight?"

"In the pantry, please. I think I've accounted for all the meals next week. I haven't planned anything for lunches, though. I figured you would be skiing and could get something in town. If not, there's makings for sandwiches."

"What do you have planned for tomorrow night?" She paused on her way to the pantry, smiling as Nic walked back through in her parka and new knit cap. "Is it something I can help with?"

"Christmas Eve? Yes, there are plenty of things you can help with. I'm going to do a Mexican buffet for tacos. I've got all sorts of things—beef, chicken, beans. I'll make a fresh batch of pico de gallo and guacamole. I've got some sprouts and shredded cabbage. Oh, and I'm making a chipotle sour cream sauce. Your father loves that."

Abby stuck her head out of the pantry. "Speaking of Dad—I know you said everything was okay, but…"

Her mother let out a heavy breath and leaned her head down, staring at the floor. Abby went over to her.

"Mom?"

"Oh, Abigail." Her mother looked at her and Abby was shocked to see tears in her eyes. "I think your father is having an affair."

"*What?* Mom, no."

"He's…he's being so secretive. He gets phone calls that he claims are from the resort. He leaves at odd times—when he's here, that is. Which, as you can tell, is rare." Her mother sat down heavily in a chair. "I did something that I'm not proud of, Abigail."

Abby sat down too. "What's that?"

"I…I followed him one day. He was on his way to work, and I followed him. But he didn't go to the resort. He went into town. He met some woman at the coffee shop. Sat right out there on the patio for everyone to see." Her mother clutched at her chest. "I was crushed."

"And you didn't say anything to him?"

"No. But I called his work. I normally call his cell, you know. But that day, I called the resort directly." She shook her head. "He wasn't scheduled to work at all that day."

"Oh my god," she murmured. She took her mother's hand. "You need to talk to him."

"It's Christmas. I am not going to talk to him about this now."

"Mom, when was this? Last week?"

"No. It's been…a while," she said evasively.

"Oh, Mom. Why didn't you tell me?"

"I didn't want you to worry."

"Fine. You won't talk to him. I will."

"Abigail Lynn Carpenter, you will not! I won't have this ruin Christmas. I will deal with it after you all leave." She tucked her hair behind her ears. "I think I knew all along that moving up here was a mistake. I knew he wouldn't be happy here. That's how I know he's having an affair. The last few months, the last six months, he's been different. There's life in his eyes again."

Abby leaned closer. "Mom, how has…I mean, what about your—" She paused. "What about your sex life?"

Her mother looked at her sharply. "What is it you're asking?"

"Are you still sleeping together?"

"Of course we sleep together!"

"Okay, there's a difference between sharing a bed and having sex." She closed her eyes and shook her head quickly. *I can't believe we're having this conversation*, she thought.

"I don't think our sex life is any of your concern," her mother said curtly.

"Well, it's not like I want details. But if he's having an affair, I wouldn't think he'd want to…you know…with you."

Her mother blushed freely. "Yes, you would think, wouldn't you?"

"What does that mean?"

"It means," her mother said quietly, leaning closer, "that our sex life has been extremely active lately."

Abby stared at her mother, trying to get the visual out of her head. "So, that's a good thing then, right? Maybe he's not having an affair."

"And maybe he is. Why else would he be meeting a woman for coffee?"

"Oh, yeah. Forgot about that." She patted her mother's hand. "You should ask him. Don't let it drag on, Mom, or you'll drive yourself crazy with it."

"We had our rough patch before, you know."

"I remember."

"I never once thought that he was having an affair back then."

Her eyes widened. "He didn't, did he?"

"No, no. What I mean is, that never even crossed my mind. We were both so busy with our work, like two ships passing in the night, as they say. But neither of us wanted to lose each other. We—as a couple, a family—were more important than our careers." She shook her head. "But now? I don't know. We will have been up here seven years in May. The time has flown by, really. But little by little, every year, I could see him getting more restless. Now—"

She stopped when the door opened and Nic came back inside, a big grin on her face. She had snow clinging to her jeans and her cheeks were red.

"There are some deep drifts out there. I sunk up past my knees."

"Did you put your tights on?"

"No, I didn't. Now I'm cold."

Her mother stood up. "Why don't you two get the fire going? I want to change into something comfortable before I start on dinner." She patted Nic's arm. "Nicole, thank you for tending to the birdfeeders. That was sweet of you."

"You're welcome." Nic eyed Abby. "Fire?"

"Yes. Come on. Let's get it roaring."

CHAPTER TWENTY-FOUR

After Abby had showered and changed, she went back downstairs. She found Holly and Aaron sitting by the fire. She shook her head, wondering at their relationship. They sat opposite each other, not speaking. They were both scrolling through their phones with rapt attention.

She nudged Aaron as she walked past. "Fire could use another log."

Holly looked up then, giving her smile. "Come join us."

Abby shook her head. "I think I'll go find Nic."

"She was helping your mother in the kitchen. Trying to earn brownie points, I guess." Holly pointed to the bar. "Have a glass of wine with me. Let's catch up."

She thought back to last year. Wasn't that how it had started? Holly offering to "catch up" over—not a glass—but a bottle of wine. That was after Christmas, though. She'd spent the first few days avoiding both Holly and Aaron. Everyone—as her mother had said—had been walking on eggshells. And then they started sharing wine, and it went downhill from there.

"I don't think so, Holly. Maybe Nic and I will join you in a bit, have a drink before dinner."

"Can't wait," Holly said dryly.

She was smiling as she went into the kitchen, but neither Nic nor her mother were around. Then she heard voices coming from the sunporch, and she went there. They were sitting near the woodstove, and it was quite comfortable inside. She was surprised to see a glass of wine beside Nic.

"I thought you didn't like wine."

"Hey, come join us." She picked up the wineglass in question. "This isn't really wine. It's a sweet and fruity something or other."

"It's a sangria," her mother supplied. "Would you like a glass? I bought a couple of bottles for our Mexican theme dinner tomorrow, but I thought Nicole and I would try it early."

"Actually, I think I'll have real wine, if you don't mind. Please say you have some in the kitchen. I do not want to have to go back out to the bar."

"No, honey, I'm sorry. We moved it all to the bar." She sighed. "I suppose we should go out and be social. William will be home any minute now."

Abby actually groaned. "Do I have to?" she asked childishly.

"Come on," Nic said. "We'll sit together and hold hands and irritate Holly."

Her mother laughed out loud at that, a hearty laugh that Abby wasn't certain she'd heard before. She looked questioningly at Nic. What had she told her mother? But Nic only smiled at her as she stood, taking her glass of wine with her.

Aaron had added another log, as she'd asked, and the fire was blazing hotly again. Since Holly was on the loveseat, Nic took the sofa. She went over to the bar, looking over the wine bottles. Holly had opened a red blend, an Apothic Red that she'd had before. She also eyed a pinot noir. Instead, she picked up the blend that Holly had opened and filled a glass an inch from the top.

Her mother came up holding the bottle of sangria that she and Nic had been drinking from. "I quite like this. I think I may have to buy it more often. A nice afternoon sipping wine."

"What is it?" Holly asked.

"Oh, it's a sangria I got for tomorrow's dinner. Something festive to go with our taco buffet." Her mother smiled at Nic. "Nicole is not a fan of wine, but I think I've got her hooked on this one."

Holly flicked her eyes dismissively. "Cheap and sweet. I'd hardly call that wine."

Her mother surprised her by her retort. "For us unsophisticated types, it goes down just fine. Uppity, snooty ones may not think so."

Abby matched Nic's smile as she sat down beside her. "So, you're unsophisticated, huh?"

"Hate to break it to you like this, babe, but yeah, I am."

Abby leaned closer to kiss her. "I love you just the way you are." Their eyes held and she wasn't surprised to find herself leaning over to kiss her a second time. God, what a rush she got from that. And when Nic's hand rested on her thigh, she felt nearly dizzy. Whatever was wrong with her?

"Have you all made your plans for skiing?" her mother asked to no one in particular.

Aaron pulled his nose out of his phone long enough to glance at Holly. "Have you decided yet?"

"I think I'd like to go tomorrow. The forecast is perfect for skiing. Then I suppose we'll skip Christmas Day, but I'd like to go daily after that." Holly turned her attention to Abby. "I bought this adorable new ski outfit. I can't wait to show you."

Abby frowned. Why on earth would she give a damn about her new ski outfit? She decided it didn't warrant a reply. It didn't even warrant a grunt. Nic replied, however.

"I can't wait to see it too. It'll give me an idea of what to look for when I go through their rental stuff."

"How often do you ski?"

"First time."

Holly smirked. "That'll be fun to watch."

"Oh, I'm sure," Nic said easily. "I'm actually looking forward to getting on a snowmobile, though. That sounds like fun."

"We'll do it," Abby said. "They have great trails for it."

"What about you, Aaron? Do you like to snowmobile?" Nic asked.

He nodded. "I do, yes. Holly doesn't enjoy it, though."

"You should come with us then. Leave her on the slopes."

"I don't despise snowmobiling," Holly said in her defense. "I'd just rather be on skis. But a group outing might be fun." Holly met Abby's gaze. "Yes, we should plan it."

"Sure. One day next week," she said with feigned enthusiasm.

By the time her father got there, they'd exhausted whatever conversation they'd forced between them. That had been draining in itself. The only saving grace was having Nic beside her. They held hands and amused themselves with exaggerated squeezes at some of Holly's comments. It was an absolute relief when her father walked in.

As she watched the exchange between her parents—the look they gave each other, the kiss on the mouth—she noticed two things. Her mother's gaze was accusatory, doubting. But the look in her father's eyes was loving, tender. Quite a contrast between the two.

"Sorry I'm late. Did I miss anything fun?"

"We've just been visiting," her mother said as she stood. "Make yourself a drink if you like. We'll eat in about a half-hour."

Holly stood too. "I think I'll freshen up before dinner."

Aaron stood on cue. "Me too."

Abby exchanged glances with Nic, both of their eyes widening teasingly. When Holly and Aaron left, she leaned closer, her voice quiet. "Do you mind offering to help Mom? I want to talk to Dad."

"Sure."

Abby went to stand by the bar, watching as her father added scotch to a glass with three ice cubes.

"Busy day?"

"Oh, yeah. Holiday crowd."

She moved closer to him, waiting until he met her gaze. "What's going on, Dad?"

He didn't appear startled by her question. "What do you mean?"

"You've hardly been around. Less than last year, even. Mom says you're gone a lot."

He glanced toward the kitchen, then back at her. "What has she said?"

"Well, mainly she said I wasn't supposed to say anything to you about it. Because, you know, it's Christmas and all and we can't have any drama at Christmas. Other than, you know, the me and Holly situation."

He smiled at that. "It's been less stressful than last year, that's for sure."

"Yes, it has. So what's going on with you?"

"You'll have to be more specific."

"Oh, come on, Dad. Don't make me ask."

He sipped from his drink but said nothing.

"Fine. I'll ask. Are you having an affair?"

He nearly spit out his drink. "*What*? Is that what she thinks?"

"You're gone a lot. At odd hours. You get phone calls. You claim to be working at the resort. A lot. But she followed you one morning. You met some woman at a coffee shop. Sat on the outdoor patio. And she called the resort. You weren't scheduled to be at work that day."

His reaction wasn't what she'd been expecting. A smile and a laugh?

"I guess I should have told her. But I'd promised and I hated to break my promise."

"What are you talking about?"

"In Dallas, when we quit, I told her I'd never go back into real estate. It had nearly ruined our marriage. I love your mother. I didn't want to lose her."

She frowned. "What are you saying?"

"I'm saying that for the last couple of years I've been working toward getting my license here. I took the broker exam in November of last year." He grinned. "Passed with flying colors, of course."

"I would hope so."

"Anyway, for the last year, I've been working."

"For a firm?"

"I thought that was too risky. I didn't want Sandra to find out. So no, I've been on my own. But it's really taken off and I'm swamped now. I already had connections in Dallas, and you'd be surprised at how many second homes up here exchange hands. Not just that, but I've become friends with one of the builders in Taos. He builds vacation homes that the owners then use as short-term rentals. What he's found is that people will keep the house for two or three years, then sell to someone else who's looking for investment property. That alone has kept me plenty busy."

"So instead of telling her, you sneak around and pretend to be working at the resort?"

"Not pretend. I do work there a couple of days a week, but not as a manager as she thinks."

"How do you find the time?" She held her hand up. "I know. You can do three things at once. Like when you used to come to my soccer games. You always had the phone to your ear."

"Yes. But that doesn't mean I wasn't watching you."

"Were you?"

"Of course I was. Did I ever miss a game?"

She sighed. "Okay. So you need to tell her."

"It'll disappoint her."

"She thinks you're having an affair, for god's sake! Telling her you got back into the real estate business will not disappoint her." She refilled her wine glass. "But why, Dad? I thought you had both pretty much burned out on it."

"We had. And we needed to get away from it. But honestly, I was losing my mind being up here and not working. I felt like I was wasting my life."

"Why didn't you tell her?"

"Because she was happy not working. She enjoys tending to this big house and she has all of her projects outside. And she's made friends with our neighbors so in the summer when they're here, she has outings with the ladies, and they take turns having lunch. She was happy."

"But you were not."

"I was bored, to be honest. And I found myself taking it out on her."

She smiled. "So to save your marriage in Dallas, you quit the business. And to save it now, you got back into it?"

"Exactly. But it's different here. Not nearly as stressful. Not the cutthroat business like when I was dealing commercial properties. This is almost relaxing."

"Okay. Daughter to father advice—after you confess to her, that is—is not to keep odd hours, don't go overboard with it again, and bring her flowers on occasion. Oh, and take her out to dinner more often."

He added a splash more scotch to his glass as well. "Do you think she'll be mad?"

"I know I would be," she said bluntly. "Not that you've gotten back into the business, but that you didn't tell me." She softened her words. "She was really hurt, Dad."

He nodded. "I think I knew she was getting suspicious. You're right. I should have told her."

She smiled at him. "Okay. So that's one drama averted. Now if we can just make it through without me and Holly coming to blows, it'll be a success."

CHAPTER TWENTY-FIVE

Nic closed the door to their bedroom and leaned back against it with a sigh. "That was actually tolerable. Much better than last night's dinner."

"She was quite subdued tonight, wasn't she?"

She pushed off the door, going to the drawers where she'd put her clothes. "I feel sorry for your brother."

"Why? He has free will."

"You think so? She seems to snap her fingers and he jumps." She took out her sleep shirt. "There's no way they're in love with each other. They both look miserable."

"I'm guessing it's their sex life that is miserable," Abby said as she went into the bathroom. "Being a lesbian and sleeping with a guy has got to be difficult."

Nic walked to the open door, watching as Abby brushed her teeth. "Is she gay or is she bi?"

Abby rinsed her mouth before answering. "If you asked Holly, she would probably say she was straight. If you ask me—and by what she said to me earlier today—I'll go with gay."

Nic raised her eyebrows questioningly.

"When she indicated she wanted to sleep with me, I asked if the sex wasn't good enough with him." Abby stopped and shook her head. "Never mind."

"No, no. What did she say?"

Abby looked away. "She said he wasn't me."

Nic smiled. "You're that good, huh?"

Abby blushed and moved past her. "I'm not answering that."

Nic was still smiling when she went into the bathroom to change and brush her teeth. She heard Abby in the bedroom, presumably changing as well. Much like last night, Abby was already in bed with only the lamp on beside the bed. Unlike last night, they weren't both dog-tired.

When she got into bed, Abby made no move to turn the lamp off. Instead, she rolled to her side.

"Did you have a good day?"

"It ended well, yes. I like your family. Your mother especially."

"Wanna tell me what you told her about Holly?"

Nic gave a quiet laugh. "Don't be mad. It just came out."

"Oh my god! You told her we slept together last year?"

"No, I didn't tell her that. I told her Holly wanted to sleep with you *this* year. I told her I caught you in the kitchen."

"Oh god," she groaned. "How did she take it?"

"She blames Holly." Nic moved her hand under the covers and found Abby's. "If we were real girlfriends and I'd walked in on you like that, I would have been pissed as hell."

"She kinda blindsided me."

"And if I hadn't been there?"

"I don't know. Right then, at that moment, I didn't feel anything for her. There was no underlying attraction that I was trying to fight. But I don't know. If you weren't here and she did that to me three, four, five times—I may have gone along with it. I would hope not, but…"

Her voice trailed off and Nic wondered what she was trying to say. "But you're lonely?"

Abby surprised her by turning the question back to her. "This morning, you said that you were lonely. Have you ever been in a relationship, Nic?"

Nic nodded. "Once. Like I said, I didn't have great role models, but I thought I'd give it a try." She thought back to the girl she'd met in college—Kayla. "I was twenty, I think, when I met her. I liked her a lot. At first. I wouldn't say I was ever in love with her. I didn't have those deep feelings, whatever that is. But I thought maybe it would grow to that. She was fun and we had a good time together. But then she got into the whole college scene and was binge drinking and partying. Stuff I wasn't into. Turns out she was a mean drunk and she liked to pick fights with me, then she wouldn't remember it the next morning. It was too much. That was my parents' relationship. Yelling, fighting. I thought, is that how all relationships were? If so, I wanted no part of it."

"Was she the same age?"

"A year younger." She rolled onto her back. "One morning, after a fight the night before, I broke up with her. She didn't remember getting hammered, didn't remember the fight. It didn't matter. I was through. She kinda turned into a stalker for a few months after that. So much so that I didn't go out at all. She finally moved on to someone else, but I was over the whole dating thing by then. Sex became so much more relaxed when you didn't have to worry about the emotional crap that comes with dating."

"And that's how you still are?"

She smiled. "I'm not in college anymore. I'm over thirty. I have a job that demands I get to work before dawn. So no, I don't cruise the bars at night, looking for a hookup. I'm with Eric and Addison a couple of times a week. I have dinner with my uncle at least once a week. I have a handful of other friends that I go out to dinner with occasionally. And yes, sometimes I get lonely, and I go to the bar. And sometimes I go home alone and sometimes I don't."

She heard Abby sigh. "I wish I could be like you. I'm not brave enough to pick someone up at the bar like that. My friend Sharon says I like to vet them first before I become even a little bit involved with them. So, I get lonely too. I feel left out. Most of my friends are couples. In fact, I think all of them are."

"Do they try to set you up? Blind dates and whatnot?"

"Oh, sometimes but not often." Abby met her gaze. "I think that's why I let Holly into my life. I remember the night I met her. I was at the bar alone. I usually go with a group or at least a couple of friends. But not that night. So I met Holly and I let her in. We don't really go together. I can see that clearly now. She's so fake. And really, we had nothing in common. I don't know what I was thinking. I didn't see past the charm, the looks. It was just nice to have someone, you know."

Nic shook her head. No, she didn't know. It had been ten years since Kayla. So no, she didn't know what it was like to have someone. And she didn't imagine she ever would. But right now, here, in bed…there was Abby. A woman who, on the surface, she hardly knew. Yet they did know each other, didn't they?

Abby was the one to move, to move closer to her. "Do you want…do you want to collect on your—well, our agreement was—"

"Abby, I shouldn't have made that offer. It shouldn't have been a stipulation. I'm sorry."

"No. But we did have an agreement. Didn't we?"

Nic rolled to her side, facing Abby, trying to read her eyes. Hell, it *was* their agreement, wasn't it? Sex. No attachments, no nothing. Just sex. Her payment for being the fake girlfriend. She leaned a little closer, touching her mouth to Abby's. It was a light kiss, just lips moving together. It felt nice.

She sat up then and pulled her shirt over her head, tossing it on the floor. She urged Abby up too, removing hers as well. Her gaze went to her breasts. They were full, the nipples taut. Then she leaned closer, kissing her again, this time with a little more fervor. She heard Abby moan quietly. She lay back down, pulling Abby on top of her. Their lips parted simultaneously, their tongues meeting, dancing together in a delicious kiss.

She cupped Abby's hips, slipping her hands inside the flannel pajama bottoms. Abby arched against her, drawing out her own moan as their centers pressed together. Abby's hair fell across her face as they kissed, and she blindly pushed the pajamas down, wanting to touch flesh. So did Abby, apparently, as her hand went inside her underwear, pushing them out of the way.

They were struggling to breathe as they kissed, but they didn't struggle with their clothing. She rolled them over, both naked now. She slipped between Abby's thighs, hearing her groan as she thrust against her. She bent Abby's knees and pushed them up, spreading her legs even further. She moved her mouth to Abby's breast, sucking a nipple inside, feeling Abby squirm beneath her.

"God, yes," Abby hissed as Nic slid fingers into her wetness. Abby rose up to meet her, her hips rocking against her hand.

Nic used her own hips to drive her fingers deeper. Abby was panting, her fingers digging into Nic's arms as she met each thrust. Nic bit down lightly against her nipple, then sucked it hard into her mouth. Abby's hips bucked wildly against her, then she turned her head, stifling her scream with her pillow as she climaxed.

Abby's legs slowly settled back on the bed, and Nic rested her face against Abby's breasts, her fingers still inside her. With her thumb, she brushed across Abby's clit, making her jerk.

"God, I thought you were the one to be compensated, not me," Abby murmured huskily.

Nic looked up and smiled, finding Abby's eyes closed. She slowly withdrew her fingers, making Abby jerk again. Abby gave a satisfied moan and her eyes fluttered open.

"I think I like the way you kiss."

Nic moved higher, doing just that. Abby rolled her over this time, resting her weight on top of her.

"I may be out of practice. As you know, it's been a year."

Nic smiled against her lips. "If you need three or four tries at it, that's fine with me."

Abby laughed quietly as she pulled her mouth away. Their eyes met and Abby's smile slowly faded as she moved to kiss her again. Nic lay back, letting Abby do as she may. Her kisses turned fiery hot before moving to her breasts. She closed her eyes, relishing the feeling of Abby's mouth and tongue on them. Yes, hopefully it would take three or four tries. How glorious would that be?

CHAPTER TWENTY-SIX

Abby's eyes were closed as she stretched her legs out. She was aware that she was smiling. Aware that the lamp was still on. Aware of how contented she felt. Odd, really, when she'd so dreaded fulfilling this agreement she and Nic had made. But god, what a glorious night it had been. She rolled over, turning off the lamp, plunging the room into darkness. Well, not quite darkness—dawn was already breaking outside.

"You're smiling."

She rolled back toward Nic. "I think I kinda like this."

"This what?"

"This having sex without worrying about dating and all that goes with it. It's much more relaxing. I'm really glad you made me that counteroffer."

Nic moved closer to kiss her. "I'm glad you picked me to be your fake girlfriend."

"Can we do this every night?"

"If you want to. I won't complain."

Abby took a deep breath and closed her eyes again. God, she felt so wanton, so shameless. And tired. She wondered how many hours of sleep they'd gotten. Not enough, obviously as she felt herself drifting off. She didn't fight it. She felt Nic's arm snake across her stomach and she pulled it tighter around her.

When she woke again, sunlight was streaming in through the blinds, and she blinked against it. She was alone in bed, and she listened, but all was quiet. She tossed the covers off, aware of her nakedness. She hurried into the bathroom, turning on the small heater there to warm it. She looked at herself in the mirror, seeing her disheveled hair. Her lips felt puffy from kissing, and her breasts felt swollen. God, Nic's hands and mouth had been everywhere on her body, and she positively loved it. Who knew she could be so unrestrained in bed with someone who was practically a stranger? But no, Nic didn't seem like a stranger at all anymore, did she? No. She met her eyes in the mirror and smiled. They would have eight more nights together. She wasn't certain she could keep the pace, but she would certainly give it a good try.

"You're so bad," she murmured as she stepped into the shower. And to think she had been dreading this. It was kinda fun being a little naughty. She nearly rolled her eyes at herself. What she considered naughty most people would probably consider perfectly normal.

After her shower, she made the bed and straightened up the room before going downstairs. She found Nic in the sunporch with her mother, chatting away as if they were old friends. Nic met her gaze and gave her a lazy smile. Abby felt her stomach turn over at the look in her eyes.

"Good morning."

Abby suddenly felt a little shy. "Morning." She glanced at her mother. "I guess I wasn't recovered from the drive up here. I slept like a log."

"Uh huh."

She hoped she was successful warding off the blush that threatened. She sat down beside Nic on the wicker loveseat. It was toasty warm in the room, and she took a sip of her hot coffee.

"Where is everyone?"

"Oh, Aaron and Holly went skiing," her mother explained. "They'll stay and have lunch in town again, then come home."

"And Dad?" She eyed her mother as a very lovely blush lit up her face.

"He had a client to meet this morning."

She smiled. "A client? I guess he told you then."

"Oh, Abigail, can you believe he's back in real estate? I was just telling Nicole about it all. And I thought he was having an affair!"

"Well, I'm glad he told you."

"Thank you for speaking to him, even though I asked you not to."

"Were you mad at him?"

"I was mad that he kept it from me, yes. But we talked it out and, well—"

"And you had makeup sex," she stated with a laugh, causing her mother to blush crimson again.

"Yes, we made up. And it was quite nice and that's all we're going to say about *that*. Now, what do you two have planned today?"

Abby looked over at Nic. "I don't know. It's a beautiful day. Want to try snowmobiling? Or we could hike along the forest road to the meadow. There's a nice gentle slope there for sledding. Or the roads are all clear—we could take a drive down to Taos or over to Angel Fire."

"Anything. You pick."

She took another sip of her coffee. "Okay. Let me think on it." She looked at her mother. "I'm starving, by the way. Is there something special for breakfast or are we on our own?"

"No, I haven't made anything yet. I was waiting on you to get up." She stood. "At this hour, it's more brunch than breakfast. I'll fry up some hash browns and do scrambled eggs."

"We can help," Nic offered.

"No, no. Enjoy your coffee. It's nothing to it."

After her mother left, Nic smiled at her. "So? Sleep well?"

"I did. What time did you sneak out?"

"About an hour ago. Aaron and Holly were already gone."

Abby found herself leaning closer to Nic. Their kiss was soft, gentle, and she nearly swooned from it. Her heart hammered as Nic deepened the kiss. She moaned quietly as she felt the tip of Nic's tongue touch hers.

She was breathing hard when Nic pulled away—her eyes that dark, smoky blue that she was beginning to recognize. She fell into them, then leaned closer again, nearly spilling her coffee as they kissed.

"God, what have you done to me?" she whispered.

Nic smiled at her but said nothing.

"I've never done anything like this before."

"Like this?"

"You're practically a stranger."

Nic shook her head. "I'm not a stranger, Abby. We've talked too much and told too many secrets for that."

She took a deep breath, nodding. "Yes, I guess we have. It's only that, I'm not used to…to just sex. So I'm a little surprised at how comfortable I feel with you. You know, the morning after and all."

The smile Nic gave her wasn't teasing. It was rather sweet. Then Nic leaned closer and lightly touched her lips, giving her a quick, fleeting kiss.

"I've always wanted to go sledding."

Abby nodded. "Okay. I know the perfect spot."

CHAPTER TWENTY-SEVEN

Their sledding adventure hadn't turned out quite the way she'd planned. Mainly because she was hoping to have some alone time with Nic. But Nic had casually invited her mother to go along and to probably both their surprises, she'd accepted. So the three of them had bundled up and trekked down the forest road, their boots crunching in the snow as they pulled two sleds behind them. The meadow, with its gentle slope toward a beaver pond, was the perfect spot if you were looking for a very tame sled ride. If you wanted something with a bit more thrill, you had to climb up the hill beyond the pond, which normally required snowshoes to make it up. When she was younger, that was a trip she made annually. The last few years, though, she hadn't given sledding much thought, opting instead to hit the ski slopes.

She was glad they'd chosen this activity, though. It was great fun and her mother looked like she was having the time of her life. Her mother did not ski so whenever everyone went to the slopes, she was left behind.

"Oh, what a fun day it's been, girls, but I am exhausted," her mother exclaimed as they trudged back up the meadow. "I need to do that more often. It's great exercise."

Abby turned to Nic. "And you?"

"I had a blast. Couldn't you tell?"

"I can see your teeth chattering," she teased.

"Wouldn't mind taking a turn by the fire."

"Oh, yes," her mother agreed. "We'll get it roaring and maybe sneak a glass of that sangria. We have an early dinner tonight, remember?"

"Yes. A tour of the lights," Abby said.

While she loved that tradition, she was looking forward to the day being over with already. She felt a little bit wicked knowing the reason why. Whatever in the world was wrong with her? She'd tried all day to keep images of last night out of her mind, to no avail. They snuck in whenever Nic looked at her, whenever they touched, however innocently. And the one time they'd ridden together on the sled, she'd been nearly on fire having Nic between her legs. Who knew she would embrace the idea of having sex…just for the fun of it? She wasn't in a relationship; she wasn't involved with anyone. There were no feelings to consider, no complications. No strings, as Marcos had suggested. If she were honest with herself, it was rather freeing. Perhaps she was discovering a whole new side of herself.

Which brought to mind last year. Maybe she'd been too hard on herself. Maybe she should have taken what she and Holly had done at face value. They had sex. They weren't involved. There should have been no emotional entanglement. Yet she'd made it out to be a much bigger deal than it had been. So they slept together? It obviously hadn't meant anything to either of them. Was it really any different than what she'd done last night? In fact, last night may have even been worse. Because in theory, last night had been a payment—compensation—for Nic's services.

She stopped walking. When she thought about it like that, it sounded kinda dirty. Cheap.

Nic bumped her arm. "You okay?"

Abby met her blue eyes, holding them. "I'm not sure all of a sudden."

Nic raised an eyebrow questioningly. But before either of them could comment, her mother had stopped, too, and turned around.

"The walk back to the house seems longer than when we came out."

Nic moved on toward her mother. "I was thinking the same thing. My feet feel like blocks of ice."

They walked on. Abby watched them for a moment, then followed. Maybe she would talk it out with Nic later. Or maybe she simply wasn't cut out for cheap, dirty sex. She sighed. So, okay, she was complicating things. That seemed to be her specialty.

* * *

When they got back inside, Sandra headed down a hallway to the back of the house without even removing her coat. "I'm going to take a nice long hot shower."

Nic nodded as she hung her parka beside Abby's coat. "That sounds great, doesn't it?"

"Yes, it does. Come on, let's get the fire going first."

Nic brought in a handful of logs that were stacked on the back deck. She put them in the rack beside the fireplace as Abby turned on the gas, catching some of the smaller limbs.

"I didn't notice that last night," she said, pointing to the gas flame.

"They only use it to get the fire going, then turn it off. Beats having to use kindling and newspaper and all that to start it."

Nic held her hands out to the fire as Abby added a bigger log. Nic watched her, noting the frown on her face. She finally took her hand, tugging her around.

"Want to tell me what's running through that pretty head of yours?"

Abby took a deep breath. "Yes, actually, I do." She shrugged. "I'm not sure how I should be feeling."

"Feeling? About last night?"

"Yes." She held her hand up. "What I mean is, should I feel so comfortable about it? Because that's *so* not me. Yet, I had, well, I had fun."

"So did I."

"Yes. And it's okay to have sex and to have fun and for there not to be any complications. We're not dating, we're not in a relationship, so there's no involvement. Emotional, anyway."

"Right. So, what's troubling you?"

Abby met her gaze. "It makes me feel cheap. And dirty."

"I see."

"I mean, maybe that's not exactly how I feel, because I really did enjoy it," she said with a smile. "Maybe what I'm thinking is that I *shouldn't* have enjoyed it so much. Does that make sense?"

"Shouldn't have enjoyed it because it's not something you normally do or shouldn't have enjoyed it because it was part of the stipulation for me being here with you?"

"A little of both, I think."

"Abby, we're adults, we're single. It's not like we're cheating on anyone. You don't have to feel guilty for enjoying sex."

"Yes! That's it. I feel guilty."

Nic smiled at her. "Guilty for liking it?"

"Yes."

Nic moved closer to her. "You know what? How about you evaluate it all again in the morning?"

Abby met her gaze. "You mean after we have sex again?"

"Yes. Maybe tomorrow you won't feel guilt or shame or whatever else you're feeling." She let her gaze drift to Abby's mouth. "Would you believe me if I told you it was one of the best nights of my life?"

Abby shook her head.

"But it was. You know why? Because we both knew up front that there were no expectations. You weren't someone who I was going to have to run away from and avoid after a date or two. I felt relaxed and I thoroughly enjoyed myself." She took a step away from her. "But it's not all about me, Abby. So, if you're not comfortable with this arrangement, if it makes you feel dirty or cheap as you say, then I'll respect that. We'll play by your rules."

"Really? But what about your compensation?"

"Well, I'll have to get by with my memories from last night." She turned back to the fire. "I like you. I certainly don't want to force myself on you. It's your call, Abby."

"Wow. Simple as all that?" Abby moved closer to her. "I like you too. I thought you were arrogant and conceited, but now—"

"What?" she asked with mock indignation.

Abby laughed. "I did. But it was only an act, wasn't it?"

She sighed. Was it? Yeah, she supposed it was. Abby surprised her by leaning closer and kissing her full on the mouth.

"Go shower. I'll help Mom get started with dinner."

She was about to comment when the front door opened. Holly was there with Aaron behind her. Holly's cheeks were red and her hair disheveled.

"Oh, that fire looks heavenly."

"You can take my spot," Nic said easily. "I'm going up to shower." She winked subtly at Abby, then leaned over to kiss her before heading up the stairs. She glanced over her shoulder once, seeing Holly standing close to Abby—far too close. Aaron seemed oblivious to it as he poked at the fire.

Before she turned away, she saw Abby say something, saw Holly laugh and lean closer to touch her arm. She was shocked by the twinge of jealousy that hit her. She wasn't certain she'd ever felt that before. She shook it away, reminding herself she was only the fake girlfriend. Fake girlfriends didn't get jealous.

CHAPTER TWENTY-EIGHT

"We'll take the back seat," Abby offered when her father backed his Suburban out of the garage.

"Are you sure? Aaron and I won't mind sitting in the third-row seats," Holly said.

"No. We got it. It'll be fine." Abby took Nic's hand and tugged her along. "That was an endless dinner and I just want some alone time," she whispered to her.

Nic wasn't sure how much alone time they would be afforded, but when Abby crawled in the back, she followed. Abby leaned closer and smiled at her. A little bit of a flirty smile that had her wondering what she had planned. She didn't have to wonder long. As soon as all the doors were closed and the lights were out, the hand that was resting on her leg slipped between her thighs, squeezing the inside intimately.

She turned her head, finding Abby's eyes in the shadows. As Abby's hand squeezed again, Nic felt her breath catch. She heard Sandra mention something about which route they were going to take, but whatever conversation followed was lost to her. She spread her thighs, giving Abby access. She heard the change in Abby's breathing, saw the rise and fall of her chest. Without thinking, she leaned closer, taking Abby's mouth in a fiery kiss, her tongue meeting Abby's for a second before pulling away.

Abby's fingers pressed into the seam of her jeans, and she only barely stifled the moan that tried to escape. Good lord, but she was turned on. Common sense told her to remove that hand before things went any further, but she was powerless to do so.

They were on Main Street now and she tried to look at all the colorful lights, tried to force her voice to comment like the others were doing. Even Abby, with her hand still firmly between her thighs, made note of the giant Santa that was in front of the bank. She remained mute, however, as Abby's fingers rubbed back and forth, making her squirm in the seat. She was breathing hard now, and she was certain that Holly or Aaron would hear her. Her hips jerked when Abby pressed against her clit.

She turned her head, seeing Abby's face again, the colors of the downtown lights flashing across her as they drove. When Abby looked at her, the fire she saw in her eyes nearly made her whimper. Abby held her gaze for a moment, then looked away as her fingers began to dance against her.

She bit down on her lip to keep quiet. She clutched the armrest with her hand to remain still, but her hips arched off the seat in near desperation as Abby's fingers continued to stroke her.

"Nicole, are you enjoying it?" Sandra called from up front.

She nearly broke out into a fit of giggles, but Abby's fingers never stilled. She cleared her throat before speaking, hoping her voice sounded normal and not like she'd been running a race.

"It's wonderful. It's definitely a first for me," she managed, hearing Abby's quiet chuckle beside her.

"Wait until we get into the neighborhoods. It's all so festive, up and down the streets."

She couldn't comment. Hell, she couldn't breathe. Abby didn't seem to care, however. She spread her legs further, letting

Abby do as she wanted. She swore her vision blurred as she tried to keep quiet. With Abby's fingers dancing against her, she climaxed with a quick jerk of her hips. She took Abby's hand, holding it between her legs, pressing it into her center.

Abby leaned closer then, her lips at her ear. "That was fun."

Nic turned, capturing her mouth with her own. She heard Abby moan into the kiss. "So, you have a little bit of a naughty side, huh?"

Abby snuggled against her with a sigh. "Yes. Who knew?"

* * *

After the tour of lights, they settled by the fire, sipping wine and cocktails as Bill took out sheet music from the piano bench. To say the least, the last thing Nic wanted to do was sing Christmas carols. No, she wanted to take Abby's hand and lead her upstairs and get her naked. Because by the time they'd finished the tour, she'd had about as much foreplay as she could take. Secret touches and stolen kisses had them both in a sexual frenzy by the time Bill had driven them back home. Her legs felt wobbly as she got out, and she and Abby had held hands and leaned against each other like the new lovers they were.

Once inside, she'd seen the longing in Abby's eyes, the desire, and she simply wanted to skip the festivities and head to bed. But no, they couldn't do that, could they? With a sigh, she turned her attention to the piano as Bill drummed his fingers across the keys, then played the opening notes to "Silver Bells." She didn't know all the words, so she only pretended to sing along. She found herself staring at Abby, who had a beautiful voice. Abby looked her way, holding her gaze. She stopped singing altogether, her mind conjuring up all the things she intended to do once they got into bed. Abby's eyes darkened and she, too, stopped singing. Had she read her mind? A tiny smile told her yes.

"Silver Bells" blended into another song. She'd heard it before, yes, but she didn't know the name. Like the holiday itself, Christmas music had never been a part of her life. She learned the most common songs in school, like "Jingle Bells," but it wasn't something she carried with her. She found herself receding to the background, watching the others as they sang. Holly was standing next to Abby now, and they sang together.

She felt those fingers of loneliness creeping in again, but she didn't let them totally take hold this time. She tried to focus on the words she heard, hoping they would conjure up some happy memory. All she felt was pain, though. Fifteen years ago, her Christmas Eve had been filled with pain—with screaming and yelling, accusations and blame. And then the blinding pain, both physical and emotional.

Fifteen years ago. A lifetime, yet it could have been yesterday. She should have stayed in Dallas. She should have stayed with people who loved her. But here she was, at this most trying of times, pretending to be happy and in love. Pretending that she was over the emotional wreck of that night. Pretending—

"Hey, you okay?"

The words were for her ears only, and she was surprised to find Abby next to her. She'd been in a lost daze, apparently. She hadn't noticed her approach. She nodded automatically.

"Sure. Fine." She met her gaze. "I…I don't know the words."

She felt Abby's hand slip into hers. "That's okay. You don't have to sing." She leaned closer. "I'm ready to sneak upstairs anyway. Are you?"

She nodded. "About four songs ago."

Abby smiled at her. "Then let's go."

Nic looked at the others, who were still singing. "Just like that? Can we?"

"Of course." Abby turned, motioning to her mother, then pointing upstairs. Sandra winked at them, never missing a beat as she sang.

Nic felt a sense of relief as she held Abby's hand and headed up the stairs. She paused at the landing, looking back down. It was picture perfect, wasn't it? The crackling fire, the carolers gathered around the piano, Bill wearing a red elf hat as he played. Then Holly turned, glancing up at them. In the brief moment that their eyes held, Nic saw regret in them and perhaps even jealousy. Jealous because Holly knew exactly what she and Abby were about to do. And regret? Maybe Holly was second-guessing her decision to leave Abby for Aaron. Most likely, yes, although she couldn't possibly see Abby and Holly together. They had no chemistry whatsoever.

Abby tugged her along, and she pushed thoughts of Holly from her mind. She pushed the whole Christmas scene away too as the door closed behind them.

CHAPTER TWENTY-NINE

When Nic closed the door, Abby turned, feeling a little embarrassed now. It was the first second they'd had alone since the...well, since the scene in the back seat. Scene? Was that a good word? She smiled, remembering the "scene" vividly. Nic smiled too and moved closer to her.

"Did you enjoy the tour of lights?"

Abby laughed quietly. "Very much. Did *you*?"

"I did." Nic touched her cheek softly, running her index finger along her jawline. "Wonder how I'm going to pay you back for that?"

Abby swallowed. "If you need some suggestions, I can think of a few."

Nic spun them around, pushing Abby back against the door. "I can think of a few too."

Abby stood still as Nic's fingers unbuttoned her jeans, then slid them down her thighs. Nic's kiss was slow and very thorough, leaving her nearly panting when she drew away. Then Nic smiled at her before dropping to her knees. Oh dear lord, she thought as she leaned her head back. Nic's hands parted her thighs, and her eyes slammed shut when Nic's mouth covered her. She nearly whimpered as Nic's tongue cut through her wetness, circling her clit several times before sucking it into her mouth. She felt her head thump against the door as she moaned, and she grasped Nic's shoulders with her hands to steady herself.

Nic gripped her from behind, holding her tightly to her mouth as her tongue continued to tease her clit. She felt her knees go weak and she gave in to her orgasm, climaxing hard as her hips jerked against Nic's face. She may very well have collapsed if Nic hadn't stood and held her, still pressing her back against the door.

When Nic kissed her this time, it wasn't slow. No, she nearly devoured her mouth the same way she had her clit. Abby found herself responding again, pulling Nic close to her as her hips arched into her. But Nic had far too many clothes on for what she wanted to do. She tugged at Nic's sweater, urging it over her head. Nic pulled away long enough to rip it off.

"This too," Abby whispered, indicating the undershirt. Nic pulled it off as well, leaving her torso naked. "No bra? God, I love that." Nic's hands slid under her own sweater, shoving it off as Abby fumbled with the zipper of Nic's jeans. "I think you've turned me into some sort of a shameless sex fiend."

It was true. She was so terribly aroused—possessed by this wild, frenzied passion that she wasn't quite sure what to do with. Well, she knew what to do, of course. She simply didn't recognize herself any longer as she drew Nic to her, finding her mouth again. Hot, wet kisses had her moaning. It was Nic who brought some normalcy to the situation though.

"Bed," Nic murmured into her ear. "Let's go to bed."

"Yes, good. I'm about to fall down."

She fell into bed instead, pulling Nic on top of her. She felt insatiable, wondering how long it would take to quench her desire. She closed her eyes as Nic's mouth covered her breast. She hoped it took hours and hours.

And hours.

* * *

She didn't know if it was the silence that woke her or the empty bed. She stretched her legs out, noting the sweet ache between her thighs. Lord, but could that woman make love or what? She reached over to where Nic had been, feeling the cool of the sheets. She sat up and grabbed her phone, looking at the time—3:12. Where was Nic?

She got up, searching for her sleep shirt, then remembered that they hadn't gotten that far. They'd simply shed their clothes. She looked around, seeing them still strewn across the floor. She went to the drawers, pulling out a pair of sweats and a shirt. She opened the door quietly, listening. Her parents' bedroom was downstairs, and Aaron and Holly's room was quiet. She moved to the landing, stopping when she saw her.

Nic was sitting on the stairs—halfway down—her knees drawn up to her chest, her arms looped around them. She was staring at the Christmas tree, the colorful lights blinking, causing shadows to ebb and flow. Nothing remained of the earlier fire except a few red embers. The coolness of the air made her wrap her arms around herself.

She moved down the stairs, sitting beside Nic. She leaned into her but said nothing. Nic shifted, finding her hand.

"It happened on Christmas Eve," Nic said quietly. "That little, pathetic Christmas tree was on the table beside the TV. There were exactly two balls on it. They were blue. No lights. There were no gifts. Nothing. I often wonder why she bothered with it at all." Nic's fingers tightened around her own. "They were drinking early that day. By the afternoon, the yelling started. Sean and I went into his room. It was in the back of the house. It was where we went to most often when they were fighting."

She turned to look at Abby. "It was raining. A cold, steady rain—one of those dreary days where you want to crawl under the covers and fade away. That's what we wanted to do. Disappear."

Abby said nothing. She simply sat and held Nic's hand, letting her reminisce. Nic's next words, however, made her gasp.

"I didn't even know he owned a gun. Not sure she did either." Nic took a deep breath before continuing. "He'd called in a pizza. It was almost dark, not quite, but almost. There hadn't been any meals on the table that whole day and Sean and I were starving. When he called us to come out to eat, I knew something was wrong. Something was different. He had this crazed look in his eyes like he wasn't all there. She was on the couch. She was holding a bottle—vodka, I think it was. She was crying, yet she was laughing, like she didn't know which one to do. She said 'merry fucking Christmas' when Sean and I came out of his room."

"Oh, Nic," she whispered, leaning her head against her shoulder.

"He shot Sean first. Twice. Shot him twice. She screamed and threw the vodka bottle at him. He shot her." Nic took a deep breath. "Shot her in the head. Then he turned the gun to me. I ran toward the back door. I don't know that I even heard the shot. I just felt this burning in my back. I fell down. I heard him walk over, heard his shoes as he stepped on broken glass. I laid there. I didn't move. I think part of me was just hoping he'd pull the trigger, get it over with."

"Oh, honey, no."

"There was one more shot, yes, but it wasn't for me. I heard him fall. I opened my eyes, but I couldn't get up. I thought I was going to die right there on that dirty kitchen floor." Nic continued to stare at the Christmas tree. "From where I was, I could see Sean. I could see my mother's arm hanging off the side of the couch, and I could see that damn little tree with the two blue balls. That's all I remember. When I woke up, I was in the hospital. My uncle was there."

Abby could feel her heart breaking, and she wasn't surprised when she felt tears in her eyes. She didn't know what to say, though. She couldn't think of anything that was appropriate at that moment. She knew that Nic didn't need words—wasn't expecting them. She wondered how often Nic relived that day. Or was it a once-a-year tradition now, to recount the events that took the lives of her parents and her brother.

"So that's why I'm not too fond of Christmas."

She wrapped her arms around Nic and pulled her into an embrace. It was then that she felt the wet tears on Nic's cheeks. She kissed them away as they fell, feeling something swell within her. An urge to protect her, to comfort her.

"Let's go back to bed. Let me make love to you."

She led Nic back up the stairs and into their room. She undressed her slowly, taking her time as Nic stood there, almost despondent. Abby drew her to the bed, holding her, her hands moving gently, tenderly across her back. She came to the scar near her shoulder blade, her fingers tracing around it. She'd felt it earlier but had paid it no mind. Now that she knew what it was from, she wanted to kiss it—kiss it and make it all better.

She kissed Nic's mouth instead, a slow, tender kiss that elicited moans from both of them. Yes, she would make love to Nic. Slowly. Gently.

She would make her feel loved on this Christmas Day.

CHAPTER THIRTY

Nic wasn't sure if it was embarrassment she felt or something else. She felt exposed, she knew that. Besides her uncle, Eric and Addison were the only two people who knew about what had happened on that fateful Christmas Eve, fifteen years ago. And now Abby.

What had compelled her to share that story, she didn't know. Maybe it was just the closeness she felt with Abby. Or maybe she wanted to unburden herself, say it out loud, and let someone else share in her feelings. Maybe it was simply the beautiful Christmas tree that drew it out of her—a tree that was in complete contrast to the little one that was stuck in her mind.

She rolled her head toward the window, hearing the water turn off in the shower. Abby would be out soon. What should she say to her? Should she apologize? Or should she thank her? Thank her for loving her so thoroughly? Abby had been so gentle, so tender with her, touching her as if she were a fragile doll that might break. It wasn't sex then. Abby made love to her. It was the first time for her, and she'd nearly cried when she climaxed. Abby had gathered her close, whispering soft words into her ear, making her feel like she was the luckiest woman alive.

She didn't remember drifting off to sleep. Abby was still holding her, making her feel safe—making her feel loved. The sound of the shower had awakened her, though, and she wondered if the others were already downstairs, waiting on them. She closed her eyes again, wishing they could linger in bed a little longer. She felt drained. Too tired to participate in a joyous Christmas, that was for sure. There was to be no respite, though. The bathroom door opened, and she sensed Abby watching her.

"Good morning," she murmured without opening her eyes. She felt a light kiss on her lips.

"Good morning." Abby sat down on the bed beside her. "Are you as tired as I am?"

"Uh huh."

When a soft hand touched her cheek, she opened her eyes, meeting Abby's gaze. The affection she saw there made her feel warm and happy and…and relaxed. It was Christmas, a time of year that held no cheerful memories, no enjoyment. Yet this year, right now, she felt content. She embraced what she saw in Abby's eyes, and she smiled at her, soaking it all in. It was Christmas. And it would be different this year.

"Will it be too hard for you? I mean, with my family and gifts and—"

"No, Abby. It'll be like the fairytale Christmas that I never had."

"But you look sad, not happy."

"Do I? I feel pretty happy right now, actually." She smiled at her. "Thank you for last night. I…I—"

"You needed that," Abby finished for her. She touched a finger to her lips. "You don't let anyone get close to you. Is that why? You don't want to have to share your story with them?"

"Partly, I guess. And there's that trap I'm trying to avoid."

"A trap?"

"Yes. My parents were caught in a trap and neither of them could get out. I don't know if the drinking caused their relationship to deteriorate or if their relationship caused the drinking. Even when I was a little kid, I knew they didn't really like each other. I don't remember a time where there wasn't fighting, yelling. They were caught in a trap. I don't want that to ever be me."

"You'd rather be alone?"

"Yes. Besides, I don't have anything to offer anyone. I'm… I'm damaged."

"Oh, honey, you're not damaged. You were the victim. All of that was out of your hands."

"I feel broken, Abby. That's why it's easier to be alone."

Abby stared into her eyes for the longest moment, then nodded but said nothing else. They heard voices in the hallway. It was Holly and Aaron, going down to see what Santa had left, no doubt. She sighed.

"Guess I should shower."

Abby didn't move from the bed. "How old were you, Nic? When it happened."

"Fifteen."

Abby held her gaze again and she saw a myriad of emotions there. Then Abby touched her face softly. "I'm going to find coffee. Meet you downstairs?"

"Yeah. I won't be long." She forced a smile to her face. "I'm anxious to see what Santa left me."

Abby gave her a real smile. "I hope I get a necklace or something. That would be super."

CHAPTER THIRTY-ONE

Aaron and Holly were sitting on the sofa, both holding coffee cups. The fire was going, and Abby automatically glanced up to the stockings, smiling as she saw that they'd been stuffed during the night.

"Merry Christmas," she said cheerfully. "I see that Santa came."

"Yes, he did," Holly nearly purred. "You slept in, even after retiring rather early last night."

"Yes. I hope no one missed us," she said easily.

"You love singing Christmas carols." This coming from Aaron. "That's normally a highlight for you."

"Yes, well, I had a different kind of highlight last night." She actually blushed as she said the words, so she turned away. "Coffee."

Her mother was in the kitchen putting what she assumed was the normal Christmas quiche into the oven.

"Good morning, dear. Merry Christmas."

"Merry Christmas, Mom."

"Where's Nicole?"

"She was in the shower. She'll be down soon." She went to the coffee pot, pouring a cup. "Where's Dad?"

"He's in his office. He's pretending to be working, but I saw him sneak in with some wrapping paper and tape, so I'm hoping he's wrapping up something special for me."

"What could you possibly need?"

"I don't need anything, of course. He's still trying to make up for keeping the news of his real estate business from me." Her mother topped off her own coffee cup. "I sensed that Nicole was feeling a little uncomfortable last night. Was everything okay?"

She didn't know how much to tell her mother about Nic and her childhood. She was actually surprised that her mother hadn't grilled both of them already. "Well, to use Nic's words, she had a crappy childhood. Christmas was an afterthought in their house and there were no decorations and rarely gifts."

"Oh, the poor thing."

"Yeah, so this is all new to her." She took a sip of her coffee, eyeing her mother. "If I tell you something, will you promise you won't say a word to Nic about it? Or anyone else, for that matter."

"Of course, honey. What is it?"

"Well, Nic's parents are…are gone. She went to live with her uncle when she was fifteen."

Her mother raised an eyebrow. "Gone?"

Abby grabbed her mother's arm. "It's so tragic. Her father shot her mother and her brother, then shot Nic too, before killing himself."

"Oh dear lord," her mother gasped. "You hear of such things happening, of course, but yes, that's so tragic."

"It happened on Christmas Eve."

Her mother put a hand to her chest. "Goodness. No wonder she looked so lost last night. Nicole is such a sweet person, too. That's such a shame."

"I wanted to tell you in case she's not acting overly excited about Christmas. I didn't want you to ask any awkward questions of her." She pointed a finger at her. "And not one word to anyone else."

"Of course not."

"And please don't act weird around her. I probably shouldn't have said anything, but—"

"I won't say a word, Abigail. I'm glad you told me. I'll be extra careful of what I say to her."

Abby sat down at the breakfast table, taking her coffee with her. "So…how are you?"

"Me? What do you mean?"

"About Dad. Do you want to talk?"

"Oh, honey, I'm okay. I guess." Her mother sat down too. "I only wish he would have told me how unhappy he was. I mean, I could tell but we just kept going as we were. And he seemed so involved with the resort that I thought everything was okay."

"He didn't want to disappoint you."

"We made that silly promise all those years ago as a means to get us out of Dallas. If he really missed the business so much, he should have said something to me."

"So you're still a little pissed about it?"

Her mother took a deep breath. "Yes. But he knows it and we've talked. It's the whole me thinking he was having an affair thing. I mean, in my heart," she said, touching her chest, "I knew he was seeing someone—the woman at the coffee shop—and I didn't have the courage to confront him. What does that say about me? How weak must I be?"

"Oh, Mom, don't do this to yourself. He *wasn't* having an affair. You've embraced living up here and you're happy with your hobbies, your friends, the house. Let him have this. You can both be happy then. I mean, I've noticed the change in him in just one day. Now that you know, he's free to express how happy and content he is finally. Last night, he was like a different person."

"So, I need to let it go?"

"Yes. Besides, you already said you had makeup sex," she said with a laugh.

"And I said we weren't going to talk about that." Her mother leaned closer. "But speaking of sex, you and Nicole look quite taken with each other. Is she a keeper?"

Abby hesitated. How in the world should she answer that? If she said yes, then she'd have to explain away their breakup, which would be coming very soon. If she said no, then that made it look like she and Nic were only in a sexual relationship. Of course, she wouldn't have to tell them that she and Nic broke up. She could drag it out for months. They would never know.

"I like her a lot." That much was true. "But it's only been a few months, Mom. We're still getting to know each other."

"Well, I like her for you. You seem much more comfortable around her than you did with Holly. Night and day difference."

"Really? I guess I don't remember much about that first Christmas with Holly other than her saying she and Aaron had slept together and she was breaking up with me. That tends to be my focal point with her."

"Well, you tell me I need to let it go...*you* need to let it go as well. You've both moved on and that's two years in the past. Nothing but wasted energy, Abigail."

Before she could reply, Nic walked in looking quite refreshed. Her eyes seemed brighter, her smile genuine.

"Good morning, Sandra."

"Merry Christmas, Nicole. Come have some coffee. We were just having a little girl talk."

"Sorry I missed that."

Abby smiled at her. "I took a peek at your stocking. It looks to be bulging. Apparently, Santa found you after all."

As soon as she said the words, she wanted to take them back. Would Nic appreciate such teasing on this day? But she smiled easily as she sipped from her cup.

"I can't wait. As you know, I've never had a stocking before."

"Then it'll be fun."

"Yes, it will," her mother agreed. "Then afterward, we'll have a very light breakfast. I have the Christmas roast all ready to go into the oven. While that bakes, we'll go outside and do our snowman competition. Nicole, that'll be a first for you too, won't it?"

"Yes, it will." Nic looked her way. "You failed to tell me about that."

"I'll help you. They're fun to build. The secret is to get old, crusty snow, not any fresh powder." Then she laughed. "I suck at building snowmen, though. Maybe you should take advice from someone else."

Aaron and Holly came in, both heading to the coffee pot. Her father stuck his head in too.

"It's time to open presents. I just put another log on the fire, and I've got Christmas music on. It's perfect."

Abby got up and went to stand by Nic, taking her hand. "Come on. It'll be fun," she whispered.

Nic met her gaze and nodded. "I think it'll be the best Christmas ever."

CHAPTER THIRTY-TWO

Nic wasn't sure if she was excited or scared. She sat beside Abby on the sofa, trying to appear as nonchalant as she could, all the while listening to her hammering heart. There was soft music in the background, the fire was blazing, the lights on the tree were twinkling, and the stockings were all bulging with goodies. There were a few gifts under the tree, and she spotted the two small boxes that she and Abby had put there for each other. There was a larger box that Bill picked up first and brought it over to Sandra.

"Got you something."

Sandra turned and winked at Abby. Abby gave a quiet laugh, then leaned toward Nic. "So other than the makeup sex, he's getting her gifts too," she whispered to her.

More gifts were handed out. Nic was surprised that, besides the gift from Abby, there was another one handed to her. Bill gave her a smile.

"We got you a little something, Nic," he explained.

"Thank you." She nudged Abby. "I didn't get them anything."

"And they didn't expect you to. Open it."

She paused, looking around. Everyone seemed to be opening something. Sandra's gift was an appliance, an Instant Pot pressure cooker. Holly had pulled out a colorful sweater from a box that looked similar to hers. Aaron was laughing at a pair of fuzzy house shoes. Abby held her gift on her lap, waiting on Nic. She finally tore off one corner of the wrapping paper carefully, and Abby laughed.

"Rip into that sucker. Tear it up," Abby encouraged.

Nic did just that, ripping the paper off the box. She was conscious of Abby watching as she opened it. Inside she found, not a sweater like Holly had, but a navy sweatshirt with a mountain peak and Red River written across the top. Also in the box was a long-sleeved T-shirt, again advertising Red River. She looked over at Sandra.

"I love it. Thank you."

Sandra smiled at her. "Just a little something."

Then Abby was leaning against her. "Open your box."

She grinned at her. "Wonder what it is."

Abby laughed quietly. "Yeah. I hope you like it."

"Open yours too."

And they did, opening them nearly simultaneously. She was aware of the others watching them, and she smiled with fake surprise at the necklace she found. Abby did as well, laughing as she held it up.

"It's beautiful, Nic." Abby leaned closer, kissing her. "I love it."

"Let me see," Sandra said as she came closer. They showed her their necklaces and Sandra nodded approvingly. "This is so unique," she said, pointing to Nic's. "Where did you find it?"

"At that silver shop in town," Abby explained. "It fits her, don't you think?"

"Yes, it does." Sandra then inspected Abby's heart-shaped necklace. "That's beautiful. And it suits you too. Perfect gifts."

"The way you two have been going on, I would have expected rings," Holly drawled with a laugh. Then she held her left hand up, flashing her diamond. "Speaking of weddings, Aaron and I have an announcement."

Nic glanced at Abby, who rolled her eyes.

"Yes. We've set a date," Aaron added. "Sort of. We've settled on June or July, up here or in Dallas."

Sandra clapped. "Wonderful news! So happy for you!"

"If we have it here, it'll only be family. So I'm leaning toward Dallas," Holly continued. "I always envisioned having this huge wedding." Her smile was positively saccharin as she looked at them. "Did you ever imagine getting married, Nicole?"

"Can't say that I have."

"Well, I for one, hope you have it here," Sandra said. "But I'm being selfish. I have no desire to visit Dallas during the heat of summer."

"That's a consideration, of course, although my mother wants it in Dallas so she can show me off to all her friends," Holly said with a flair. "If she has her way, it'll be extravagant." Then Holly's gaze landed on Abby. "Abigail, I'd love for you to be my maid of honor. If not for you, I would never have met this wonderful man here. You deserve all the credit."

Nic felt Abby stiffen beside her.

"I believe it's all you, Holly. Afterall, you cheated on me with him. No need to give me credit for that."

The room became deathly quiet as Holly and Abby stared at each other. Nic wanted to applaud Abby for speaking up, finally. Nevertheless, Holly didn't seem fazed by her statement.

"So, is that a yes? Aaron and I would both love for you to accept."

Aaron nodded but said nothing. Abby slowly turned her gaze to Nic. As their eyes met, they both smiled.

"What do you think?" Abby asked.

"Well, if it were me, I'd probably tell them to kiss my ass."

Abby laughed loudly and so did Bill. Sandra, too, let out a laugh but recovered quickly, covering her mouth with her hand.

"But it's not me," Nic continued. "So, what do *you* think?"

Abby shrugged and looked back at Holly. "I'll have to let you know."

Sandra stood quickly. "Wonderful. Now let's see what Santa left in our stockings."

Abby leaned against her. "That was kinda fun," she whispered.

"I thought so too."

They sat close together, and Abby found her hand, their fingers tightening. For a second, she forgot they were pretending. It felt natural to be holding hands with Abby. It felt real. She quite liked it.

"Here you go, girls." Sandra handed them each their stocking.

Nic still marveled over the name—Nicole—painted on the front. Abby turned, watching her.

"So? What did you get?"

Nic looked at the stocking, then back at her. "I've never had a stocking before. What do you do?"

Abby's eyes softened. She leaned closer, kissing her lightly on the mouth. "You stick your hand inside and pull something out. Hopefully, there'll be lots of fun things in there."

So, she did, tentatively reaching inside. The first thing she felt was cool and round. She wrapped her fingers around it and took it out. She grinned as she saw it. It was the snow globe she'd been fascinated with when they'd shopped. She shook it now, the little gingerbread house getting buried beneath the falling snow.

"When did you sneak back and get this?"

"I got Dad to get it for me. You like?"

"Yes. It'll be a great reminder of the very best Christmas," she said honestly.

"Good. That was my hope."

As Abby fished things from her own stocking—a pretty glass candle holder, for one—Nic stuck her hand back into hers. There was an assortment of trinkets—from Sandra, no doubt—a Red River keyring and a Red River bottle opener among them. She was also surprised to find a stack of lottery scratch-off tickets in it.

"Everyone gets them," Abby explained, holding up her own. "Twenty dollars' worth of tickets. We'll sit at the table before we eat and have a scratch-off party." Abby leaned closer. "Holly thinks it's beneath her."

"It'll be fun." She put the tickets aside and picked up the snow globe again, shaking it once more. "I never had one of these before. It looks so peaceful, like you wish you were standing there on the porch or something."

"I'm glad you like it."

Before long, Bill was tidying up the discarded wrapping paper and everyone was gathering their loot.

"We'll eat in twenty minutes," Sandra announced. "I just have to get the hash browns on the griddle. Oh, and don't forget to bring your scratch-offs."

"Come on. Let's take this upstairs."

Holly and Aaron had the same idea. The four of them stood at the bottom of the stairs, as if trying to decide who got to go up first. Abby smiled charmingly at them.

"Age before beauty, please," she said with a wave of her hand toward the stairs.

It was Aaron who spoke. "I hope you'll seriously consider being the maid of honor. It would mean be a lot to us."

"Would it? Or would it be just another way to humiliate me?"

Holly looped her arm with Aaron's. "Let her think on it, honey."

They stood at the bottom watching as Holly and Aaron went up. Abby turned to her.

"I think I hate her."

"I wouldn't waste even that emotion on her." Nic headed up the stairs after them and Abby followed.

Once in their room, Abby closed the door, putting her gifts on the bed. "So? Was that okay for you? Not too bad?"

"It was fun."

"You think so? There was a little tension."

"Was there?"

"It was like everyone was faking being happy."

Nic put her things on the dresser, then went closer to Abby. "Were they? Like you and I were faking being girlfriends?"

Abby met her gaze. "Having you here has been the highlight of Christmas, Nic." Then she smiled. "For a number of reasons.

But like we said, Holly and Aaron don't really look happy. My mother is still a little miffed at my dad. I'm obviously still angry with Holly and Aaron."

"Are you?"

"Aren't I? Shouldn't I be?"

"I don't want to tell you how you should or shouldn't feel. I think you *think* you should still be angry. At some point, you have to get past it, though."

"You're right. It's almost like I have to remind myself that I should be angry with them. If you weren't here, I think I would be. I would still be focused on that. I don't like Holly. I can see her for what she is, and I don't like her. I wouldn't even want to be friends with her. It's just appalling that she—*they*—think it's perfectly acceptable to ask me to be in their wedding. I mean, who does that?"

"So say no, you won't do it and be done with it."

"My mother will push me to do it. Less drama that way." Abby came closer. "But you know what? I don't want to be in their freakin' wedding. So, I'm not going to." Abby slid her hands up to Nic's shoulders, then looped them around her neck. "Have I thanked you lately for being my girlfriend?"

Nic pulled her closer. "Not lately, no."

Their slow, leisurely kiss turned heated, and Nic was surprised to find herself being pushed down onto the bed. She moaned into Abby's mouth as Abby settled her weight on top of her. She forgot about Christmas brunch as her hands pushed Abby's sweatshirt up, her fingers touching warm skin. She spread her thighs, feeling Abby press hard against her as she shoved her bra aside.

Through her lustful haze, she heard voices outside in the hallway, heard steps on the stairs. A few seconds later, Sandra called out.

"Come down, girls. Everything's ready!"

Abby groaned as she pulled her mouth away, then rolled off her. "God, the last thing I want to do is have breakfast." She rolled her head to look at her. "I'm kinda turned on, in case you can't tell."

"I kinda am too."

Abby laughed. "Who would have thought I'd enjoy this compensation thing so much."

She smiled at that. "I'm quite enjoying it too."

"Girls!"

Abby sat up. "She'll be beating on the door soon if we don't get down." She leaned over and kissed her. "We'll finish this later."

CHAPTER THIRTY-THREE

"No, no, no."

"Why not?"

Nic shook her head. "Nope." She pointed to the chairlifts. "Not getting me on that thing. Nope."

Abby smiled at her. "You won't fall."

"Not doing it. You go on. Have fun. I can walk the streets in town. Window shop. Stop by the brewery for a beer. Anything." She shook her head again. "I have a tiny fear of heights."

Abby laughed. "Tiny?"

"Okay. More than tiny. I'm sorry." She wasn't really. She hadn't been looking forward to skiing anyway. She didn't know how, and she was afraid she'd make a fool out of herself.

"I don't have to ski then. We can—"

"No, Abby. You were looking forward to it. Go ahead. I don't mind. Really."

"Are you sure?"

"I'm sure. Call me when you're done, and we'll meet somewhere."

Abby fished her keys from her ski pants. "Here. In case you want to drive around or something. I'll call you and you can pick me up. We'll grab lunch in town."

Nic took the keys, nodding. "Deal."

Abby grabbed her arm before she turned away. "There's only three more days left. We can do snowmobiles again tomorrow if you want."

"Yeah, that was fun. But you don't have to entertain me, Abby. I'm fine. Go enjoy your skiing. I'll see you in a few hours."

"Okay. Don't get lost."

"Don't break a leg," she countered.

No, she'd not been looking forward to skiing. She should have told Abby that upfront. Nevertheless, she'd thought she'd give it a try, at least. She looked up to the chairlifts now, seeing legs and skis dangling in the air, seemingly hundreds of feet off the ground. She turned away with a shudder. *No thank you.*

They'd spent the last few days doing rather tame things. They'd gone sledding again, this time to the higher hill. It had been great fun. They'd gone snowmobiling too. It had been with a guided tour group, though, so Abby had informed her that they couldn't get "wild and crazy" on the machines. It was still fun, as they'd gone deep into the backcountry. Yesterday had been a warm and sunny day and they'd taken the scenic drive— the Enchanted Circle, Abby had called it—to Angel Fire, then down to Taos, where they'd had lunch, then back to Red River. They'd seen the elk herd near Angel Fire and stopped to watch them. After lunch, instead of heading back, they'd walked to a couple of old missions and had spent a leisurely hour mingling with other tourists.

It had been a perfectly normal day, but she wasn't sure what normal was anymore. They looked at each other like new lovers do, smiling in a secretive way that only they could. They teased and flirted and stole kisses. It never once occurred to her that there was no reason for any of that. No one from Abby's family was around so there was no need to pretend to be girlfriends.

She shoved her hands into her pockets as she made her way along the street, absently glancing into the shops that she passed. At the corner, there was a nook—a small picnic area—with park benches and two tables. She thought maybe she'd take this time to call Addison and check in, even though she'd texted her on Christmas Day to let her know that she'd made it through another Christmas Eve.

She went over and sat down, lifting her face toward the sun. It wasn't a brutally cold day but certainly not the warmish one they'd had yesterday. She'd learned over breakfast that there was a storm coming that would bring more snow. She wouldn't mind that. She enjoyed watching it fall, much like she enjoyed the little snow globe Abby had given her.

The thought of that made her smile. Such a simple, trivial item, yet when she held it, shook it, it brought a peace and happiness to her that was unfamiliar. She liked the necklace, sure. It was unique. She reached a hand up, touching it now. It was the snow globe, though, that would always remind her of this trip. This trip and Abby.

She sighed, wondering how she'd let herself get so involved with Abby—and her family. Her whole adult life had been lived with the certainty that she would not let anyone get close to her—and she would not get close to them. So far, that had worked out perfectly. She dated and she had sexual relationships, that was it. That was what she was used to. That was all she wanted, all she needed. She was perfectly fine with that arrangement. She didn't want anywhere near that trap that she'd told Abby about. Her parents' life was a living hell and, therefore, that's what her childhood had been. She was adamant that she would stick to her conviction and not ever let anyone close enough to control her. Her parents' dysfunctional codependency had ruined their lives. Literally.

Yet here she was, falling into a companionable, close, and intimate relationship with Abby Carpenter. She couldn't even say she was only pretending. Because she wasn't. She enjoyed Abby's company. She obviously enjoyed having sex with her. Abby had made Christmas—her most dreaded time of year—fun and even special.

And in a handful of days, they'd head back to Dallas—back to their lives—and say goodbye to each other. Oh, she might run into her at the courtyard, if she made it a point to go there, but that was it. Here, with just the two them, they were allies. But back there, back in the real world? No. They ran in different circles. They might be friendly enough here, but she couldn't see that being sustained in Dallas.

She shook her head, then got up and walked on. What was she thinking? That maybe she and Abby could continue this… this pretend relationship once home? That maybe Abby might want to get together occasionally? And do what? Have sex? Go out to dinner? Hang out?

"Don't be stupid," she muttered to herself. No. None of those things were going to happen. She didn't *want* them to happen. She was perfectly happy—content—with the way things were. And the sooner she got back to it, the better it would be, and she could push these crazy thoughts aside for good.

Yes. That's exactly what she would do. Three more days here. Then the New Year would be upon them and one long drive back to Dallas would put an end to this pretense.

She looked up into the sky as she walked—the blue, blue sky. It was bright and sunny and the snowcapped peaks surrounding Red River were nearly dazzling. It was picture-perfect. With a sigh, she pulled her gaze away. The blue she was feeling didn't match the sky. No, it was dark and gloomy…that place where she was. She didn't even chance a call to Addison. Addison would sense her mood and be full of questions.

So she walked on alone, trying to find some cheer on this suddenly gloomy day.

CHAPTER THIRTY-FOUR

Abby bit down on Nic's shoulder as she climaxed, trying to stifle the scream that wanted to come out. She rested her weight on top of Nic, smiling against her skin. Who knew she had such a passionate side to her? And who knew she'd become obsessed with sex? Because that's what it was, wasn't it?

"Are you tired of me yet?"

Nic laughed quietly beneath her. "Tired of you? Should I be?"

She lifted her head. "You know, you said you only have affairs. Quick ones at that. I took that to mean you slept with them one, two, maybe three nights at the most."

"Ah. And this is what? Seven?"

"I think it's eight. I don't know anymore." She shifted off Nic, resting on her side now. "Even though I agreed to your counteroffer, I still had no intention of sleeping with you, you know."

"No? You planned to renege on our deal?"

"Yes. I didn't think you were the type to force yourself on me and I didn't imagine you'd tell my family about our little charade to get back at me. I figured you would be stuck up here and there would be nothing you could do about it."

"That was your plan, huh? Sorry that didn't work out."

Abby touched her breasts, her finger moving from one nipple to the other. Instead of answering, she lowered her head, gently kissing the nipple that she'd just been touching. At Nic's sharp intake of breath, she closed her mouth around it. Oh, but they didn't have time for this. Not again. They'd come upstairs to shower before dinner. Her parents were taking them out to eat this evening, an hour earlier than usual. The snowstorm—with near blizzard conditions—was expected to hit by nine and her father wanted to be home and off the roads before then.

With a groan, she rolled away from Nic. "Shower. We're supposed to be showering."

But Nic rolled toward her and gathered her close, kissing her hungrily. Abby returned the kiss, letting her tongue dance with Nic's. God, she felt like a horny teenager. She moved her fingers between Nic's thighs. Maybe they had time, she reasoned. Because when she felt Nic's wetness, she had no intention of stopping. She circled her clit with her finger, feeling Nic writhe against her. Their kisses were frantic now—frenzied—as if they couldn't get enough. And no, she couldn't get enough. She wanted Nic to swallow her up, she wanted to drown inside her, she wanted to devour her.

A loud knock on their door made her jerk her head up, staring at it in disbelief. Surely to god they locked the damn thing.

"Hey…Mom said we're leaving in ten minutes."

"Jesus…ten minutes?" she whispered. She pulled away from Nic. "Yeah. Okay," she called. "Be right down."

"No, no, no, no," Nic murmured. "I'm dying here."

Abby smiled at her. "Come on. I'll take care of that for you. In the shower."

CHAPTER THIRTY-FIVE

The fancy steak place had had a waiting line and, much to Holly's chagrin, they opted for the barbeque joint instead. Either one would have suited Nic—she'd been starving. It was a fun place and it had been hopping. A corner was reserved for dancing, and it was crowded as people took advantage of the live band playing country music.

The brisket was tender, the ribs had been falling off the bone, and the sauce had just enough of a bite to take the edge off the sweetness. It wasn't Scooter's Pit Barbeque, but it was damn good. Holly seemed to be the only one not impressed with the food or ambiance, but Nic simply ignored her complaints as she practically wolfed down the ribs on her plate.

"Waiting for the storm?"

Nic turned, finding Sandra watching her from the doorway. She nodded. "Hope you don't mind, but I figured the sunporch was the perfect place to see it."

"Of course not. I'll put the corner lights on outside. You'll have a better view then."

She moved to a wall switch and did just that. Lights illuminated the snow that was already on the ground, and in the beam, she could see small, gentle flakes falling.

"The prelude," Sandra explained. "To hear the weathermen tell it, it'll be quite fierce when it blows in."

"Do you ever lose power with storms like this?"

"Oh, it's rare. A blowing blizzard like this is common. At least once or twice a season, we'll get a good one, but the wind is rarely strong enough to topple trees. That's when we'll lose power." Sandra sipped from the cup she was holding. Coffee or tea? "I hope you two didn't have plans for tomorrow. I would imagine you'll be stuck here for the day."

"Abby thought we could try sledding again." She smiled. "Maybe talk Aaron and Holly into going along."

Sandra smiled too. "Good luck with that." She sat down and offered the other chair to her. "Have you enjoyed yourself, Nicole?"

"Very much." She looked over at her. "I don't know how much Abby has told you, but I didn't exactly grow up having any sort of traditional Christmas. In fact, none." She stared outside into the light, wondering if it was her imagination or was the snow starting to get thicker. "Your home is beautiful, Sandra. The tree is…well, it's perfect." She looked at her again. "Truth is, I always hated Christmas. Abby and your family have shown me a different side to it." She was surprised when Sandra reached over and touched her arm, squeezing it gently.

"I'm so glad Abigail brought you, Nicole. It's been a joy to get to know you." She smiled. "I hope this is the first of many."

Nic felt a twinge of guilt as she nodded at Sandra. "Me too."

"Only a few more days, then you'll be heading back to the city. It's always so quiet here when the kids leave."

"What about your parents? I thought they were coming."

"So did I." Sandra's tone indicated her disappointment. "When they owned this house, we always spent our Christmas up here with them, from the time Aaron and Abigail were babies. They've never known anything else. Since my parents moved to Arizona, it's them who make the trip up here now." Sandra let out a heavy sigh. "A cruise apparently sounded better to them and now this storm," she said with a wave toward the windows. "When I spoke to them this morning, they were going to wait and see how bad it was." Sandra turned to look at her. "That means they won't come. The storm is a convenient excuse. To hear my mother talk, they are absolutely exhausted from their trip."

"They just got back?"

"They flew in yesterday afternoon. And I can't say I blame them. If I'd just spent nine days on a ship, the last thing I'd want to do is travel." Another heavy sigh. "I miss them. We don't get to see them nearly enough and they're getting older." She waved her hand again. "Sorry, Nicole. I didn't mean to go on so."

Nic smiled but said nothing. Her gaze was still on the snow. Yes, it was definitely getting thicker. She could almost feel her anticipation.

"I was wondering where you'd slipped off to." Abby walked behind her and rested her hands on her shoulders. "It's started?"

"Flurries," Sandra supplied. "You want to sit with us?"

"Let me make a cup of tea first. Just watching the snow makes me cold." Abby tapped Nic's shoulder. "You want some?"

"Sure. Thanks."

"Be right back."

The quiet was broken a short time later when Aaron and Holly came in. Nic tuned out the conversation going on around her as her gaze was fixed on the snow. When Abby handed her a cup of hot tea, she smiled her thanks. It was laced with honey, and as she took a sip, she realized it was the very first time she'd had hot tea. She quite liked it.

When the others erupted in laughter, she still paid them no mind. She didn't want to miss a second of the snowstorm. She absently acknowledged that Abby and Holly appeared to be getting along better. That was good. Maybe Abby would agree to be in their wedding after all. That thought brought a bit of sadness to her. She wouldn't be around to see it.

CHAPTER THIRTY-SIX

Nic was sound asleep, and Abby took that opportunity to snuggle even closer to her. In sleep, Nic's arm tightened for a moment, then relaxed again. Abby closed her eyes and let out a contented sigh. Never in a million years would she have thought she'd enjoy sex this much. Maybe Nic was right—sex *was* better without all the emotional attachments that come with dating.

She opened her eyes then, seeing Nic's face in the shadows. They obviously weren't dating, no, but could she say that she had no emotional attachment to her? Would she consider Nic a friend? Well, yes. But that, too, was temporary. Once they got back to Dallas, back to their respective lives, that wouldn't be the case. They'd have no reason to see each other, to talk, to hang out.

Did they need a reason, though? Her sigh this time was no longer contented. What was she thinking? That she and Nic could still get together every once in a while and have sex? Like fuck buddies? She nearly cringed at the thought. Lord, she didn't have *fuck* buddies. No. That was too far out there for her.

No, she would go back to her normal routine, she imagined. In fact, Beth had texted her yesterday, saying Jenna had met a friend of a friend—a doctor. A doctor who was thirty-five and just starting to date again after a brutal breakup last year. Beth said that Jenna said that the doctor would be perfect for her. She'd even included a photo of the woman.

So yeah, that's probably what she'd do. Back to her normal routine. But instead of vetting them—as Sharon called it—she might throw caution to the wind and be more open to casual dating and casual sex. Because if these past eight or nine days had taught her anything, it was that casual sex was quite fun.

She shifted a little, resting her face against Nic's breast for a moment, noting the softness of it, before moving to her shoulder. Nic's shoulder made an awesome pillow, she decided.

* * *

She awoke hours later to an empty bed. She opened her eyes, knowing she was alone in the bedroom. She heard the wind howling outside and she glanced to the window. It still appeared dark outside. She tossed the covers off, then reached for her clothes, pulling on sweatpants first, then a shirt.

Other than the Christmas tree lights that still blinked, the downstairs was dark and quiet. She found Nic in the sunporch, standing near a window looking out. It wasn't quite daylight, no, but it wasn't full dark either. It was that moment in time that was in between—the night hanging on for a few more seconds as the day tried to push it aside.

"Good morning," she said quietly and Nic visibly jumped. "Sorry." She moved beside her. "You okay? Watching the storm?"

"Yes. I haven't been up long. Too dark to really see anything."

"It's cold in here. How about a cup of coffee? It'll be daylight soon." Then she paused. "Unless you'd rather be alone."

"No, no. This is just all so fascinating to me. My one and only blizzard, I guess. I doubt I'll ever see another one."

Yes, their time up here was coming to an end, wasn't it? Tomorrow would be New Year's Eve. Since they were planning on heading back on New Year's Day, she doubted they'd even make midnight.

By the time the coffee brewed and she brought back two cups, the sky had lightened. She stopped in the doorway.

"Good lord!"

The landscape was dressed all in white, head to toe. There didn't appear to even be a single pine needle that had been spared. It seemed that—now that they could see—the wind was blowing with more power, the snow coming down in thick waves.

"This is pretty cool," Nic said, her voice tinged with awe. "Look at your mom's picnic table. It's practically buried."

"And so is my car, no doubt." She handed Nic a cup. "When this is over, you'll get your first taste of shoveling snow. Then we'll see how excited you still are."

They sat down on the wicker loveseat, both staring out through the windows. A gust of wind seemed to rattle the panes and she felt Nic jump beside her. She leaned closer, touching her shoulder.

"You haven't said. Are you getting homesick?"

"Homesick? No. I actually haven't really given it much thought. I've thoroughly enjoyed my time here." She wiggled her eyebrows. "Some things more than others."

Abby smiled at her. "Yes, there were definitely some parts I loved more than others." Her gaze dropped to Nic's lips. "I'm going to miss you."

"Yeah?"

"Yes. I wouldn't have thought that at first, you know, but now…"

"Well, you might see me out in the courtyard someday. We're super busy in March getting the spring flowers out. I usually always help out in the field that month."

March? That was two months away. After spending nearly every second together for ten days straight, were they really going to part company and say goodbye with no intention of even talking? That was the original plan, of course. She reminded herself of her thoughts from last night. She was going to get back into her routine. She was going on a blind date with a doctor. And Nic would go back to doing whatever it was she did. Best not to draw this out any longer than necessary. She leaned back with a sigh.

"I got a text from Beth the other day."

"She's your best friend?"

"Yes. She and Jenna. Jenna met someone." She waved her hand. "A friend of a friend."

"Someone for you?"

"Yeah. She's thirty-five. A doctor."

"Wow. That's an upgrade. I think a doctor trumps an attorney. Maybe next year at Christmas, you can really put Holly in her place."

Abby wondered how Nic could be so casual about it all. But then, why not? Nic was only the fake girlfriend. At least Nic hadn't lost sight of that, even if she had. She pulled her phone out.

"You want to see her picture?"

Nic hesitated just a moment, then nodded. "Sure."

CHAPTER THIRTY-SEVEN

Nic kissed her way down Abby's smooth skin, relishing the taste of her. It was their last night together and she wanted to make it memorable. Truth was, she was trying to memorize the feel, the taste, the sight of Abby's body.

Abby moaned quietly as she nibbled at the hollow of her hip. Every night had been an adventure into drawing out as much pleasure as possible while still keeping in mind that Aaron and Holly were sleeping just across the hall. She smiled against Abby's skin, imagining her screaming out without care as she climaxed.

"Why are you smiling?"

She lifted her head, trying to see Abby's eyes in the darkness. "I was picturing us in bed without people next door."

Abby's hand touched her face, gently caressing her cheek. "That would be nice, wouldn't it?"

"Mmm," she murmured as she bent her head lower.

Abby's hips raised up to meet her mouth and as her tongue circled her clit, Abby's quiet moan sent chills across Nic's body.

She cupped Abby's thighs, lifting her legs and pressing her hard against her face. She wanted to devour her as Abby writhed beneath her, her moans louder now.

"God...*Nic*."

Hands held her face tightly, bringing her even closer, and Nic got lost in the pleasure she was giving to Abby—a pleasure that ended all too soon as Abby turned her face into her pillow to stifle her scream. She rested her cheek against Abby's thigh, eyes closed. A few moments later, Abby's fingers brushed through her hair, but she said nothing.

Nic finally raised her head, moving back up to lay beside Abby. They both sighed at the same time.

"Gonna be a long drive tomorrow," Abby said quietly.

"We can take turns. Driving and sleeping."

Abby rolled toward her, resting one arm across her waist. "What will you do when you get home? Do you have to go to work right away?"

"On Monday, yes. Uncle Jimmie was in Vegas over the break. He texted me two days ago, I think it was—when he got back. He's anxious to get the crews back out. This time of year, it's mostly maintenance and clearing out dead plants and stuff, though. Our workdays are much shorter. Some days I'll leave the office by noon."

"What do you do then?"

"I try to hit the gym every day. If the weather's good, I'll take a run outside."

"I hate to run."

Nic moved her hands across Abby's thighs, noting the firmness of them. "You must do something."

"I go to the gym at least three days a week. I'll usually do the elliptical. It's not quite as torturous as a treadmill." Abby scissored her legs between Nic's. "What else will you do?"

"I'll go see my uncle tomorrow. And Addison invited me over for dinner on Wednesday. They want to hear all about my Christmas."

"Do they...well, do they know about your family?"

"Yes. No one else. Well, other than you now. But I mean, other than Uncle Jimmie, no one knows. I don't normally make new friends so there's no one to tell."

"I'm glad you shared that with me, Nic. It makes this year even more special, I think, knowing it was your first real Christmas."

"Yeah. I think I might be more receptive from now on. I'll probably take Addison up on her offer next year, especially since there'll be a baby now."

"What is she having?"

"Don't know. They wanted to do it the old-fashioned way and not find out ahead of time. Eric and I are hoping for a girl. Addison actually wants a boy." She reached her hand up, running her fingers across Abby's nipple. "What about you? What will you do? I mean, other than your date with the doctor."

"I'll have a ton of work to catch up on, I'm sure. Quarterly reports will be due by the fifteenth. It usually takes me about a week to get back into my routine after a long break like this." Abby rolled them over, resting her weight on top of her. "I'm tired, but I don't want to go to sleep."

She smiled against Abby's lips as they kissed. "We'll pay for this in the morning."

"I know. But right now, I don't care." Abby kissed her again. "I just want to make love one more time."

One more time. Yes. For the last time. Then back to Dallas. Back to their real lives. And their real lives did not intermingle.

And she would miss Abby. Miss her a lot, she realized.

CHAPTER THIRTY-EIGHT

Yes, she was exhausted, but she wouldn't change it for anything. She glanced over at Nic, who was leaning her head against the passenger window, her eyes closed. She smiled at her sleeping form, then sighed. They'd agreed to change drivers every two hours and she had another thirty minutes to go before she could wake Nic.

They'd gotten away an hour later than she'd planned. It was her mother's fault. She'd made breakfast for them—scrambled eggs and fried potatoes and crispy bacon—and had chatted away as if they were staying another day. Her mother really liked Nic, she could tell. It was going to be harder to break up with her than she thought. Of course, she'd probably go with her earlier plan—drag it out as long as she could.

Then there was the awkward goodbye hug that Holly gave her. A hug and a whisper into her ear—*let's get together sometime.*

Good lord, would the woman ever give up? Thankfully, neither the words nor the hug made an impression on her. She could honestly say she was completely over Holly. It was probably clichéd to say, but what in the world had she ever seen in her?

Had she been that lonely, that desperate for companionship that she'd convinced herself that she'd fallen in love with her? She nearly shuddered now, thinking what could have been. What if Holly hadn't cheated on her with Aaron? What if Holly hadn't broken up with her? Would they still be together? Would they be planning to build a big-ass house? Would they be making wedding plans?

She shuddered again. Surely to god she would have come to her senses. Yes, surely. Because even if she thought things were good with them, she knew now that they weren't. Being with Nic told her that. She never knew she had such a passionate side to her until Nic. An unquenchable thirst that hadn't been satisfied until the early morning hours. It had never been like that with Holly. Not even close.

She looked over at Nic again, her eyes lingering on her lips. Oh, she would miss her, wouldn't she? And not just the sex. She enjoyed Nic's company, enjoyed being around her. Maybe she should reconsider her plans. Maybe she should just come right out and ask Nic if they could remain friends and—

No, no, no. *Fuck buddies.* Nope. She wouldn't do it. It wasn't her, she reminded herself. Just let it go. They had fun. Now it was over with. Simple as that.

* * *

Nic absently watched the lights of the city as Abby drove them to her apartment. As they got closer and closer to Dallas, their conversation had all but ceased. They'd taken turns driving and sleeping, but by three o'clock, they'd both been slept out. At first, they talked of trivial things—their work, the weather—but never once mentioned the approaching separation. By the time they'd hit Decatur, they'd both become increasingly silent and when they hit the city limits, there was nothing more to say.

It was nearly eight when Abby pulled into the parking lot of Nic's apartment complex. She was about to open the door when Abby turned the engine off. She turned to her. Her face was in shadows, preventing her from reading her eyes.

"So…"

Nic nodded. "Yeah. Here we are."

"Well, I can't thank you enough for going with me. You made the whole situation with Holly bearable. And, of course, made me realize that she was never the one for me. So, thank you for that."

"Thank you for giving me a real Christmas. I'll remember it always."

Abby reached a hand over and touched her arm. "My mother loved having you there. She'll be crushed when we break up."

Nic smiled at that. "I really liked your mother. Maybe you should wait a few months before you tell her. That way you can just say we grew apart or something. Or tell her we realized it was just lust and not love."

Abby squeezed her arm then released her. "I hope you find someone someday, Nic. Someone you can let in. You're too nice—*good*—of a person to be alone."

"Thanks. Maybe I will."

She opened the door finally, getting out. From the backseat, she took her backpack, then waited while Abby popped the back door. She took out her larger bag and set it on the sidewalk. Abby closed the hatch, then walked over to her. They said nothing as Abby's arms went around her shoulders. She drew Abby close, relishing this last hug. Then, after a lingering kiss on her cheek, Abby pulled away. Their eyes met for a brief second, and Abby looked like she wanted to say something, but she didn't. She went back to her car, but before she got inside, she turned back to her.

"Goodbye, Nic. Take care of yourself."

She nodded. "Goodbye."

She stood there long after the taillights disappeared into the night. With a heavy sigh, she picked up her bags and headed to the stairs. Once inside her apartment, she flipped the lights on. It was as she'd left it—empty and quiet.

She stood there, looking around for a long moment, listening to the quiet, then she opened her bag. She carefully unwrapped the snow globe. She shook it, watching the tiny snowflakes cover the gingerbread house. When the snow settled, she shook it again, then set it down, reaching inside her bag once more. This time she pulled out the red stocking. *Nicole.* She smiled as she stared at it, then put it on the bar beside the snow globe. She pulled out a barstool, sitting down and resting her chin in her palm, her gaze going between the globe and the stocking. She was shocked to feel tears in her eyes, even more surprised when they ran down her cheeks.

She couldn't ever remember feeling lonelier than she did at that very moment.

CHAPTER THIRTY-NINE

Abby grinned as Sharon waved at her across the courtyard. She hurried over to their table, pausing to give Sharon a quick hug before sitting down.

"Did you have a good break?"

"I only had a few days off. Remember, I worked between the holidays. But you look good," Sharon mused.

"Thanks."

"So, spill it. Did you sleep with Holly?"

"God, no." She opened up her sandwich. "You were right. We never did go together. We're nothing alike and she was quite the bitch at times. That doesn't mean she didn't want to sleep with me. I'm not even the least bit interested." She looked up shyly. "And then there was Nic, you know."

"Oh my god! You're blushing. You went through with it?"

"God, it was so fabulous. And I really liked her. She was perfect. No one ever suspected that she wasn't my real girlfriend. In fact, my mother fell in love with her."

"That's good, then. Are you going to like, date now?"

"Date? Me and Nic?" She shook her head. "Nic doesn't date. She…she has some personal issues and stuff," she said evasively. "Old family drama that she's carried with her. So no, we won't see each other again. She's not interested in that." Saying it out loud made it seem true, even though all day yesterday she'd tried to find a reason to call Nic, a reason to see her.

"That's too bad. So now you've got to break up with her?"

"Yeah. I'll probably wait a few months before I tell my mother. It'll break her heart. I think she had us getting married." She rolled her eyes. "Speaking of weddings, yes, they really did ask me to be the freakin' maid of honor."

"Are you going to do it?"

"I don't want to, no. My mother will pressure me to do it. And Aaron was completely sincere when he asked." She bit into her sandwich. "I just don't know why they want me. There's so much animosity between us already."

"Maybe they think this could be the bridge to get you back."

She motioned to Sharon's salad. "Are you back on your diet?"

"Of course. I had a protein shake for breakfast. Salad for lunch."

"And you'll be ravenous by dinner." She sighed. "I have a date."

"Tonight?"

"No. Friday. You know my friends Beth and Jenna?"

"Right."

"Jenna met someone. A doctor. They're having us over for dinner Friday night."

"A doctor? Ooh la la," Sharon teased.

Abby put her elbows on the table. "I'm a little nervous. You know I haven't been on a real date in ages."

"Not since Holly, I believe."

"No, no. There was that woman—what was her name? Monica, yes. That was last spring, so nearly a year. And a doctor? What in the world are we going to talk about? It's going to be a disaster, I can already tell."

"You're trying to talk yourself out of it, aren't you?"

She blew out her breath. "It's…it's because of Nic. I really liked her. And I miss her already." She leaned closer. "And the sex was *really* good."

"So tell her."

"Tell her the sex was good? I'm pretty sure she already knows that."

"You know what I mean."

"I don't want to get hurt. Or disappointed. And if I went to her and told her that I wanted to see her—to date—then I'd be crushed when she said no. And she would say no. She's got some childhood issues." Was that a good way to put it? "She made it clear she doesn't want anyone in her life, but I think, deep down, she wants someone. She's just afraid."

"And you want to be that someone?"

She met Sharon's gaze. "I think…I think I fell a little bit in love with her, yes. Crazy, isn't it?"

"Oh my god! So tell her."

"No. Like I said, I'm not going to set myself up. We talked a lot and I understand her reasoning. I respect that. I don't want to place any sort of guilt on her. It is what it is."

"But maybe she's changed her mind."

"No. There were ample opportunities for her to suggest we see each other again. She never did. I even hinted at it a time or two, but she didn't." She put her sandwich down, realizing she'd only taken a couple of bites. "It doesn't matter. You can't base a relationship on sex, and we did a *lot* of that. So yes, I'll go to dinner with the doctor and see how it goes. I'm just saying, I don't have high hopes." Because she couldn't seem to get Nic out of her mind. She picked up her sandwich again, wanting to change the subject. "So…tell me about your Christmas. What did Michael get you?"

CHAPTER FORTY

Addison's hug was hard and tight—well, as tight as a very pregnant woman can hug you.

"Wow. You've gotten bigger," Nic exclaimed.

"I know. I swear, my boobs are like cantaloupes already. I can't believe I have three more months of this." Addison drew her inside. "Eric's got the grill going. He decided to hook up the rotisserie and do a chicken. Grab a beer for y'all. Let's go out. It's so nice this evening."

"Yeah, it was like spring today." She went to the fridge and pulled out two beers. "What will you have?"

"I've got a bottle of water out there. Come on. I'm dying to hear about your trip."

"What about you? Did you have a good Christmas?"

"We missed you being here, but yes, it was nice. My mother even asked where you were."

"Really? Was it with relief that she asked?"

Addison laughed. "A little. Come on."

Eric grinned at her when they went out to the patio. "There's my girl." He pulled her into a hug. "Missed you, Nicky."

"I missed you guys too."

He took the beer from her and twisted off the top, then clinked his to hers. "Damn glad you're back."

"Sit down," Addison urged. "Tell us all about it."

"It was fun. I never did brave skiing, but I did get on a snowmobile. That was a blast. And we did some sledding. Built snowmen. I came in second place in that contest."

Addison touched her arm and smiled. "Good, good. Sounds like fun. Now tell me about the girl."

Nic nodded. "Abby." It was the first time she'd said her name out loud all week. It certainly wasn't the first time she'd thought of her, though. "She was...she was great, actually." She finally sat down and took a swallow of her beer. How did she tell her two best friends that her cold, cold heart had melted a little over the holidays? "I...I liked her a lot."

"So? What does that mean?" Eric asked.

"Tell us about Christmas. How was it?" Addison added.

"It was my fairytale." She smiled at Addison. "The house was this huge, two-story mountain cabin, and Sandra—that's Abby's mother—had it decorated to the hilt. Even our bedroom had a little tree in it." She laughed. "And she got me a stocking with *Nicole* written on it."

"Why Nicole?"

"Because when Abby told her she was bringing me, her mother wanted to know my real name. She doesn't do nicknames. Abby assumed Nic was short for Nicole." She laughed again. "So I was Nicole the whole time."

"Oh, that's too funny." Addison laughed. "Did you get gifts and stuff?"

"I did. Her parents got me this sweatshirt, in fact. And Abby and I went into Red River and picked out necklaces." She pulled the collar of her sweatshirt down, showing off hers.

"Oh my god. That's gorgeous. And so unusual." Addison touched it. "It fits you perfectly."

"Thanks."

"I want to know about sex. As in, did you get any?"

Nic grinned at Eric. "What do you think?"

"You dog! So she paid up, huh?"

Nic's smile faded a little. "It really wasn't like that. We sort of, I don't know, bonded or something." She glanced at Addison. "I told her about my family, about what happened."

Addison's eyes widened. "You did?"

"Yeah. You know, Christmas Eve, I never can sleep worth a damn. I went down to look at the tree. The lights were on, and I was sitting there, letting in all those old memories. Abby came to find me. I just...I just told her. And she was so good about it all."

"She didn't freak out?"

"Not at all. At least not in front of me. I had already told her some, about their drinking and stuff. And how we never had a real Christmas. She knew all that already."

"Wow, Nicky, I didn't think you'd ever tell anyone that story." Eric sat down beside her. "I think it's good. You keep it locked away, you don't ever want to talk about it." He shook his head. "Not that I blame you. Hell, I don't know how you didn't lose your damn mind over it all."

Nic smiled at him. "Is that your way of saying I'm stubborn or strong?"

"A little of both."

"So, you really liked her? This Abby?" Addison asked gently.

"I did." She leaned back in her chair with a sigh. "If I was inclined to let someone into my life, she'd be the one."

Addison took her hand. "Then why don't you, Nicky?"

Nic squeezed Addison's fingers. "I'm a little out of her league. Holly, the ex who is now engaged to her brother, is an attorney. And she's got a date lined up with a doctor. Probably this weekend."

"But—"

"Doesn't matter anyway. I don't think I'm emotionally sound enough to let someone in, to let someone get close. I don't think I'm mentally equipped to handle a relationship. I wouldn't even know how to begin."

"You begin by asking her out on a date. A real date."

"What if she says no?"

Addison's eyes softened. "What if she says yes, Nicky?"

"If she said yes to anything, it would be for sex. That was really good between us. But to date? No. I don't think so. I told you. Attorneys, doctors. That's her thing. Not me. I'm damaged goods with a lot of baggage."

"Oh, hell, Nic, you know that's not true," Eric said.

"It is true."

Addison shook her head. "You are the only one who thinks that, but I won't argue with you. Now, did you take pictures? I'd love to see."

Nic pulled out her phone. "I took a few. Mostly snow and stuff." She flipped through them, pausing when she came to the one of Abby. It was on their second sledding trip and Abby had just landed in a snowbank. She was laughing, her cheeks were red, and she was absolutely gorgeous. She showed it to Addison. "That's her."

Addison's eyes widened. "Wow. She's cute."

"Let me see."

Nic handed her phone to Eric, listening to his wolf whistle. "You're out of your mind if you don't ask this one out."

CHAPTER FORTY-ONE

"What's wrong? You're being awful quiet."

"I'm sorry." Abby glanced to the living room where Jenna and Kate were talking. Kate was nice, she supposed. Certainly attractive. She turned back to Beth. "I don't guess I have anything in common with her."

"I'm not sure you've had a long enough conversation to find out." She lifted the lid on the sauce, slowly stirring. "And you've been very evasive about your trip. Was it that bad that you don't want to talk about it?"

"Oh, Beth, no, that's not it. It was actually quite fun having a fake girlfriend along." She sighed. "Too much fun, actually."

Beth looked at her sharply. "What does that mean?"

"I'm almost embarrassed to say, but her stipulation for going with me was…well, it was sex." She laughed quietly. "Okay, I *am* embarrassed to say it."

"Are you serious? And you went along with it?"

"Did I have a choice? She was my last resort." She waved a hand in the air. "Anyway, the whole situation with Holly was actually bearable having Nic there." She leaned against the counter, watching as Beth slowly stirred the marinara sauce. "All in all, it was a good Christmas. And they're still getting married, and they still want me to be the maid of honor."

"That's just crazy. Are you going to do it?"

"I say no now, but my mother still has six months to talk me into it. And of course, I have to break up with Nic at some point."

"Why? See if she'll go along with you to the wedding." She put the spoon down. "Did you *really* sleep with her? That's so not you, Abby."

"God, I know." Then she smiled. "It was actually fun being with her. I kinda miss her." Well, "kinda" was kinda an understatement, wasn't it? Truth was, this had been the longest week of her life.

Beth eyed her. "Is she why you're not interested in Kate?"

"I never said I wasn't interested in her. I said we didn't have anything in common." She looked across the bar, watching as Kate laughed at something Jenna said. She really was attractive. Blond hair, greenish eyes. And a doctor, she reminded herself. Maybe she should make more of an effort. With a sigh, she pushed off the counter. "I guess I should go back out."

"Take the wine bottle with you, please."

CHAPTER FORTY-TWO

Abby stood at her office window, looking down on the courtyard, something she did nearly every day after lunch. She was hoping to have a Nic sighting. She no longer lied to herself about that. It had been over a month. Five weeks and two days, to be exact, and she still scanned the courtyard each day. She didn't know what she'd do if she saw her. Would she go down to talk to her? Would she stay here and stare at her as she worked, afraid to go down?

Oh, god, she needed to get a life. She was in such a freakin' rut, wasn't she? With a sigh, she moved away from the window and back to her desk. She couldn't seem to get into a groove. Even here at work, her enthusiasm was lacking. She'd been going through the motions, getting her job done and nothing else.

And personally? She stared at the far wall as her hand rested on the mouse. Her personal life consisted of two dates with Kate—the second of which she was certain would be the last—and dinner out with Marcos once. She didn't think she liked Kate well enough to even be friends, much less become romantically involved with her. Besides, Kate was still very much hung up on her ex.

Other than that, she hadn't even seen Beth and Jenna since the dinner date with Kate. They'd invited her over last weekend, but she'd wanted to wallow in her loneliness alone. On top of that, her mother had called on Sunday and inevitably she asked how Nic was. *Nicole*, she corrected. And they'd managed to get through the conversation without even once mentioning The Wedding.

She let out a deep breath, then shook the mouse, revealing the analytics report she'd been reviewing. It was tedious and mind-numbing, which was a good thing, she supposed. At least it kept her occupied. Before she dove back in, though, her office phone rang. It was her admin assistant.

"Yes, Julie."

"Abby, there's a Ms. Welch here to see you. She doesn't have an appointment, but she was hoping you could find time for her."

Abby frowned. Welch? It didn't ring a bell. "What account is it in regard to?"

"She says it's personal."

Personal? She had no clue what it could be about, but she nodded. "Okay. Send her in. Thank you." She got up and went to the door, opening it just as a very pregnant woman was about to knock. "Ms. Welch?"

"Thank you for seeing me."

She closed the door behind her. "Do I know you?" she asked bluntly.

"No. I'm Addison Welch. A friend of Nicky's. Nic Bennett."

Abby's eyes widened. "Addison and Eric, yes." Then she frowned. "Is something wrong? Is Nic okay?"

"Let's just say Nicky would kill me if she knew I was here."

She motioned to one of the visitors' chairs. "Please. Sit." She didn't know if she should assist her or not. "And forgive me, but I thought Nic said you had three months to go. Of course, that was a month ago, but—"

Addison laughed. "Oh, I know. I'm huge. Each time I go to my doctor, I'm like…are you *sure* I'm not having twins? I'm due mid-April or so she keeps saying."

Abby laughed too as she sat down, waiting for Addison to explain her visit. Addison unconsciously rubbed her protruding belly.

"Do you know that you're not the only Abby Carpenter who works in the towers here?"

"Really? No, I had no idea. Is that how you tracked me down?"

"Yes. And I hope you don't mind. It is about Nic, actually. She's been in such a blue mood, we're starting to worry about her. She hasn't been herself since she came back from Red River."

Abby met her gaze. "I miss her. I do. And in the last five weeks, I've thought about calling her practically every day. But she made it clear that she doesn't want someone in her life. I didn't feel like it was my right to intrude."

"Those are her words, yes. I don't think they hold true any longer. Nicky is, well, she's always come across as strong, a little cocky even. She's both attractive and outgoing. In college, all the girls would fawn over her. She just didn't want anything to do with a relationship. She was adamant that she would not fall into that 'trap' as she called it."

"Yes. She told me that too. She said that her parents were in a trap and couldn't get out."

"We were shocked that she told you about her parents. She doesn't ever talk about it. It's all she can do to get through the anniversary of it each year." Her hand jumped and she smiled. "He's active today."

Abby watched as her hand again moved affectionately across her belly. "Nic said you were hoping for a boy."

"Yes. And she and Eric want a girl. I fear they will be disappointed." She took a deep breath. "I think Nicky is a little bit lost right now. For the first time, someone got in, probably without her consent. You. You got in."

"Yes, I think I did. We had this crazy chemistry between us. And not just in bed," she said, feeling a little embarrassed to admit that to this stranger. "I like her. But still, she wasn't receptive to anything other than what we had."

"She's afraid of a lot of things, Abby, but mainly, I think she's afraid of getting hurt. She told us that if she were ever going to let someone in her life, it would be you. Only I don't think she can bring herself to admit that you'd already gotten inside. She thinks she's still in control."

Abby smiled at that but said nothing.

"I told her to call you. She said you were out of her league. The attorney. Now a doctor." Addison looked at her pointedly. "I hope you're not seeing someone now. I guess that should have been my first question when I got here."

Abby shook her head. "No. I've been out with Kate a couple of times, but no, there's nothing there. In fact, I found myself comparing her to Nic and…"

"Why don't you call her? Please?"

"I don't know, Addison. I don't know if she'd be receptive to it. She thinks she's damaged and has nothing to offer. Her words, not mine."

"Yes, damaged and she has baggage and all that," she said with a wave of her hand. "Yes, she said those very words to me too. That's why I thought it was time to intervene." Addison smiled at her. "What are you doing Saturday night?"

Abby's eyebrows shot up. "Umm, I don't have any plans."

"Good. Because she's going out to the bar. Outlaws. It would be such a coincidence if you ran into her there, wouldn't it?"

Abby smiled at her. "Yes. Yes, it would."

CHAPTER FORTY-THREE

Nic almost turned around and left. Almost. A part of her wanted so badly to get Abby out of her mind—and sleeping with a stranger would hopefully do that. But another part wanted no such thing. She didn't *want* Abby gone. She held on to those precious moments, reliving them one at a time—each touch, each kiss, each look. She didn't know how or when, but Abby had gotten inside her heart. Hell, she'd gotten inside without even trying. She'd knocked down walls and climbed right over them as if they'd never been there.

So, she didn't want her gone. She'd become a friend—or at least her memory had. She remembered bits of conversation and it made her smile. She remembered the secret looks that they shared whenever Holly said something ridiculous, and she smiled even more. She remembered laughing with her as they'd tumbled down the slope, the newly fallen snow nearly swallowing them. All memories that remained fresh in her mind, not fading in the least.

She almost turned around and left. But she could hear the music, could feel the beat. She heard laughter and singing. So she went inside, heading to the bar. Maybe she'd stay for a drink or two. Maybe she'd dance. Maybe not. And maybe she'd find someone to go home with.

She sighed. Probably not. Six weeks since she'd seen Abby. Six weeks today, actually. Abby had left her standing in the parking lot, left her to watch the taillights fade away. She remembered it as if it were yesterday. She shook that thought away. Maybe she would find someone, take them home. Maybe it was time. Maybe it was time to say goodbye to Abby Carpenter and get on with her life.

She looked around as she went up to the bar. It was barely nine. At one time, she would have thought it was far too early to be out. By ten, the place would be packed. Outlaws was a gay bar that attracted a mixed crowd. It was one of the few clubs that played exclusively country music.

"What can I get ya?"

"Shiner on draft."

"Blonde or Bach?"

"Blonde, please." She took a handful of the peanuts in a jar and absently cracked the shell before popping one into her mouth.

He slid a frosty mug her way. "Three-fifty."

She handed him a five-dollar bill. "Keep it."

"Thanks."

She took a sip of her beer, then glanced around, not seeing any familiar faces. Truth was, she hadn't been out to a bar in more months than she could recall. Last summer, she supposed. She couldn't for the life of her remember who she'd gone home with. She was blond if she recalled, but the woman's face was a blur.

She jumped when she felt two hands resting on her shoulders from behind. She turned, her eyes widening. She wouldn't have been surprised to find that her heart had stopped beating.

"Abby. My god, what are you doing here?"

Abby didn't say anything for the longest, she simply stared at her, their eyes locked in a tight embrace. Then Abby smiled and came closer, leaning over to kiss her cheek.

"What a nice surprise."

"Yeah, it is," Nic said with a nod, then looked past her, wondering if she was alone. Abby seemed to read her mind.

"I'm here with Marcos, a buddy. You?"

She met Abby's eyes again. "Yeah. I mean, I'm alone."

"Good." Abby pointed at the barstool next to her. "Do you mind?"

"Of course not."

Abby sat down, then leaned closer, their shoulders touching. "How have you been?"

Nic stared at her. Was Abby really here, talking to her? Or was she dreaming? "I've...I've been okay. You?"

Abby shook her head. "No. Not really." Abby reached for Nic's beer and took a swallow. "Let's dance."

Nic's eyebrows shot up. "Dance?"

"Yeah, dance. You know how, don't you?"

"I do, yeah."

Abby smiled at her and took her hand. "So, let's dance."

Nic found herself being pulled onto the dance floor. She suddenly grew another left foot as she stood there stupidly. Abby's smile was sweet and nearly melted her heart.

"We're going to get run over if we don't move, you know."

Nic finally pulled Abby into her arms, and she did melt, just as she knew she would. She still didn't move as Abby's arms went around her shoulders and her body pressed close.

"God, I've missed you, Nic."

Nic closed her eyes at the quiet words. All sorts of memories flooded her brain as Abby got them moving ever so slowly. They were in no way keeping pace with the song or the others who danced around them. She didn't care.

"I missed you too," she heard herself say.

Yes, surely, she was dreaming. There was no way Abby was in her arms again, no way they were dancing. But it felt real, didn't it? Fingers at her neck, threading into her hair. Thighs brushing hers. It certainly felt real.

"This is my first time coming here in months. You?"

She nodded. "Yeah. I was thinking earlier that I hadn't been here since last summer." She pulled away enough to meet Abby's eyes. "How was the doctor? Your date?"

Abby shook her head but didn't say anything. She merely burrowed closer and Nic let her. One song turned into three, then four. She knew they weren't *really* dancing. They were simply moving together, letting their bodies touch. What did it mean? What did Abby want? When an actual slow song came on, they stopped moving altogether. Abby's mouth found hers, and Nic was embarrassed by the moan that left her lips.

They pulled apart as they got bumped from behind. Abby's eyes were on fire and Nic just wanted to drown in them.

"Can we...can we get out of here? Please?" Abby asked almost shyly.

Nic didn't pause to consider the question, didn't take into account whether it was a good idea or not. She took Abby's hand and led her out of the bar. Her mind was muddled, though, and she couldn't remember where she'd parked. The street was lined with cars, and she looked up, and then down.

"What is it?"

Nic laughed lightly. "I don't remember where I parked."

Abby slipped her hand around Nic's elbow, and they started walking. "The doctor was very nice. Attractive. We had two dates."

"Oh, yeah?"

"Uh huh. She called me yesterday. Wanted to have dinner. Like tonight. I said no."

"Why?"

"There wasn't any kind of a spark there, and we really didn't have anything in common. She's a movie buff. Never misses a new one, regardless of the genre. Me? I can't remember the last time I've been to a movie." She sighed. "Besides, she's still hung up on her ex. She talks about her all the time."

"Sorry that didn't work out."

Abby stopped walking. "Are you?"

Nic swallowed, stalling. No, of course not. She wasn't sorry at all. But she nodded. "Yeah. I mean, I know you were looking forward to going out with her."

"Was I?"

They walked on and Nic finally spotted her truck. She hit the remote to unlock it and Abby nodded.

"Yes, I pictured you driving a truck, not a car."

She opened the passenger's door for Abby, who lightly brushed her stomach as she got inside. That innocent—or maybe not so innocent—touch sent her heart racing. What were they doing? She walked around to the driver's side, pausing before getting inside. She knew what they were doing, didn't she? She was about to drive them to her apartment. They were about to get naked.

Kind of ironic, she thought. Here she'd come to the bar, hoping to meet someone, someone to make her forget about Abby. Instead, the very woman who'd been roaming—at will— through her dreams for the last six weeks was now sitting in her truck, waiting on her. Waiting on her to take her to bed.

She got inside, glancing at Abby before the light dimmed. Abby's eyes were full of desire, a desire she remembered well.

"Should we…talk or something?" Nic asked quietly.

"Do you want to talk?"

Did she? Hell, she didn't know what she wanted. *Liar*. She started the engine. "Let's go to my place."

"Good. And hurry."

CHAPTER FORTY-FOUR

Abby nearly stumbled as Nic led her up the stairs to her apartment. God, yes, they should talk, shouldn't they? She had thought they would. At the bar. Visit. Catch up. But no. One look into Nic's eyes had chased away any plans she'd had. The look in her eyes, yes, but the dance had been her undoing.

So, no, she didn't want to talk. Not now. They could talk later. Like in the morning. Because right now, she just wanted to strip her clothes off and get into bed. But when Nic unlocked the door and turned the light on, she stopped. Her gaze swept across the room, finding the snow globe, the stocking, and the sight tugged at her heart.

"I...I haven't gotten around to putting that up yet," Nic said, clearly embarrassed.

Abby looked at her, meeting her gaze, holding it. Then she reached out, moving Nic's sweater down, revealing the necklace she'd given her for Christmas. She met Nic's eyes again before gently cupping her cheek with her palm.

"Did you think of me?"

"Yes," Nic whispered.

Abby nodded, then moved closer, touching her lips lightly. "I missed you," she said again, echoing the words she'd told her while they'd danced. "Take me to bed. Please?"

Nic didn't move, though. No, she reached out, shifting the collar of Abby's blouse aside, revealing her own necklace—the Infinity heart.

"You wear it?" Nic asked quietly.

"Always. And yes, I think of you."

Nic's eyes darkened as she pulled her close, claiming her lips with a possessive passion that ignited her own. It was so familiar, yes, yet it seemed like it had been an eternity since she'd felt this way. Her arms went around Nic's shoulders, holding her close as their mouths and tongues became reacquainted. Hands tugged at clothing as they shuffled toward Nic's bedroom. By the time they reached it, they were both naked.

She realized it was relief she felt as Nic rested her weight on top of her. Relief in that she'd been so afraid she'd never have this again, never know the feelings that Nic's touch brought her. The handful of sexual partners she'd had in her lifetime were but fuzzy images—Holly included. It was Nic—her mouth, her lips, her fingers, her very breath—who seemed forever etched in her mind now.

And as Nic parted her thighs, the relief turned to fear. Fear of rejection, fear that Nic didn't want this as much as she did. Fear that nothing had changed at all. Was she simply a woman Nic had picked up at a bar?

Those thoughts faded too, however, when Nic's fingers slipped into her wetness, filling her. Right then, she no longer cared what her fears were. She would confront them tomorrow. Because right now, as Nic's mouth settled over her nipple and her fingers stroked her, she was in too blissful a state to worry about what it all meant. Nic brought out a side of her—a sexual, passionate side—that no one had before. And she simply wanted to embrace it.

"Yes," she breathed.

CHAPTER FORTY-FIVE

The bedroom was dark, quiet, cold. Abby moved, snuggling closer to the warm body lying next to her. Nic pulled the covers up and tightened her arm around her. Oh, it was all so familiar, wasn't it? The sex, the cuddling afterward. The utter contentment she felt.

"You know, I didn't think I'd ever see you again," Nic said quietly.

"No? I thought you said you might pop in at the courtyard someday," she reminded her.

"Yeah, but I didn't think I'd actually do it." Nic shifted a little. "To be honest, I was afraid to see you."

Abby lifted her head off Nic's shoulder. "Why afraid?"

"I was afraid I'd see you and want this," she said with a smile.

"And what's wrong with this?"

Nic let out a deep breath. "I told you, I don't have anything to offer you."

Abby leaned up and met her gaze in the shadows. "And what makes you think I want something?"

"Because you're not the type of person to have casual sex. You want the relationship, the commitment. You want stability."

"Yes, I thought I did. Now I'm not so sure. I kinda like this. I told you that when we were in Red River. It's kinda freeing."

Nic raised an eyebrow. "So did you sleep with the doctor?"

"Of course not."

"Why not?"

"First of all, I hardly know her. And secondly, I told you, there was no spark."

Nic laughed. "See? You don't do casual sex."

"I must. I slept with you on the second night."

The smile left Nic's face. "I can't offer you anything, Abby. Emotionally, I mean. So if you want to get together occasionally, like this, then I'm okay with it. But don't expect anything else."

Abby tried to read between the lines—tried to read her eyes. She knew Nic believed it when she said she had nothing to offer. And she knew Nic believed that she didn't want a relationship, didn't want to be involved with anyone. Emotionally. But if they saw each other, slept together, how did Nic propose to *not* become involved? And what about her? Did she really want to do this? Hadn't she said that this *wasn't* her? Wasn't Nic right? She wanted the relationship, the commitment. She didn't want someone she only had sex with and nothing else.

But she liked Nic. She was attracted to her. And as she'd told Sharon, she fell a little bit in love with her. If they did this, would she get in over her head? Would she end up with a broken heart?

None of that mattered, she realized. Nic could say what she wanted, what she thought, but when they made love—and yes, it was making love, it wasn't just sex—the look in Nic's eyes said something completely different. Nic was lonely, yes. So was she. But Nic was also attracted to her, and if she had to guess, Nic was falling a little bit in love too. And she imagined Nic was plenty scared by that feeling.

She leaned closer and kissed Nic gently, quietly. When she pulled away, Nic's eyes were closed, and Abby smiled.

"I accept."

Nic's eyes opened. "No counteroffer?"

"Nope. On your terms." She lay back down. "On one condition."

"What's that?"

"Breakfast in the morning. A nice breakfast." She lifted her head again. "Or am I being presumptuous?"

"About?"

"Well, staying the night. I'm not sure how this is done. Am I supposed to leave now?"

"Leave?"

"What do you normally do?"

Nic smiled at her. "You act like I do this every weekend. I don't."

"Okay. So in the past then."

"I would leave, or she would leave, yes. There was no breakfast."

Abby met her eyes. "So, you want me to leave?"

"No. But what constitutes a nice breakfast?"

Abby lay her head back down, feeling relieved that Nic wanted her to stay the night. "Omelet?"

"How about a scrambled omelet and hash browns in the waffle maker?"

"Mmm. Okay. I don't know what a scrambled omelet is, but okay."

* * *

She was in a deep sleep, convinced she was dreaming when soft lips moved across hers. She finally opened her eyes, surprised at the brightness of the room. Nic was smiling at her. Nic was also fully dressed.

"What time is it?" she asked sleepily.

"Seven thirty."

"It's Sunday," she yawned. "Isn't that kinda early?" Then she smiled. "Because I distinctly remember being woken up—what

time was it? Two?—with your tongue in all sorts of nice places."
She was surprised by the blush that crept onto Nic's face.

"I don't recall you complaining."

"God, no." She stretched her legs out. "When did you get up?"

"Five thirty. Habit." Nic slid the sheet lower, revealing Abby's breasts. She saw Nic's eyes darken. "I've...I've started breakfast."

"I guess that means I can't drag you back into bed then, huh?"

"I've got the veggies sautéing." Nic straightened up, clearly fighting with herself. "There's time for you to shower, if you want."

"Do you mind?"

"Of course not. I've already put a towel out for you."

She got out of bed, pressing her naked body against Nic's clothed one. She kissed her, almost wistfully. Pity they couldn't go back to bed. Of course, she didn't know what the rules were. Were there rules?

"Give me ten minutes."

The shower felt so good, ten turned into fifteen, but Nic was still preparing breakfast. The scrambled egg concoction was on the stove, and she was just taking the hash browns out.

"Can I help with something?"

"I'm good. Grab you some coffee. Everything's about ready."

They sat at the bar and Abby noted that the snow globe had been moved, slid down to the end against the wall. Nic followed her gaze.

"I couldn't bring myself to put it away somewhere. It makes me feel...at peace, I guess."

Abby patted her thigh affectionately. "You don't have to apologize for it, Nic. That's why I gave it to you. I had hoped you wouldn't shove it into a dark closet and forget about it." She stabbed a forkful of eggs. "This is delicious, by the way."

"Thank you. It's the cheese that puts it over the top."

"Mmm."

"So, who were you with last night?"

"Marcos? He's a friend from college. We have dinner occasionally."

"Do you think he's worried about you? I mean, you just kinda disappeared on him."

Abby blinked at her stupidly. "I...I texted him," she lied. *Damn.* She hadn't considered that Nic would remember Marcos. She couldn't very well tell her that Marcos had been in on the plan all along. The plan to find her and then go home with her. And that plan had worked to perfection.

Nic stared at her. "Oh. I guess I don't remember you getting your phone out."

"Yes, yes. It's fine," she said quickly. "So? How's work? Have you been busy?"

"It's starting to pick up. I've been busy with lining up our orders for spring. We've got three commercial nurseries that we order our flowers and plants from. I've been doing that for the last week." Nic gave her an apologetic smile. "Sounds kinda boring, I know."

"Boring? No. If I described my day of poring over sales reports and analytics and such, it would put you to sleep. Which is what it's been doing to me." She picked up her coffee cup. "I'm actually quite bored with my job. It's challenging and stressful—both things that should keep you on your toes—but I think I've lost interest."

"How long have you been there?"

"Since college. My first job."

"You've got job security, at least."

Abby shook her head. "No, job security doesn't exist in today's world. Maybe at mom-and-pop shops but not when you work for a multi-million-dollar corporation. There's no loyalty. You can be the biggest asshole in the company, but if the profit margin is on target, you're gold. And the reverse is true. You could be the most-loved person on your floor, but that doesn't hold any weight when it comes to the bottom line."

"So, it's like looking over your shoulder all the time?"

"Kinda, yes. And truthfully, now that I've become a manager, some of the stress has eased. Because if things go wrong, you have underlings to blame," she said with a laugh. "Of course, that only works for so long. Ultimately, it's your team. If it continues to fail, it has to be you and not the team. I've got a good one, though, so there's never any problems."

"Who picks them?"

"When I became manager, the team was already there. After a few months, I knew who I could work with and who I couldn't. And those were either reassigned or fired. It's a cutthroat business and you must leave emotions out of it. That was the hardest thing to learn."

"You have to be a bitch?"

She laughed. "No, that's not what I mean. But even if you like someone personally, you can't let that cloud your judgment on the job. And I've lost friends because of that. And it's taught me that I'm the boss and they're my team. There is no room for friendships." She paused. "I miss that. When I was one of the underlings, I had friends. We'd do Friday happy hours nearly every week." She held her hand up. "Sorry. Didn't mean to go on and on about it. I guess I didn't realize how lonely my workdays are."

"You still have lunch with Sharon?"

"Oh, yes. She's my outlet and we've become great friends. But in all these years, we have never done one single thing outside of our lunches, yet I know all about her life and she mine." She raised her eyebrows. "What about you? Do you ever hang out with any of the guys?"

"I'll grab a beer with them sometimes after work, but no, we're not really friends."

"Just Addison and Eric?" she asked gently.

"Pretty much." Then Nic smiled. "And you."

Abby returned her smile. "Thank you. And thank you for breakfast."

Nic nodded. "Guess I should run you home, huh?"

"I suppose. I have laundry to do, my normal Sunday chore." She got up and took Nic's plate with hers to the sink. "I'll do the dishes."

"You don't have to."

"You cooked. I'll clean up." She leaned across the bar, pulling Nic to her for a kiss. "I had a *really* good time last night."

Nic held her closer for a second kiss. "And this morning wasn't too bad either."

CHAPTER FORTY-SIX

"Do you want to come in?"

Nic hesitated—yes, she was curious to see where Abby lived—then shook her head. "No. I better not. I've got a couple of hours at the gym planned. Then grocery store. And we have an early dinner on Sundays."

"Okay." Abby opened her door. "Dinner? With your uncle?"

"Eric and Addison. I pretty much go over there every Sunday."

Abby got out, then leaned down to look at her. "Well, enjoy your dinner. Maybe I'll get to meet them someday."

Nic very nearly invited her to go along. She knew Addison wouldn't mind. Hell, Addison would be thrilled. But no. That would be too much like dating, something she didn't do. So she kept quiet and simply nodded at her.

"Maybe so."

Abby stared at her for a long moment, then gave a quick smile. "See ya later."

Nic watched as she walked away, disappearing behind a hedge. She tapped the steering wheel, feeling a sense of loss.

It was suddenly too quiet, the truck too empty. With a twist of her wrist, she turned the music up loud and pulled away. She was no longer in the mood for the gym but drove there anyway. It was her Sunday routine. Two hours. Then off to do what little shopping she needed. Home to shower. Relax a bit before heading out again. Routine. Nearly every Sunday was the same.

This one felt different, though.

She hit the phone icon on her console. The music died as her call list came up. A call list of three numbers. Her uncle, Eric, and Addison. With a sigh, she pushed Addison's name.

"Hey, Nicky. What's up?"

"Yeah, hey. Listen, do you mind if I bring a friend to dinner?"

There was a long silence, and she pictured the quizzical look on Addison's face.

"I don't mind at all." Then, "Anyone we know?"

"It's…it's Abby. I ran into her last night at the bar."

"You did? That's great."

"Yeah." She cleared her throat. "She kinda spent the night with me."

Addison laughed. "Kinda?"

Nic laughed too. "Okay, yeah, so I just dropped her off at her apartment. She mentioned that she'd like to meet you sometime, so I thought maybe tonight…"

"Absolutely. We'd love to meet her."

The enthusiasm in Addison's voice made Nic shake her head. "No, no, no. I know what you're thinking. This is not a date or anything. We're not seeing each other. Nothing like that."

"Of course not. You don't date. Remember?"

"Right. So don't forget that."

"Uh huh. See you about four, Nicky. Burgers."

The line went dead, and she shook her head again. Mistake. This was most likely a mistake. Maybe Abby wouldn't go. Maybe she already had plans. Hell, maybe she wouldn't even call her.

But as she sat in her truck, staring at the entrance to the gym, her mind went back to last night, this morning. In bed, yes. But not only that. Just being in Abby's presence, looking into her eyes, watching her smile—all things that made her just a little bit happier inside.

"Oh, hell," she murmured. She picked up her phone. Maybe she should add Abby to her favorites. She picked up on the second ring.

"Hey you. What a surprise."

Nic found herself smiling at the sound of Abby's voice. "Hey. So, I was wondering, if you don't have plans, maybe you'd want to join me for dinner tonight. Well, not really tonight. About four, actually."

"No, I don't have plans. I would love to."

"Great. I'll pick you up about a quarter to four. Will that work?"

"I'll be ready. I'm assuming casual?"

"Oh, yeah. Burgers." She cleared her throat. "So, this isn't like a date or anything, you know. Just—"

"Oh, I know. And you don't have to spend the night with me tonight if you don't want to." A pause. "But I'd love for you to."

Nic's breath caught as she tried to swallow. "We'll see," she managed.

"Okay. See you in a few hours. Looking forward to meeting your friends." Another pause. "Looking forward to being with you, Nic. Bye."

She stared out into space, wondering what was happening to her. Wondering where those walls were that she'd so carefully constructed over the years. She'd built them strong and built them high.

Or so she thought.

CHAPTER FORTY-SEVEN

"So nice to meet you," Addison said with a friendly smile. "Nic has told us so much about you."

Abby looked at Nic. "You have?"

"Have not."

Abby gave a subtle wink to Addison. "She's told me a little about you too. When are you due?"

"April seventeenth. I can't imagine I won't burst by then." Addison held the door open. "Come in, please. Eric is out on the patio already. Go visit with him. I was just washing the tomatoes."

"Oh, I can help," Abby quickly offered. She smiled at Nic. "I'll be right out."

"Grab a couple of beers," Addison added.

Nic stared at them, looking at first one then the other. "I can help too."

"No, no. We got this."

Nic pointed her finger at Addison. "No talking about me."

Addison dramatically rolled her eyes. "Now why would we talk about you?"

Abby patted her arm. "I'm just going to help slice tomatoes and onions and stuff. I'll come out to meet Eric in a second."

"Okay." Nic opened the fridge and took out two beers. "I'll go supervise him cleaning the grill."

As soon as Nic closed the patio door, they looked at each other and grinned. "I see you found her last night."

Abby nodded. "The plan worked like a charm. Thank you." She grabbed a tomato, then paused. "I told you I'd missed her, but I had no idea just how much until I saw her again."

"So did you talk?"

"Yes. She reiterated that we weren't dating and that she couldn't give me anything other than what we shared last night."

"And?"

Abby smiled. "And I'm falling in love with her, and I have no intention of letting her run from this. She can pretend—can tell herself—that she feels nothing for me, but I know she does. It'll catch up with her sooner or later."

"And in the meantime?"

"In the meantime, I'll let her believe that she's in control."

Addison laughed. "Oh, I think our Nicky has lost this battle already. I tell you, she was in such a gloomy state. Today? Her eyes are bright and lively." She slid a cutting board and a knife toward her. "And she's out there watching us, probably so afraid I'm telling secrets or something."

"I'm so glad she invited me along today. I wanted to officially meet you. I was afraid I'd say something out of line."

"You know what? Even if she finds out that I reached out to you, I don't think she'd be angry."

"No, I don't suppose she would. But still, let's keep that to ourselves for now, huh?"

* * *

"So, from what I can see, she looks really cute," Eric said as he peered over her shoulder.

Nic nodded. Abby and Addison were chatting like old friends as they sliced the vegetables. She'd been a little nervous, wondering if they would hit it off or not. She didn't know why, though. They were both likable women.

"I swear, Addison gets bigger every time I see her. You think she's going to make two more months?"

"She was at the doctor on Thursday. The date hasn't changed." Eric laughed. "Addison is convinced she's having twins."

"When are you going to settle on a name?"

"I like Sarah for a girl. Addison likes Shelby," he said as he wrinkled up his nose, indicating he didn't care for it. "And for a boy, I want to go with a normal name, like Michael or something. She wants something different, like Grayson or Carson. Those are her two favorites."

"It's gonna be a cute little girl. I just know it." She nudged his arm. "I like Shelby."

"Yeah. I'm only pretending I have a say in it." He sat down at the table, and she joined him. "So, you broke down and called her or what?"

Nic grinned. "I went to the bar last night. She found me."

"So, it's like fate or something, right?"

She shook her head. "No, it's not fate, Eric. I don't believe in that stuff. We just, you know, hooked up. Nothing more."

Eric studied her. "You know there's nothing wrong with having someone, Nicky. Maybe it's time you gave it a chance."

"I don't think so. Besides, I don't think Abby is looking for anything either. She seems fine with our current arrangement."

"Which is?"

Nic shrugged. "Which is no commitment, no relationship. Just sex."

Eric laughed. "Well, I guess there are worse things in life."

CHAPTER FORTY-EIGHT

"Okay, so I don't know anything about pregnancies, but Addison is going to have that baby any day now," she said as Nic drove them back to her apartment. "The poor thing looks miserable."

"She is. She's been sleeping in the recliner. She says she just plops down and pushes the button to lay back."

Abby laughed. "She told me." She reached across the console and rested her hand on Nic's thigh. "I really like them. It was a fun evening."

"Yeah, they're the best."

When they pulled up to her apartment, Abby squeezed Nic's thigh. "I forgot my remote. You'll need to put in the gate code." She waited for Nic to lower her window. "It's eight-zero-four-seven-three."

"Pound sign or something?"

"Nope." Nic put in the code and the gate opened, allowing them to drive through. "Will you stay?" she asked almost shyly.

"Yes. That is, if—"

"Yes. I've been dying to kiss you all evening."

She got her chance a short time later when the door closed behind them. She found herself being pressed against the door. Her mouth met Nic's in an urgent kiss, and they moaned simultaneously as Nic's thigh pressed between her legs.

God, but Nic could get her into a heated state, couldn't she? Warm hands shoved her bra aside, fingers brushing over her nipples. Then Nic's tongue moved past her lips, circling her own. She moaned again, letting Nic have complete control. She felt the zipper of her jeans go down and soon fingers found their way inside. She braced herself against the door as Nic found her clit, rubbing lightly across it. Then those fingers dipped into her wetness for just a second before returning.

"I love how you touch me," she murmured with her eyes closed.

Nic's mouth nibbled at her neck, one hand at her breast, fingers rubbing her nipple, the other hand down her jeans. Abby was nearly breathless as Nic held her against the door, hands and mouth driving her arousal to a feverish high. Just as her orgasm was about to envelop her, Nic dropped to her knees and shoved the offending jeans down in one motion before her mouth claimed her clit, sucking it hard into her mouth.

Abby jerked once, then stilled as Nic's hands cupped her from behind. A mere five seconds later, she climaxed, a loud "ohh" leaving her mouth as she pressed Nic closer to her.

"I'm going to fall down."

"I won't let you fall," Nic said quietly as she stood again, kissing her with an exquisite softness, a kiss that told her just how much Nic cared for her. It melted her heart.

"Let's go to bed, huh? I have all sorts of things I want to do to you." She smiled as they kissed again. "Lovely things. It'll probably take hours."

"I've got nowhere to be."

"Good. Because tonight...you're mine."

CHAPTER FORTY-NINE

"I think it's corny when people say you glow, but I believe it now. You're freaking glowing," Sharon said with a laugh.

Abby laughed too. "I know I am. I've been so blissfully happy these last few weeks."

"So let me get this straight. You're not dating. You're not in a relationship. You're just…having sex?"

Abby bit into her sandwich. "On the surface, yes. That's what she wants to believe."

"Yet you've seen her nearly every night?"

"Yes. And I don't push, I really don't. Yesterday, for instance. I hadn't spoken to her all day. We had no plans. And I was fighting with myself about calling her. Then the doorbell rang, and she was there." She grabbed a chip from the bag. "She's scared, so I'm letting her work at her own pace."

"I don't understand her whole phobia about dating."

"It's a childhood thing having to do with her parents," she said evasively. "I know her story and I completely understand where she's coming from. That's why I'm letting her make the rules."

"But you're falling in love?"

"God, yes. And so is she. She just doesn't know it." Or did she? Hadn't there been an almost terrified look in Nic's eyes that morning as they'd cuddled in bed? Abby had smiled at her, had kissed her lightly, chasing that look away. Yes, Nic knew it. That's why the look of fear was on her face.

"So, you're going to pretend you're not dating when you kinda are?"

She nibbled on another chip. "I'll go as slow as she needs. I don't want her to run, but I think she'll try. When she realizes how entangled we've become, I think she'll run. And then I'll have to convince her to come back."

She saw movement a few tables over and she looked up, nearly gasping. Sharon followed her gaze.

"Who is that?"

"It's…it's Holly."

"*Your* Holly?"

"Yes."

Holly was dressed rather casually today. Jeans—designer jeans, to be sure, but still jeans. A burgundy button-down shirt was covered by a sweater that was a shade or two lighter. Even her lipstick matched.

"I was hoping I'd find you out here." Holly glanced at the gold watch on her wrist. "Do you have a few minutes to chat? Alone?"

Abby glanced at Sharon, who was busy gathering up her lunch, but she reached out a hand, stopping her. "No, don't leave. We'll go up to my office. I'll see you tomorrow."

The walk through the courtyard was made in silence, but her mind was jumping to all different kinds of scenarios as to why Holly had come to see her. The most obvious one—she wanted to "get together"—came to mind.

At the elevator, she could stand the silence no more. She offered a smile, albeit a fake one.

"So…how have you been?"

"I've been missing you."

The doors opened and she stood back, waiting while two guys got off. Just before the doors closed, someone called to hold the elevator and she stuck a hand out, stopping the doors. An older man carrying a briefcase came inside and nodded at her.

"Thanks."

"No problem."

Silence again. The man got off on the third floor. They rode up to the sixth without speaking, her mind reeling as she tried to figure out why Holly was there. She went into their suite of offices, nodding quickly at her admin assistant before going on to her own office.

She closed the door, then leaned back against it. "What in the world are you doing here?" she blurted out.

Holly gave her one of her practiced smiles. "Does that mean you've missed me?"

"Not for a minute." She moved around Holly to her desk, opting to sit behind it. Holly took one of the visitor's chairs, crossing her legs and resting her purse on her lap.

"Well, I thought we could talk. Visit."

"Whatever for?"

The smile left Holly's face. "I think I made a mistake, Abigail."

Abby arched an eyebrow but said nothing.

"With you."

"Which time?" Abby shot back.

The smile Holly gave her was actually a little sad-looking, and again, she wondered what was going on.

"I should never have ended things with you."

"Of course you should have. We were so wrong for each other, Holly. I can see that clearly now." She waved a hand in the air. "Besides, I think you said you preferred men. Remember?"

"As I tried to tell you over Christmas, I was wrong about that. Aaron—while a very sweet man—doesn't get my..." She paused. "Well, to be blunt, he doesn't get my juices flowing, if you know what I mean."

"Oh good lord, I do not need to hear this."

"Sorry, but it's the truth."

"And it took you two years to figure this out?"

"I thought it was something I could live with. Turns out, I don't think I can. Seeing you again at Christmas, I realized that what I have with Aaron is not enough."

She frowned. "Wait a minute. Surely you're not suggesting that you and I...what? *Date* again?"

"That's exactly what I'm suggesting."

Abby laughed. "Oh, can you imagine how *next* Christmas would be if you and I started dating again?" Her smile disappeared. "But I guess you forgot that I'm seeing someone. Remember Nic?"

"Is she still in the picture? My god, Abigail, you can do so much better than that."

Abby stared at her. "I can do better? What? *You*?"

"She doesn't even have a real job. She works for her uncle, for god's sake, doing who knows what." Holly leaned closer to the desk. "Aren't you embarrassed to introduce her to your friends?"

"Wow."

"Wow?"

"My relationship with Nic is just between us. I couldn't care less if my friends don't like her. Don't care if my parents don't like her—which I know they do. Now, whether this is a forever thing or not, I don't know. We're still getting to know each other." That much was certainly true. It was also true that she could very well end up with her first truly broken heart. But she'd be damned if she'd run to Holly with it.

She stood up. "I guess our discussion is over. I'm sorry that you're having second thoughts about Aaron and the wedding and all. But I can't help you."

Holly stood too. "Why won't you give us a chance, Abby? Please?"

"A *chance*?" She slammed her fist on her desk. "Do you know how humiliated I was that Christmas? How depressed I was? Sleeping with you then was probably the low point in my life, Holly. You used me and I *let* you. And that's on me. But that will never happen again." She squared her shoulders. "I've fallen in love with someone. And I realize now that it's the first time

I've really been in love. Giddy in love and it feels so good. It's completely different than what I ever felt with you. So, I'm sorry, you'll have to find yourself someone else to screw over."

She walked purposefully to the door and jerked it open. "Goodbye, Holly."

Holly paused beside her and met her eyes. Abby could see embarrassment there and confusion.

"I'd appreciate it if you wouldn't say anything to Aaron about our visit."

"Aaron and I no longer have a relationship, as you well know. Besides, if there was anything I should have told him, it's that you crawled into my bed last year." She paused. "Then you slithered right back to him. That's what I should have told him."

Holly's eyes never wavered. "I made a mistake, Abby."

"Again...which time?"

CHAPTER FIFTY

Nic sat in her truck, the smell of the pizza making her stomach rumble. She stared up to the second floor, wondering if she should call first. Hell, wondering what she was even doing here in the first place. Oh, that was a lie, though, wasn't it? She'd told herself all day that she wasn't going to see Abby tonight. Wasn't going to call her, certainly wasn't going to pop over again. Because she thought she'd be absolutely crushed if there was someone in her apartment—a date, for instance. It was Friday, after all. Since there were no commitments in their relationship, Abby could date if she wanted. And surely, at some point, she would. But during these last few weeks, Abby had made no mention of it, and they'd seen each other nearly every night.

And here she was. Again. After her workout at the gym, she'd gone home to shower, thinking she'd call in a pizza instead of cooking. By the time she'd finished her shower, however, her mind had been full of Abby, and she couldn't shake the need she had to see her. She was too embarrassed to call, though, afraid that Abby might say no. Afraid that Abby already had plans. Afraid that she was getting in too damn deep.

Yet, here she was. Again. She took a deep breath, pushing down her insecurities, hiding them. She picked up the pizza box, then got out. It was a windy, damp evening, and she felt the misting of rain on her face. She hurried up the stairs, pausing to catch her breath before punching the doorbell.

The door jerked open, and Abby stood there, a big smile on her face. "I'm so happy it's you. Come in."

"You are? Not sick of me yet?"

"Are you kidding?" Abby took the pizza box from her and leaned in for a kiss. "And you brought dinner. You get bonus points. I had absolutely nothing here to eat."

She followed Abby into the kitchen, noting how roomy it was compared to her own. Of course, Abby's apartment was much larger than hers too.

"Oh goody," Abby said when she opened the lid. "You got, like, everything on this."

"I thought if there was something you didn't like, you could toss it over to my side."

"No. I love it all." Abby came closer and slid her arms around her neck. "Thank you."

"For the pizza?"

"For coming over. I wanted—needed—to talk."

Nic felt a bit of panic set in. "Okay," she said carefully.

Abby drew her into a hug, then kissed her before pulling away. "I realized that of all of my friends, you are the one I wanted to talk to."

She let out a relieved breath. Okay, Abby just wanted to talk. It wasn't about *them*. Because she didn't even know what the hell it was they were doing, and she certainly didn't want to talk about it.

"Do you mind if we sit on the floor in there?" Abby motioned.

"My favorite spot to eat pizza," she agreed.

Abby was in sweatpants and a T-shirt, and Nic wished she was too as she looked down at her jeans. Abby must have read her mind.

"Want something a little more comfortable?"

"Do you mind?"

"Of course not. Grab some plates and napkins and the pizza. I'll be right back."

Nic did as instructed, taking the pizza box to the coffee table and kicking her shoes off. Abby came back with a pair of navy sweats.

"Feel free to change right here."

Nic laughed. "I don't know. Can you control yourself?"

"Only because I'm starving."

By the time she slipped off her jeans and put on the sweats, Abby had two slices of pizza on each plate and had already taken a bite of one of hers. "Sorry, but my lunch was interrupted, and I didn't even eat half of my sandwich."

"That's okay." She sat down beside her and leaned back against the sofa. "I was hungry after my workout and didn't feel like cooking."

"You're so dedicated to the gym. If I make three times a week, I'm proud of myself."

"And this week?" she teased.

Abby leaned closer and bumped her shoulder. "Once." Abby put her pizza down. "I had a visitor today. At lunch, thus my sandwich going uneaten."

"Unexpected?"

"Quite. It was Holly."

"Really? Maid of honor talk or—"

"If only it was that. But no." Abby met her gaze. "She said she'd made a mistake. By ending things with me," she clarified.

"I see."

Abby pounded her fist against her thigh. "The goddamn nerve of her. Can you believe she came to my office with a proposal? She wanted us to start dating again. Good lord, can you imagine my mother's reaction to *that* news?"

Nic sat back, eyes wide. "And…and are you?"

"*What*? No. Why would you think that?" She held her hand up. "You and I aren't dating and I'm technically single, but Holly doesn't know that. She expected she could just snap her fingers and I'd break up with you and fall back to her. I was so angry with her. The nerve!"

"Did you tell her?"

"Oh, she knew I was angry. I told her I was in love with you and that I finally knew what real love felt like." Abby held her gaze. "And I told her it was so very much different than what I'd ever felt for her." She picked up her pizza again. "Anyway, she came there saying that it wasn't working with Aaron, that he didn't get her juices flowing." She laughed. "She actually said those words."

"My god."

"I know. After I turned her down, she asked me not to say anything to him. As if I was going to call him up and tattle on her."

"So even though she's not in love with him, she's going to stay?"

"That was my assumption."

"You don't think you should warn him?"

"Warn him that he's marrying a lesbian? Unless she's a really good actress when they're in bed, surely he knows. Maybe he doesn't care. He's thirty-four years old. Maybe he's just ready to get married."

"And kids?"

Abby shook her head. "I can't see them having kids, can you? They're both self-absorbed. They're going to build the big-ass house. I don't think kids are in their plans."

"That was it? She asked you to take her back, you said no, and she left?"

"Pretty much." Abby pounded her thigh again. "Can you *believe* she asked me that? I'm still floored over it."

"Do you think it has to do with love, or is it just the sex part?" Nic asked hesitantly.

Abby smirked. "Holly doesn't know what love is. And sadly, neither does Aaron apparently." She squeezed her arm. "And I don't want to be in the middle of it." Her cell rang, and Abby smiled. "That's my mother."

Nic took another piece of pizza as Abby answered.

"I'm having pizza with Nic." A pause. "Really?" A shake of her head. "I'll call you tomorrow. You can fill me in then." Abby met her gaze and smiled. "I'll tell her. Bye."

Nic arched an eyebrow when Abby put the phone down.

"She said she's looking forward to seeing you again. At the wedding."

"Oh?"

"Aaron called her. They've set an earlier date. In April. Here in Dallas. I'll get the details when I call her tomorrow."

"So, you were right. She struck out with you so she's going forward with Aaron." Nic looked at her, holding her gaze. "I think you should tell him."

"Tell him what? That his fiancé propositioned me? That we slept together Christmas before last? That he doesn't excite her in bed? What should I tell him?"

"If it was me, I think I'd want to know."

"Oh, Nic, I don't want to be that person. For one thing, he probably wouldn't even believe me. And secondly, it's none of my business. It's their thing, not mine." She took another slice of pizza. "Besides, I doubt he's going into this blindly. I mean, she was sleeping with his sister when they met."

"Are you going to tell your mother?"

"Oh god, no." Then she paused. "Do you think I should?" Then she shook her head. "No, no, no." She took a bite of her pizza, then looked at her as she chewed. "Will you stay tonight?"

She should go. They'd been together nearly every single night and it was becoming too...too comfortable. Too familiar. So she should go.

"Please?"

"It...it kinda feels like we're dating."

Abby smiled at her. "But you don't date."

"No. But you do."

"Well, I think we agreed that you and I *weren't* going to date. Right?"

"Those are just words, Abby." She could feel panic starting to set in and she stood, needing to...to what? Escape? Run? Hide? And to that, hide from what?

"Nic? What's wrong?"

She held her hand up when Abby would have come closer. "I should…I should go."

"Why?"

"Because we're not dating," she said firmly.

"Is this where you run? Is it getting too real, Nic? Are you starting to feel things?"

"No. I don't feel things. Remember? I don't date. I don't get involved with people. I don't *feel* things. I don't…"

"You don't love?"

Nic met her gaze without flinching. "Right. I don't love. I'm not capable of it. I told you, I have nothing to give you. *Nothing.*"

Abby tilted her head. "Yes. You told me. You warned me about all of that. I fell in love with you anyway, Nicky."

Nic felt her breath choking her, felt her heart squeeze painfully in her chest. "No. No, Abby."

"Yes, Nic. Surely you can see that—*feel* that—when we make love."

"No," she said forcefully. She stared at Abby, then shook her head before bolting for the door. She was only dimly aware that she was wearing Abby's sweats and not her jeans. She didn't care. She had to get away.

The rain was falling outside as she stood beside her truck. Her keys, her wallet, her phone…all in her jeans. She felt small pebbles dig into her feet. Her shoes were up in Abby's apartment too.

God, what was she doing? She looked up into the sky and, as if triggered by her doing so, the rain fell harder, soaking her.

In love? Was it true? No. They had sex. That's all. They weren't involved. They weren't dating. They were just…what? What were they doing?

She stared straight ahead, seeing nothing. No. In her mind, she saw them together, talking, laughing, being together. She saw them making love. She saw the way Abby looked at her. She saw—

"Nic?"

She turned slowly. Abby was there, out in the rain. Her feet bare. She stared at her, seeing the concern in her eyes, seeing… yes, love. She swallowed, trying to find her voice.

"My…my mother, my parents…they never once told me they loved me. Not even once." She felt tears well in her eyes and she tried to blink them away. "No one has ever said those words to me. And in turn, I've never said them to anyone else." She put a hand to her chest. "I…I don't know *how* to love, Abby. I don't know how to trust."

Abby moved closer, still holding tight to her eyes. "Just because you've not said the words doesn't mean I haven't seen it, Nic."

"I don't know what love is."

"I think you do. I think you feel it with me and you're afraid." Abby came closer still, pulling her into a hug. She didn't resist. "I love you, Nicky. I feel that. I don't want to hide from it even though I'm scared too."

"Why are you scared?"

"I'm scared that you won't accept it. That you'll run from it." She pulled back enough to look at her. "I'm afraid that you're going to break my heart. But I'm not so afraid that I don't want to give it a try."

"I don't know what to do."

"You don't have to do anything, Nic. You just have to live life and whatever happens, happens." Abby squeezed her hand. "Please don't run. Please don't leave me. Take a chance on me, Nic. Let me be the one to love you. Won't you please let me?"

The sky opened up, and the rain came down in a deluge. Neither seemed to notice the downpour as they stared at each other. Nic finally nodded.

"I am scared. I do want to run. I just don't think that I can. It hurts to think about leaving you."

They kissed there in the parking lot, with the rain cascading around them. It was one of those long, slow kisses with mouths and lips, nothing more. When Abby pulled away and looked at her, what Nic saw there nearly made her stumble. She'd never seen love before, but she knew without a doubt that she was seeing it now.

Abby looked up into the sky, the rain stopping as if someone had turned off a faucet. Abby reached out, wiping the rain from her face.

"You'll need to be patient with me," Nic managed. "This is all uncharted territory for me. I don't know how to act or what to do."

"There are no rules. You don't have to act a certain way, Nic. I like you just the way you are." Then she smiled. "Although you're not quite as cocky as when I first met you."

"Cocky? Me?"

"Yeah, you. You know, with your counteroffer and all. You were so certain I'd agree to it, weren't you?"

"You had such a desperate look in your eyes when you came down and found me, I was sorry I'd made the counteroffer."

"But you didn't take it back."

Nic smiled and wiped at the dampness on Abby's face. "That's because I knew you were going to agree."

"See? Cocky." Then Abby's face turned serious. "If you hadn't made that stipulation, do you think we would have still slept together?"

"Yes."

Abby smiled at her and nodded. "Yeah, me too. I was very attracted to you. It just hit me. One minute I'm trying to keep my distance and the next, I wanted your hands on me." She laughed lightly. "Speaking of that, let's get out of these wet clothes, huh? I'm thinking a hot shower sounds good. Share?"

Nic nodded numbly. Her life was changing, wasn't it? She didn't feel in control and that scared her a little. A *lot*. At the same time, it comforted her. Abby was her safe haven. She wouldn't let her fall.

Because Abby said she loved her.

CHAPTER FIFTY-ONE

It was a beautiful, sunny spring day. Perfect for a wedding, she had to admit. The grounds were flawlessly manicured, flowers were blooming, and birds were singing. The chairs were set up in neat rows, curving around a small amphitheater which was bursting with white flowers.

Her mom and dad, along with Aaron, waited. Holly's parents would escort her down the walkway. There was no best man or maid of honor. For that, she felt only a small twinge of guilt. It wasn't Holly, but Aaron who called and once again asked her to participate in their wedding. While she had said a firm "no," she did take that opportunity to speak to him about Holly. She didn't actually tell him word-for-word what Holly had said to her, but she did let him know that Holly had blatantly hit on her. He laughed it off, saying Holly was just playing around.

"Are you sure this is what you want to do, Aaron? Maybe you should at least talk to her about it."

"We're getting married, Abby. It's obviously not what you want, but it's what we both want."

She let it be, not wanting to argue with him. She knew it was not what Holly wanted even if Holly had convinced Aaron that it was. She told herself it was none of her business and she washed her hands of the whole thing. Or so she told herself.

And now here they were, sitting among a handful of guests. There was no big, elaborate wedding as Holly had predicted. It was a small, intimate affair, as they say. Even her grandparents hadn't made the trip. She guessed twenty people at the most. She and Nic were sitting in the front row, holding hands. Nic was wearing her "best dress-up clothes" she'd told her. Neatly pressed khaki pants and a lovely navy blouse made her eyes a deep blue today. She had chosen to wear pants too, one of her nice suits.

She sat up a little straighter when the soft music changed to the traditional "Here Comes the Bride" chorus, a violin version that was very soothing. She glanced at her mother, who was smiling broadly. Her father stood beside her, his gaze on Aaron and not on the bride coming toward him. Did her father suspect that things weren't all sunshine and harmony with them?

Then Holly and her parents brushed beside them, going up to the front. Holly's dress was beautiful, she had to admit, although the long, flowing train was more suited to an indoor event. While Aaron was smiling, she wouldn't say he was beaming with happiness at this most joyous moment in his life. Was he having second thoughts?

As the ceremony began, she squeezed Nic's hand. Yes, a joyous occasion, yet it seemed depressing. At least to her. It was like they were going through the motions, just trying to get it over with. Maybe they were simply in a hurry to get to their honeymoon—the Cayman Islands. She could picture Holly in a bikini, on the beach. She could *not* picture Holly in the water, however.

All none of her concern. It was their life. And maybe someday, she and Aaron might have a relationship again. But as she'd told Nic, they'd never been close, and she certainly didn't see Holly being the one to pull them together.

"You okay?" Nic whispered to her.

She turned, finding Nic's eyes. "I'm blissfully happy, yes." She gave her fingers a tight squeeze. "I love you."

She saw the darkening of her eyes before Nic turned her gaze back to the ceremony. Nic had yet to say those words to her, but that was okay. She didn't need to hear them to know how Nic felt. Still…it would be nice if she did. She closed her eyes for a moment, being thankful that Nic was in her life. Yes, she was blissfully happy. They had integrated their lives so easily, she found it hard to remember her life before Nic was in it.

And while they weren't technically living together, they spent most nights at one or the other's apartment. She'd introduced Nic to Beth and Jenna and they all got along famously. They'd shared dinner three or four times now. And they had a standing dinner date on Sundays with Eric and Addison. She liked them both, and she and Addison were becoming good friends. She was nearly as excited as Nic was for the upcoming birth, which would be any day now.

Cheers erupted and she brought her thoughts back to the wedding, staring as Aaron and Holly shared a quick kiss. As they turned, Holly's eyes found hers. Abby simply nodded at her, noting the lack of enthusiasm in Holly's. How sad. How very, very sad.

Then, just like that, it was over with. There was no formal procession. Aaron shook hands and Holly stopped to hug a few people. Her mother came over to them, smiling brightly.

"That was beautiful, wasn't it?"

"Was it?" she asked quietly.

"At least no one protested," her mother said pointedly.

"Oh my god! Are you talking about me?"

Her mother winked at her, then went to Nic, hugging her quickly. "You look lovely, Nicole."

"Thank you."

"Well, I hope when you two get married, we can do it in Red River. A casual setting out in the forest. Wouldn't that be great?"

Nic's face had turned nearly white, and Abby couldn't contain her laughter. "I think you're getting ahead of yourself, Mom."

Her mother patted Nic's face lovingly. "When you two look at each other, it is true love." Then her mother's voice lowered. "I wish I could say the same for those two." Then she backed away. "Now, I should go mingle. Let's have some champagne together, girls."

"You know, we *really* need to tell her that your name is not Nicole."

Nic smiled. "Then she'll know we were faking it at Christmas."

"I don't care. We're not faking it now."

The others had all left, heading to the large white tent that had been set up for the luncheon. She could already see bottles of champagne being brought to tables. Holly was standing in a group of smartly dressed women—some of her colleagues, maybe. Aaron was chatting with their parents, looking very handsome in his tuxedo. He turned then and met her gaze. He nodded at her, and she returned it.

Nic took her hand as they walked. "Maybe we should invite them to dinner sometime."

"Aaron and Holly?"

"Yeah."

"Why on earth?"

"Because he's your brother."

She was about to protest but realized the meaning behind those words. Nic no longer had a brother. Nic had mentioned a few times now that she and Aaron needed to reconcile. Her response was always that there wasn't really anything to reconcile—they simply weren't close. But Nic was right. Yes, she and Aaron had never really talked about the whole Holly thing. Never. They had swept it under the rug where it stayed and festered. Yes, she felt a sense of betrayal by him. She'd been deeply hurt and humiliated. That had stayed with her.

"You're right. Aaron and I need to talk. By ourselves."

"Yes. And then you need to let it go."

"You think I haven't?"

"You've gotten over Holly cheating on you because you don't love Holly and you know that she wasn't the one for you.

You haven't gotten over Aaron's part in it because he's your brother and you do love him. You may not like him, but you do love him."

Abby met her gaze, knowing she spoke the truth. "When did you get so insightful?"

"I would give anything to have a brother."

Abby felt tears in her eyes, and she hugged Nic tightly. "Oh, honey. I'm sorry."

"Don't take it for granted."

"No, you're right. When they get back, I'll make it a point to talk to him. Maybe have lunch with him or something."

"Good." Nic reached out and wiped the corner of her eye. "Don't cry."

"Oh, I love you, Nic."

Nic didn't look away from her. No, she looked deep into her eyes.

"I…I love you, Abby."

Abby stood there, soaking in the words, letting them echo over and over in her mind, in her heart. Then she leaned closer, kissing Nic on the mouth.

"I vote we sneak away and go somewhere private."

Nic smiled at her but shook her head. "No, no, no. I'm starving. I want to see what kind of fancy stuff Holly is going to serve. Besides, we have a champagne date with your mother."

"Really? You finally tell me you love me and we're not alone. And I want to be alone. Because—"

Nic silenced her with a kiss. "I'll tell you again tonight. When we're alone. Deal?"

Abby linked arms with Nic. Yes, she was so blissfully happy indeed.

"Deal."

Bella Books, Inc.

Women. Books. Even Better Together.

P.O. Box 10543
Tallahassee, FL 32302

Phone: 800-729-4992
www.bellabooks.com